BRIEF

The problem with having an identity crisis, is that you don't know who you are. One minute, you're playing at hero. The next, you're regaining consciousness, covered in blood. With dead bodies strewn all over the place, wondering what just happened.

When Ash finds out about a plot to destroy the Earth, his first impulse is to be the hero. But heroes don't lie. Least of all, to themselves. Can he be trusted to save the day, or has he been the bad guy all along?

TWIN TORN

Pangea Saga: Book One

STEPHAN F. ROGERS

VENERATED
SAGE

Twin Torn is a work of fiction. Names, places, and occurrences are either the product of the author's imagination or are used fictitiously.

For information contact: Venerated Sage,

651 N Broad St, Suite 205 #3439

Middletown, Delaware 19709

ISBN 978-1-7357161-0-7

eBOOK ISBN 978-1-7357161-1-4

Cover art: by Wyndagger

For Karolyn Kuonqui
Valued author and friend

FOREWORD

When I first wrote *Twin Torn* it took me about 6 months to put together. On the first draft I thought I was finished and I was ready to publish my story. Then I thought, wait, I should probably check for spelling mistakes. After that, I was definitely done. That was just me writing off instinct, based on other books I must have read over the years.

Then I started taking some creative writing classes at Hunter college. I thought it was probably a good idea to get some real experience, to see if what I'd written was as good as I thought it was. My brain was like, what do you mean you want me to rewrite stuff? What do you mean, do it over again in a different style? A different voice?

One particular Professor, Elizabeth Nunez, who's an accomplished author (you should search her up on Google), she said she rewrote her novels like 11-12 times. I was like W H A T? She totally blew my mind. Up until that point, I assumed second drafts and the like were just for getting rid of spelling mistakes, and maybe fixing some punctuation here and there. The concept of putting any more effort into writing was foreign to me. Thanks to her, I developed a bit of a work ethic in my writing. I felt I was already good, but I'd also been resting on my talents, without really exerting myself.

A few years ago, I joined an accelerated teaching program, and I had the privilege to teach English to middle schoolers for a few years. I got to see first hand, I'd like to think, the effect that a teacher can have on their students. How they could really take to heart what you were trying to convey to them. Sometimes. Kids are an ornery bunch, more often than not, but that's sort of what being a kid is about. They aren't always forthcoming with praise necessarily. They might benefit more by getting it from us anyway. Ha!

Let me be honest. This book was getting made no matter what. But because of a certain professor (in my case Professor Elizabeth Nunez) it's at a higher standard than it might have otherwise been. I had thanked her after the semester was over, but I don't think she knew how sincere I was. I thought maybe if I thanked her as an author, she'd take it a little more to heart, and know I wasn't just throwing some lip service her way. Who knew that adult students could be as inspired or enlightened as young kids? That feeling actually allowed me to understand what my own students might be going through, so double kudos to Professor Nunez. Thank you, Elizabeth. I had a blast in your class and learned a lot.

As far as *Twin Torn* goes, it's a little all over the place compared to typical conventions, but I think it comes together rather nicely. You get to see into the minds of a bunch of different characters, which I think isn't done as much as it should be. I think that makes it more fun. It's my sincerest hope that you enjoy the novel, and please consider adding a review on Amazon, or wherever it's popular to do so these days.

—Stephan F. Rogers

THE NEAR FUTURE

The three of them drove around for an eternity in silence. Eventually, the car came to a complete stop and the driver got out. After a while, the back door was opened by her head, and she was uncomfortably man-handled, and slung over someone's shoulder. It was a man. Probably the driver. He had dark black hair and a black leather jacket.

The ground was made of tar, and she thought she saw a motel sign for a second. The door to their room swung open and she was tossed down onto a bed.

Hopefully they would take the gag off and untie her, but if not, at least let her know what was going on. Either it was going to be slavery or they were going to kill her right here in the hotel room. That's where they always killed people in the horror movies.

Not knowing was so hard. She couldn't even explain it in her head. All she could do was feel it.

Crying until the salt of her tears formed a desert on her face, that mirrored the desert inside, of her hopes and dreams. All those little voices that told her everything was going to be alright, gone.

The uncontrollable shaking. Wanting to scream until her vocal cords snapped, but still scream and never stop, with broken strings flapping around, destroyed and useless in her throat. Begging the world for just one more chance. PLEASE! Because she would do anything. ANYTHING!

CHAPTER 1
A BEGINNING

I t was difficult to know how long he sat where he was. A deep
dark crevice in the bowels of humanity. Weak. Tired. But more
than that. Beaten.

Perhaps some battle long ago, whether of mind or body. He could
not remember. All he knew was that he must have lost.

It mattered only in the abstract. A distant cloud on the winds of his
troubled mind. For as sure as he knew he lived, he could not recall a
single detail but the now. His former thoughts were a whisper just
beyond hearing.

The damp. The cold. Mildew. Spiders. Rats.

Within the deep dark that was his prison he could smell, almost
taste it all. To the granite walls and metallic plates on its surface. Down
even, to the thin sheet of dust caked to the surface of his own body.

It was almost a game, in some simple disinterested way. Plates
connected to links of chain, connected to manacles. Thus, as an extension, to him around his wrists. They were long enough so that his arms
hung down at his sides, limp and devoid of purpose. This melancholy
was shared by neighboring legs. Free, but as disinclined to motion as
their northern counterparts. They all lived here on the floor with the
rest of him.

He took inventory of this with eyes that refused to look, locked in their protective lids. Not unlike a blanketed man in bed. As if it were too early or cold to come out from under the covers. There was no shivering or fear, just a shroud of malaise.

As for the rest of him, he could not be sure anything would change at all. A never-ending spec of time, frozen in an amber of now. His state of being. Until at last, he began to slip back out of focus, to completely embrace wherever he had been before now.

Drifting. But for a sound!

A single unsure—unwelcome—unfamiliar sound snapped closed his reverie and opened his eyes. As crisp and sure as a captain salutes his general. Nothing else of him moved. As things slowly came into focus, he saw cobwebs and dust eddies, glistened dew on un-kept walls, and the ants marching.

These elements were all part of an orchestra of sound, that was a constant in the background. Always in perfect harmony. Now this? One wrong note, and the sweet lullaby was destroyed.

As though the conductor, he looked around for the offender. Searching.

A little patience and there it was. His focus found the source of the disturbance, and it was unsettling. His sanctuary had been violated.

Rhythmic steps joined the orchestra that played itself out before him, but they did not belong, and they were getting closer. It was a baby crying in the theater, whining and carrying on, and throwing fits.

Panic set in.

The only thing he allowed to move were his eyes. They alone could be trusted, not to make a noise that might betray his existence. His ears listened as hard as they could, to the ever-approaching footfalls of something getting closer.

"Point that damned flashlight in front!"

"Sorry Simon, I was just trying to have a look around."

"Then look in front," said Simon. "What's the point of pointing that thing where we've already been, Thomas?"

"Who's to know what's down here?"

"I do," said Simon. "I know exactly what's down here. Absolutely nothing! Now do as I say and don't give me no back talk!"

The silence almost returned, but hidden in the darkness, he knew they were still inside his territory. Loud and clumsy footfalls betrayed their presence, despite failed attempts at stealth.

"What did I tell you about that damn flashlight?"

"Well, why don't you walk in front then?" asked Thomas.

"Me? Why? I'm already in the back. You know what? Come here." There was a loud slapping sound intermingled with a scuffle of sorts and the rapid shifting of feet.

"Hey, cut it out you jerk. I'm going to tell my sister."

"Okay, okay. I'm sorry."

"What are we doing down here again?"

"This woman Chanovalle hired us. She's paying more than enough. Trust me."

~

THE WORLD BEGAN TO SPIN.

A whispered memory blazed to the forefront of his mind's eye. Chanovalle.

Could it be the same one?

Chanovalle. A woman. Dark gray piercing eyes. Murderous.

Always hunting. Again and again.

She had found him. He was afraid of her without knowing why.

All he knew was that he had to run. Now!

~

"LOOK THOMAS, I DON'T KNOW WHY YOU'RE MAKING EVERYTHING so difficult again. It's like you're addicted to drama or something. You said you needed a job and I got you one. Didn't I? Let's leave my wife out of this, okay?"

"Susan said you're not allowed to hit me."

"Okay, okay. Didn't I say I was sorry? You know I didn't mean it."

"Didn't mean that you were sorry?"

"Oh brother! There you go again. You know what I meant."

"I hope so."

The duo continued in silence, flashlights beaming all over the place, as they searched for something that might interest their employer. Until something caught the younger one's attention. He shuffled towards it with the eagerness of a golden retriever.

"Hey Simon, look at this over here. What do you suppose this is?"

"Chains? Thomas, you idiot. Are you kidding me? You scared the bejesus outta me just now."

"So, we're not looking for these then?"

"Thomas, what are you going on about? It's just some old rusty chains on the floor. Nothing to worry about. They look like they've been here forever and a day, even. Let's keep moving." When Thomas didn't budge, he added "Quit being peculiar and lets get back to work."

"Okay, okay. I was just wondering what coulda done that, is all," he shook his flashlight for emphasis.

"Done what?" Simon wiped the back of his sleeve over his sweaty forehead, to try to hide eyes that were darting all over the place. His own flashlight, momentarily darting around as well.

"Pulled the chains off the wall like that. You can tell they used to be on the wall here, not on the floor. And how come there's no dust only right here? The whole rest of the place is full of the stuff?"

There was an uncomfortable silence that stretched on for a long time. Both men stood back to back, looking everywhere at once. Eventually Simon remembered that he was in charge.

"Aren't you just a regular Sherlock Holmes?" Simon gave Thomas a gentle shove from behind to get him moving again. "Let's keep looking."

CHAPTER 2
IDENTITY CRISIS

H e rode the terror like a rush of water from a broken dam. Pushing through the maze of corridors as fast as his legs would carry him. Only when it was too dark to see, did his gait slow to a crawl. Fumbling around for what seemed an eternity, searching for walls and doors like the blind. The accidental release was as surprising as it was jarring.

The small confined space with its stale air and darkness, turned fresh, starry, and expansive in an instant. One side of the single doorway, threatening to blot out infinite possibility. Rather than rush through, he took a moment to take it all in. All the while, holding the door open as if his life depended on it.

In the span of three breaths, he took in the aroma of salt mixed with the moisture of the water, a few feet away. The breeze caressed his face and he heard the wind, the waves, and the flutter of a bird's wings. His sight was gifted with heavenly lights in the sky. Man-made lights that were an equal distance, and great architectural structures that stood wherever there was land.

Easing the door closed behind him, a few steps to the left and he discovered the moon. It was full and beautiful and blurred his vision. When he looked away tears were falling freely down his cheeks.

This was it. He had done it. He had returned to the world.

The strength of his legs began to wane, thoughts muddled, and the whole world spun. He sat on the ground exhausted and on the verge of sleep, crawling to hide himself in some bushes next to a small castle. Consciousness faded away as soon as he reached his destination.

HIGH IN THE SKY, IN A MIASMA OF DARKNESS, HE FLOATS. A FLASH OF light. A loud bang. He shudders, covering his ears with shaking hands. Suspended as if by a string—that is cut—he falls. He screams.

Hurtling down, sometimes diverted by strong gusts of wind, pelted with cold rain against his naked skin. Lost. Unable to hear his voice over the tempest, blinded by sun-like brightness, spinning and plummeting down...

EYES OPEN TO STARE AT DIRT AND GRASS, AND RAPID BREATHING AND fear subside, as thoughts fogged with sleep begin to organize. A dream. It was only a dream.

Drops of water began to fall from the night sky, motivating him to seek better shelter, but he opted for reconnaissance instead. A sign read 'Ellis Island Immigration Museum Statue of Liberty National Monument' by the entrance of the castle he had slumbered beside. The doors were locked, but within the glass they were made of, he did not recognize the reflected face that was clearly his own.

A white male of indeterminate age, with light brown eyes, and sharp features; wearing a black shirt and black pants, caked in a layer of dust; mimicked his every movement. "Who are you?" he asked, staring into his own eyes for any hint of familiarity. There was nothing.

Tears streamed down his face and his body sobbed and shuddered. Weak legs forced him to sit. His spirit folded in on itself and he lay on his side curled up like a fetus. The whole world spun uncontrollably, as if trying to shake off the unwanted.

He placed a hand on the stone ground for support. The touch of something solid began to slowly ease his fears and he slept.

HE WAS THE KING OF A CASTLE. HE SAT ON HIS THRONE. HIS EMPIRE was vast and powerful. He had a room of wenches whose sole purpose was his pleasure. He possessed jewels and gold coins of endless supply. Any comfort or demand was met with haste and brought into being, immediately upon his request to servants.

He sat back in his empty throne room and even though he was indoors, it began to rain. This did not strike him as odd, and he continued to lounge on the mighty chair. As the drops gathered on the floor, he absently noticed a red hue to them, but this too bore no change in his calm demeanor. Soon, the entire throne room was filled to waist level in red water, and still he sat unperturbed.

When the red liquid had risen to his neck, he looked up lackadaisically, to see that hundreds of bodies had somehow been impaled into the ceiling on spikes. All of them dripped down their red blood. It was not rain at all. Even this discovery came as not the slightest shock, nor did it illicit the slightest alarm.

Still, he sat at ease. Even when he found himself so completely covered in blood, that he would have had to stand in order to breath. He remained seated and even smiled.

When blood filled the entire room, all the way up to the ceiling, he noted it in passing. He felt himself to be rather satisfied, but he couldn't understand why that might be.

ANOTHER DREAM. IT WAS STILL NIGHT WHEN HE WOKE, FOLDED IN on himself with arms wrapped around legs. He rolled onto his back, unfurled his limbs and stretched and yawned. His mouth began to salivate, and it wasn't long before the emptiness of his stomach overwhelmed all thought. Driven by instinct more than anything else, he searched for food.

Eating the flowers put together for decoration purposes—he knew not their names—the yellow, reds, and blues; they did not help. Without a boat, getting to the other island—the one with the giant green statue with an arm pointing to the sky—getting over there to look for food was out of the question. Making it to any land farther away was impossible.

He had stayed in the same relative space, unwilling to venture out past what he could readily see, before returning to square one. When his entire body ached from head to toe, he decided the time had come to expand his search. As a distraction, he tried to think up a name for himself. What sounded nice?

He found writing entitled 'The New York Times' and skimmed through its pages, only looking at samples of names. The one that stood out—that he liked the most—was Robert Davis. Every so often throughout his surveillance, he would pretend to introduce himself to an imaginary person. "Hello, my name is Robert Davis. Nice to meet you," he would say, trying out different smiles and affectations of geniality.

When the rain began to fall so rapidly and in great amounts, so that he was pelted by it, the time had come to give up the search and seek shelter under an overcropping, near a wall of the castle. The rhythm of the drops were soothing as they moistened the ground, and it did not take long for him to be lulled asleep.

THE MOON SHONE IN THE NIGHT SKY AND CLOUDS DRIFTED BY TOO fast. Legions of birds circled in the air. The wind was cold and biting, but the birds were fine with their warm feathers.

The wind howled. It called out his name, but he could not make it out, no matter how hard he strained to listen.

The lush grass and trees that surrounded him were unaffected. Someone was screaming out his name. His mind told him that he should know what was said. It was on the tip of his tongue—on the very precipice of awareness, but he couldn't be sure. He tried to concentrate.

He opened his eyes. He must have been dreaming again. He turned his head to make sure that he still had his bag full of supplies and saw a big dog staring at him.

Maybe it had come to relieve itself, as he had seen other domesticated animals do before. But why by him? Was there not a more appropriate place, away from where he lay?

That is not a dog you fool, his mind told him. It's a wolf. You're dead for sure you idiot. It is going to eat you.

The wolf growled at him for an instant and stopped, silently staring right into his face. There was an intelligence behind those eyes. Something very unusual.

He began to think that maybe this creature somehow knew who he was. Then, out of nowhere, he was overrun. Swarmed over by other wolves. It was an ambush!

The man who called himself Robert Davis fought for his life, punching and kicking at the dogs, as they overwhelmed him. All the while, he sensed the lone wolf doing nothing more than staring at him. The others bit and tore at his clothing, narrowly doing more than scraping his skin, as he flailed about. Until finally, a dog bit into his shoulder, causing agony to shoot through his body.

"No!" he screamed at the top of his lungs.

Amidst the anguish, something odd happened. The fear evaporated as if it had never been, and in its place, there was nothing—nothing but white-hot anger.

Enraged, he bit the dog's neck. How did it like a taste of its own medicine? His attack was vicious and feral. Savage.

~

ROBERT DAVIS WOKE UP COVERED IN SWEAT, DESPITE THE CHILL night air. It had all been a dream, and this time he was finally awake.

"Hey buddy, you're not supposed to be here." Looking up he saw a man in an all-blue uniform and black shoes. The glare from one of the tall lights obscured his face. "Hey, I'm talking to you." The man kicked Robert Davis in one of his ribs.

In an instant, he tackled the aggressor, knocking him off his feet and slamming him onto the ground. He pinned both his arms down and bit into the man's neck.

The first taste of blood that hit his tongue, sent him into a swoon, and his hunger could not get the nectar into him fast enough. He pulled from the draught as strong as he could, oblivious to everything until it dried up. Only then did he return to the present moment of the rain's downpour, and what was now a dead body underneath him.

"Oh my God. What have I done?"

As the horror of his actions began to settle in, those feelings were eclipsed by sensations that resided both inside and outside of himself, simultaneously.

The world crawled to a halt.

Each drop that touched the ground exploded like a tiny bomb. People could be seen standing in the streets at a distance far across the water, that should have been beyond his scope. The last vestiges of the aroma of his prey's fear touched his nose. He felt rejuvenated and powerful, where he had been frail and weak mere moments ago. His mind absorbed all the material he had glanced in the newspaper as though studied in earnest.

The world returned to normal.

He was whole once more. Whole but not complete. New instincts told Robert Davis that everything was in tip top condition. Everything except his memories. Those were as barren as the corpse beneath him was devoid of life. "Who am I?" he asked the night. "What am I?"

CHAPTER 3
MONTICELLO

They were the last ones through the Shimmering Gate. Commander Azure, her sister Magistrate Margaret, and the slave girl Kayala. Fifty of her troops awaited them on the other side. She stepped through.

New York. It was good to be back. She loved Pandoria with all her heart, of course, but home was a simple place; where New York with its technology, was something else entirely.

"Commander," Major Gordon greeted her with a salute. "We await your orders."

"As you were, Major," she said, with a return salute of her own. Azure surveyed the soldiers at her disposal, with eyes the color of blue skies, but a hardness that captured that beauty in ice. Each one of them stood in their black leather uniform, ready to receive her orders, without hesitation.

"Major," she continued. "Organize them into groups."

"Okay everybody!" he shouted. "Listen up!" Major Gordon was a veteran of war who had lost one of his eyes a long time ago, to a dead man lucky with a blade. Gordon wore an eye patch to cover up whatever remained, but that did nothing to undermine his authority. If anything, it enhanced it.

His battle prowess was legendary, and if you asked any one of the troops, they would be able to recite the tale of at least one of his many exploits. This put him in their hearts. Azure kept him as her second in command because of that and his wisdom.

At first glance he appeared a venerable old man, with gray hair and one good eye. It did not help that he kept a dog at his side, as if he were truly blind. But if you looked closer you would see that his posture was not stooped. That his lone brown eye burned with an alertness fit for two. And that the old man's dog, was a breed of wolf, trained to kill foes in battle. Add to that, the fact that the Queen had granted him Initiate status, and he was a force to be reckoned with, worthy of the respect she had bestowed upon him.

"We will be splitting up into three groups," he said. "First group: Kip, Herin, Rojen, Id, Prattle, Timkins, Wilner, Bran, Fann, Lenna, Sarlin, Dap. You lot will be with Commander Azure. Second group: Nelfo, Pimmo, Karn, Cimran, Ellis, Needles, Leon, Pinker, Mancus, Pepper, Kimmy. You lot are with me. The remainder of you are following Magistrate Margaret.

"Those with the Commander, you will be acquiring camouflage clothing, cell phones, and GPS devices, among other things. My group will be acquiring food and drink, money and supplies, and transportation. Those of you with the Magistrate will be securing us all a base of operations and sleeping quarters. Are there any questions?"

"Yes," said Specialist Vixl. "How long do we have to complete all that stuff?"

"Everyone has three hours before we regroup back here, except for you, Vixl. You have got fifteen minutes."

"That is a copy, big cheese," said Vixl with a smile.

"Anything else?" asked Major Gordon, pausing for effect. "Okay, then. Three hours. Move out." He proceeded to walk off with his squad.

"My squad, to me," said Azure, as she walked off in the opposite direction.

∾

It was not long before they came across a nearby town. Judging by the sky, they probably had a good four hours or so until daylight. The streets were all but deserted, except for her soldiers. It would be more than enough time to get what they needed.

This place, Monticello, New York, was not up to meeting her standards. Either the population was too small, or the shops were in a different location than she had anticipated. Right now, the only thing she had seen was the small neon sign that said 'Diner' on the side of a little building, a short distance ahead. Time to improvise.

Making the hand signal that everyone should gather around her, Azure communicated her assessment. "Okay, here is the situation," she said. "This town is not cutting it. We are going to have to accelerate the process, to get our mission done within the parameters. Where is Specialist Id?"

"Here, Commander," replied the young man, stepping out of the shadows. He looked no more than twenty-five years old with brown hair and eyes. It was a kind face full of compassion, whether he possessed the attribute or not. Id wasn't much for battle, but he did not have soft hands either. His expertise lay in another area.

"You are my tech guy. There are thirteen of us in total. Take Sergeant Kip and Sergeant Dap with you, and secure two vans. That should be enough to hold us."

"On my way, Commander," said Id. He turned to leave, with his partners falling in beside him.

"Captain Pratle?" she asked.

"Yes, Commander," replied Captain Pratle. He had been standing directly behind her. Hair and eyes the color of deepest night, Pratle had an angular face that seemed carved of granite. He looked about middle age.

Where Id appeared innocent, Pratle was his opposite. His strong point was that he had a very good understanding of social dynamics, admittedly born out of his penchant for having a good time.

"Take Initiate Fann and Specialist Bran with you. See about finding us supplies nearby. Try that diner up the block. Maybe the patrons know something."

"Permission to slip into something more comfortable, Commander?" he asked, tapping his chest with two fingers.

"Granted, but keep it Sweet, Captain," she said. It was her way of reminding him to keep his profile low.

"As always," he smiled, and walked off towards the diner.

The remaining seven, including herself, sat on a nearby sidewalk, waiting. The only thing they had to fear in a small place like this, was drawing attention to themselves. Here in the cover of night, everything was going like clockwork, with minimal risk of discovery.

Before long Pratle, Fann and Bran returned.

"We are in luck," said Captain Pratle. "There is something called Walmart less than twenty miles away. It is supposed to have anything that anyone could want, and it is opened day and night. Initiate Fann has the directions."

"Excellent," replied Azure. Pratle had found a donor for a new set of clothing, as had his two companions. He had his uniform slung nonchalantly over his shoulder, while the other two had neat little folded packages of the same. She did not much care what they did with them, as long as they were immaculately perfect when worn, and were not lost. Anything else might be forgiven, depending on her mood.

About ten minutes later, the others returned with the two vans. One said Ford on the outside and the other said Dodge. Other than that, aside from the gray color of one and brown of another, she really could not tell the difference.

"The six I had on assignment, in the gray van. Navigate us to this Walmart. The rest, with me in the brown van," she said, seating herself in the front passenger seat. "Come on people, move it. We have a schedule to keep."

Walmart Proved to be all that Captain Pratle said it would be. The inside of it was large enough to hold a small town. It was filled with all the clothing her troops would need, all the cell phones, and all the GPS devices. Before they got started though, she decided everyone should sit down to a meal at the tables inside. Pratle said they could purchase food with a credit card he had gotten, off the man who gave him his clothes. (Forcibly taken from, but why split hairs?)

That way they would be sufficiently rested and fed, when it came time to steal everything else. It would also add to the element of surprise, making them all seem a bit more normal. Afterwards, they could split up and reconnoiter the place to see about disabling the security cameras and alarm system, rounding up the employees and patrons, and stealing all the available money. She had charged Gordon's group with acquiring enough local currency for what lay ahead, but more of it would not hurt anything. Hopefully they were doing just as well as she.

Major Gordon walked at the head of his group, with his faithful companion Caymon, pacing alongside him. He had raised him from a puppy, abandoned in the southern forests of Pandoria—for whatever reason—and they had been inseparable ever since. Even going into battles together, torturing prisoners, and partaking in Gordon's fitness regimens. They did everything together. When it came time for the Queen to bestow the honor of Initiate on Gordon after years of faithful service, she even Initiated his wolf.

It would not do to outlive his best friend in the whole world, and now, he would not have to. Though canine, Caymon was as much a vampire as Gordon, with the long life to prove it. So, barring direct sunlight or a life-ending assault, the two of them might be around forever. When it came time to die, they would do that together too.

Coincidentally, they were early enough when they reached the bus station, or its schedule was so full, that only a single bus sat in the lot. Just enough to carry all of them on their little journey, together as a squadron. It smelled empty, like they were the only ones there, but his was not the best nose.

"Caymon, scout," he said, and the command sent the wolf off immediately. He began sniffing about for anyone who might cause them trouble by notifying the local police. After he thought enough time had passed, he said "Caymon, report," and he heard the wolf running on the concrete before he saw him. Caymon's calm demeanor and happy smile told him that the coast was clear.

"Captain Ellis," he said. "Get your butt out there and make sure that piece of junk works."

"On my way, Major," came the response.

"Initiate Kimmy. Sergeant Azon. You two keep him company and make sure nothing untoward happens."

"Roger that," the two of them seemed to say in unison, as they walked out to join Captain Ellis, who had sprinted out and was now halfway there.

"The rest of you, move out," commanded Major Gordon, taking the lead once more, with Caymon pacing him as usual.

It was a quiet night, with a brisk chill to it, so that there was not a cloud in the sky. The lighting in a small town like this, made it seem like there were more stars out tonight than there might be elsewhere. Gordon knew it was just a difference in the level of saturation. In some big cities he had seen, for example, it appeared as though there were hardly any out there at all. But how could that be, when it was all the same planet? It was just all the damn lights.

As they continued on, they passed a series of one-story houses, for about a mile or so, before they came upon one of the central locations of the town. There was a small convenience store that was still open, and an Army and Navy store, a bookstore, and a computer store, which were all closed for the night.

"Initiate Pepper, Sergeant Nelfo, Sergeant Jindle, Specialists Karn, Cimron, and Needles," called off Gordon. "I want you lot to empty out that store of every piece of food and drink it has. Take the clerk's money and knock him out. No casualties. The rest of us will be right next store, in that Army and Navy place, getting some gear together. Move out!"

He kicked the window in at his objective and led the way inside, with Caymon right behind him. "Sergeant Mancus, grab as many bags as you can and bring them next store, so they have something to put all that stuff in," he said.

"Roger that, Major," said the Sergeant, running farther in the store.

"Everyone else," continued Gordon. "I want all the bags that are not getting used by next door, and I want them filled with every weapon in this place. I want every piece of rope and climbing equipment they have got. Every flashlight, pack of batteries for those flashlights, compasses, and if they have rations, I want those too. Move on it!"

"Roger that," they all called out in unison, storming into the store.

Gordon set himself to work looking for other items that might catch his eye. He grabbed twenty face masks, twenty t-shirts, and a few sunglasses. Tossed them into a small bag he grabbed off of Sergeant Mancus, on his way back outside. One less would not hurt anything, and Mancus was bound to come back for more anyway. These were for another part of his plan he had not shared with the others yet. "Let's go people!" he shouted. "I want to be out of here in the next five minutes. Grab what you can. If you cannot carry it, leave it."

Gordon stepped back outside to see how the others were doing, with Caymon shadowing him as usual. The clerk looked like someone had worked him over, but he was still breathing. So far, so good.

"Look what I found, Major!" exclaimed Specialist Needles, excitedly brandishing a 357 magnum. "I found it behind the register. Neat, huh?"

"Yes, neat," said Gordon, as he snatched the weapon out of Needles' hand.

"Oh, come on, Major," he whined.

"Don't Major me nothing. I still remember what you did last time."

"Last time?"

"When you shot that man in the face right in the middle of a huge crowd."

"Oh yeah. But that was different. I just wanted to see if it worked."

"And this one here?" asked Gordon, waving the gun about. "You want to check that this one works too?"

"Can I?"

"No. It is mine now. Quit clowning around."

"Yes, Major." Needles resigned himself to standing outside without his new toy.

"I want everyone out here in two minutes, Specialist," ordered Gordon.

"Yes Major, you can count on me," said Needles, with a quick salute.

Gordon returned the salute and then stalked into the Army and Navy store window. "Time's up! Everyone out, now!" he yelled, stepping back outside to wait.

When everyone was back outside on the sidewalk, Gordon ordered them to hoof it back to the bus lot, sure that the vehicle would be ready by now. The usual grunts and complaints sounded, but everyone fell in line as expected and got underway. When they arrived, he was glad to see that Captain Ellis had the vehicle running. The Captain explained that everything was in working order and that the vehicle was all gassed up and ready to go.

"Alright, load her up," said Gordon. "Put it all in the cargo hold at the bottom and get your butts inside." He checked that everything was secure when everyone was done, and that they were all aboard as ordered.

"Captain Ellis," he said.

"Yes, Major?" asked the Captain, sitting in the driver's seat.

"There's a building up the road a bit that I want you to drive past. I'll show you the way."

"Not a problem," said the Captain, and pulled the vehicle out of the lot.

Driving past the scene of their latest crime, Gordon was happy to see that no police were about with their flashing lights. That meant they still had time for the last leg of his plan. In another two beats, they were directly in front of his last objective. He had Ellis drive the bus two blocks east from it and park at the curb.

"Okay squad, here's the last exciting bit for the night," he announced. "Initiates Kimmy and Pepper, Specialists Pimmo, Leon and Needles, and Sergeant Azn. You lot are up at bat." He paused a bit to enhance the suspense, and then he said, "It's a bank robbery, folks."

There was a great uproar in the bus, as some chimed in their excitement, while others let out cries of disappointment at not being included. When the volume had died down sufficiently, he continued.

"As you may or may not remember, we're still on low profile. That means we cannot all just run in there like the army that we are and wreck everything around us, because we're not trying to get undue attention." Gordon took a deep breath and let it out. "It is about the bigger picture and following the dictates of the Queen, like it or not. So, try to stay focused, okay?"

The usual hollering and hooting followed, and again Gordon waited for it to die down sufficiently before continuing.

"So, it is you six. I am going to wait on the bus with everyone else. The plan is simple. Go in, bust into the ATM devices, take all the money. If there is money behind the teller booths, take that too. You can even bust in a back door or two, to see if anything's around there. Under no circumstances is this a big vault job. I want you lot in and out like the wind. Do I make myself clear?"

Gordon waited until they all seemed to understand, using his silence for emphasis.

"Worst case scenario, we will come in to back you up, but that had better not happen, because I will not be happy about it at all. I can guarantee your Commander will not be happy, and we all know that shit runs downhill. Do I make myself clear?"

"Yes, Major," reverberated throughout the bus.

He pulled out his small bag and tossed it at Initiate Pepper. "I want you all in these face masks and t-shirts before you even cross the street to the bank. Shades too. I don't want any hassles when we get to our new location, in case there is a camera that spots you lot. This is non-negotiable."

"I will make sure of it, Major," said Pepper, and then she looked through her bag.

"Good. You six, move out," he said, and then nodded to Captain Ellis to open the front door. When they had left, the door was closed, and Gordon sat in the front seat stretching out to relax. Caymon sat in the seat beside him, and he reached down and scratched behind his left ear. It would not be long now. Soon, they would meet up with the entirety of their squadron, settle in for the day, and be off on the road headed out for the real adventure.

MAGISTRATE MARGARET SAT ON THE CURB, WAITING PATIENTLY FOR her scouts to return. She had the slave Kayala in tow at her side. The chain in her hand was fused to the slave's collar at the other end. The slave sat beside her as calm and serene as ever. It was almost too easy.

This one—this Kayala had a reputation for being a real bad ass, despite appearances to the contrary. Margaret was not about to look the fool. She tried to seem laid back herself, on the surface. But underneath, she was on the alert, as ever she had been in any war situation. Sure, she was an Initiate herself, which meant that she was far stronger than the little slip of a girl beside her; with senses far keener, and reflexes sharper. She outclassed the slave in every conceivable way, except for one, which was the most important.

This was the Queen's personal slave that sat next to her, and if anything happened to her—anything considerable, then Margaret's head would roll. Of that she had no doubt. Worse, given to extremes of temper like she was, it wouldn't be out of character for the Queen to have the entire squadron killed.

Normally, such a thing wouldn't bother Margaret as much. Perhaps she could run away and hide someplace in this world and never return home to Pandoria, though she was loath that such a thing should ever come about. But her sister, Azure, was the Commander of the entire army, let alone the squadron, and she couldn't bear the thought of endangering her life as well.

Azure wasn't the type to run off, no matter what. Margaret knew it with a certainty as sure as she knew her own mind. And she would not —could not condemn her sister to death because of her own negligence. She owed her sister too much for that, even beyond the regular duties of blood.

It was Azure who had used her reputation to bolster Margaret to the level of Initiate, only a couple of months past, at most. It was Azure who had recommended that she be entrusted with the care of the Queen's most prized possession. Who trusted her enough to guard the slave without direct supervision, even though Azure's life was also at risk.

Because of these things, Margaret's loyalty to her sister was more important than the great loyalty that she held for the Queen.

She kept a sharp eye on Kayala. With even the slightest hint of betrayal, she would have her subdued so fast, it might seem a hallucination to the poor girl. Just because the girl was human, was no excuse to let her guard down.

She was pulled out of her thoughts as the last of the scouts returned.

"What do you have for me?" she asked, still seated.

They conferred with one another a bit, and then it was Captain Zephyr who spoke. "We think we have the perfect location," he said.

"Go on."

"There is a bar in town that is at the base of a small three-story building. We figure, we can storm the apartments and bring the occupants down into the bar, undetected for the most part. The initiates can stay down there and have a meal ready when they awake. The rest of us can shack up in the apartments upstairs, and keep lookout as necessary," said the Captain. "With your approval, of course, Magistrate."

"Sounds good. You have it, Captain. Let us move on this," she said. "It will be dawn before you know it."

Her squad made its way towards the bar, with Captain Zephyr in the lead, and the Brute trailing as usual. They numbered twenty-five, without including the slave, but it still gave her comfort to have the Brute with them.

It was a regular force of nature. Perhaps stronger than a vampire in some respects, but completely mindless without an original thought of its own. It was programmed, for lack of a better word, to do exactly as she told it. Too bad it smelled like a walking pile of sewage.

When they got to the bar, she saw that it was called McGreely's

Tavern. It seemed as good a name as any, and upon her own brief inspection, she found that it would do the job nicely. Everyone would fit inside easily enough, and bars usually did not open until the night anyway, so if it was closed, the local militia would not think anything of it. Very nice.

CHAPTER 4
INALIA EDWARDS

"**N**o, get away! Let me go!" A mass of swirling bed sheets tumble to the floor amidst the thrashing of a lone woman. All eye-catching movement ending with a loud thud. At first, she lies completely still, then her disjoined thoughts begin to crystallize into a semblance of coherence. A struggle for her life with unknown captors is slowly replaced with the cold hard reality of her bedroom floor. She shakes her head to clear the cobwebs of sleep out of her thoughts.

Her name was Inalia, and she was safe at home in her bedroom. Everything was just fine. Or was it?

Still on the floor, it was a simple matter to grab her aluminum Louisville slugger bat from under the bed. Gripping the handle tightly with both hands, she went from room to room making sure they were all empty. She checked all the windows and the front door to make sure everything was still locked. Even the closets were opened and inspected one by one. Inalia also stopped to listen for any strange noises a few times for good measure.

Only after she was one hundred percent sure everything was secure, did she toss the bat back under the bed, and her sheets (still on the floor), back on top. A glance at the nightstand showed four in the morning on her alarm clock.

Could it really be that early?

Turning on her laptop confirmed the early hour and erased any wishful thinking of more sleep. The computer was kind enough to beep a reminder of a big test today as well. She could still feel the sting of Mr. Fincher's words.

"This is your last chance," he had said. "You've been doing poorly in my class up until this point, but you can still turn it around. Do good on this next test. Get your act together. And you'll pass. Fail the test. Like you failed the last one. And that's exactly what your final grade is going to be."

What a jerk. That guy was acting like his class was the most important thing in the world. Social Studies. Another name for history class. Big deal. Fincher thought it was so important to know who ruled China or Japan, or whatever, and who the rulers were and other lame crap. Boring and redundant enough to put you to sleep in five minutes flat.

Memorize all that timeline history mess for what? Oh, that's right, because your fat teacher with his horn-rimmed glasses, with a superiority complex said so. Worse was that the school had his back on it too. Know it all or get stuck in sophomore year again. Become a super senior.

Basically, whether she liked it or not, she had to pass his stupid class, which meant passing another stupid test. Fine. Whatever. She had already studied for it anyway. Passing it was going to be a cakewalk. Another easy A. It was just that on principle she shouldn't have to take it, but she needed to keep her GPA up to get into a good college.

It was, after all, what her parents had been grooming her for all these years. In between business trips, they had both managed to squeeze in some form of brainwashing or another; whoever turned up as the stay-at-home parent. Up until now, anyway.

Now that she was old enough, there would be no more passing on promotions for their precious only daughter's benefit. Mom and dad were finally free to pursue their illustrious careers as diplomats for the

United Nations. No more need for stories about how she could be anything she wanted. They were busy saving the world overseas somewhere. Completely oblivious to the fact that said only daughter was completely and utterly alone.

"I need a shower," she announced to her bedroom, and then stripped out of her pink pajamas. Worn out from oppression and loneliness, she dragged herself into the shower in search of solace.

A few hours later found Inalia at her usual spot on the train platform, with the number four train rolling into the station. She had opted for an all-black ensemble today, to mourn her resignation to conformity. Knee-high skirt, pantyhose, blouse, even down to her combat boots. She even fancied herself a shadow with powers of invisibility as she stepped to her left a bit so people could get out first. No sense getting run over to test out her new imaginary powers. The intercom speakers began to crackle.

Click. "Due to an emergency earlier today, this train will be going out of service—kzzt.. Please wait for the next available train. We apologize—kzzt.. Inconvenience." Click.

A train's worth of people spilled out onto the platform, along with the usual epithets. No big deal. All just background noise to Inalia. It really was a very simple matter to wait for the next train. This was New York City after all, and another would be along before she knew it.

After an indeterminate amount of time and the passage of an equal amount of five trains, another four train finally pulled into the fifty-ninth street station. The speakers blared to life again.

"This train is going out of service due to dispatch. There is another four train behind this one," droned the garbled announcement.

As another set of train castaways merged with what was already there, the anxiety began to mount. Inalia saw people already jockeying for position to make sure they made it on the next train. There were nervous glances from some people, at other people's casual attempts to stay close to the edge of the platform. The general tension and distrust of everyone standing next to each other, was weakly veiled by a communal anger at the errant behavior of their train schedule betrayal, which in turn was secretly directed at those in charge of the train system. But no one voiced the dissension.

The next four train that came never even stopped. It just blew right by with people already on it and everything. Some guy way down the platform somewhere screamed out something about somebody's mother. A lot of people seemed to agree with him, as his sentiment echoed across the entire station.

"Come on!" somebody yelled.

"I can't believe this!" screamed another.

It wasn't as much as she had expected. Maybe people weren't willing to get too distracted. The feelings of anger and dismay were still there, even when there wasn't outright cursing. She could feel it in the air. She could see it with shifts in posture and associated body movements. What little there was room for. All in all, she felt like everyone wanted to hold onto a false sense of hope that told them it would all work out because it just had to.

When it came right down to it, they were all in this together. Everyone had to be somewhere: school, work, home, whatever; and in that they shared a common ground. But she got the feeling also, that the primal cut-throat stuff was still really close to the surface anyway. In fact, there was a little voice in her head just like it that said "I don't care who you are. I'm getting on this God damn train and you better not get in my way. Even if I have to stand inside with my face pressed up against the glass, I'm getting on that train!"

And so it was that Inalia found herself like a sardine in a can, pressed into her rescue of a four train. Finally safe and secure, amid the stench of sweat, body odor, bad breath; cheap perfume, hair gel, and more. The assault on her senses, pressing in and overwhelming her where the physical press of bodies had not.

She wasn't even standing as much as compressed between people. Had they suddenly moved away she would have fallen.

"Education is where it's at Inalia," her father had often said, using that hip and cool routine of his. But somehow, she didn't think this was what he had in mind and—

"Get off the train so the doors can close you fat bastard!" some woman yelled.

A contagious stream of laughter rippled through the train car. Even though she was mad, Inalia cracked a smile, in spite of herself.

~

"PLEASE STAND CLEAR OF THE CLOSING DOORS," CAME THE TRAIN'S farewell call.

"Thank God," she said, as she made her way out of the station.

Inalia reveled in her new-found freedom. Stretching out in over-exaggerated movements. Surrounded by nothing but glorious space.

Pure and clean, without the foul odors that had assaulted her. Sweet nectar of the Gods. At long last she could drink endlessly with each breath, the taste of justice.

The birds were singing, and the flowers could be smelled on the breeze. Walking to school today, it was all she could do to stop herself from skipping like a little girl. In fact, the only thing that stopped her was that she was a Sophomore in high school now, and it would be unbecoming of her stature. The last thing she wanted was to be mistaken for a freshman. Talk about social suicide.

Inalia allowed herself another smile, but made it dignified this time. She made sure that her posture was extra straight. Even with her stylish black canvas bag weighing her down, with the loose strap across her chest. Not as comfortable as a regular book bag, but very Sophomore. She was also careful with how and where she stepped. Wouldn't want to trip on something and mess up her presentation.

Inalia was so engrossed with her appearance: Fluffing up her long golden locks. Making sure that her clothes didn't make her look all disheveled. Checking her makeup, with an emerald-eyed wink from her compact.

So much so that she failed to realize that she had overlooked the most important nuance of all. Time.

It wasn't until she double-checked herself that she realized another lateness might mess up her grades. And not until a third check and a reapplication of lip gloss, did she even remember that she had a test today. It was the most important thing in the world, now that her looks were taken care of, but somehow it had slipped her mind. The nonchalant attitude she had adopted evaporated.

Inalia wasn't even remotely surprised to have to sign the late roster. She was rather shocked, however, when she saw the clock on the lobby wall. 10:45 a.m. was what it said. She responded by running off down the hall, Sophomore composure be damned.

Her first class had started at 7:30 a.m., and it was now homeroom. Homeroom! Three whole classes were flushed down the toilet. She was even late for the fake one for fourth period.

The test. Missing it was an automatic failure.

When she took a seat in homeroom, she didn't even hear what the teacher had to say. She saw his lips move but she couldn't bring herself to care anymore.

Everything was falling apart.

CHAPTER 5
ASH

He sat in a dark little corner and stared out at the world of men and women, and saw things play out between them. On his little cushioned couch, hiding in the shadows, he watched what he could not have for himself. Some bar, some music, anywhere USA.

Once upon a time he had called himself Robert Davis, but that was another life from a year ago and it meant nothing to him now. Now he was called Ash. The symbolism of a phoenix rising from its own remains. Something he was always trying to accomplish.

Ash felt a strange detachment to the environment. It was 'him' alone, with everyone else grouped together as 'them.' That didn't stop him from feeling compelled to drink it all in as one might quench a desert thirst.

What was it that drew him in, though he sat frozen, to lust after every detail with such intensity? Loneliness.

A year ago, he killed an innocent man. It was an accident.

It had been a full moon that night. He remembered because it marked his first day. Of life. Of death.

A secret he carried with him every day, but not his only one. Every week since, he'd killed another person.

Never on purpose. Never premeditated.

He'd start getting hungry. Then really hungry.

Eventually, he'd kill someone.

It was never out of anger and he always drank them dry. Not out of any moral code, but because it wasn't until they were empty, that he could ever stop. Then it would reset his hunger and he would be normal again for another week.

Lately there was a different sort of hunger building up inside him. One that might not kill people.

He wanted friends. Maybe even a girlfriend.

He had started reasoning that he probably wouldn't kill them all. Even though he hadn't been able to ever stop himself before.

His mind was trying to lull him into it.

Friends. A girlfriend. Was it possible?

He needed a distraction. To get out of his head. A drink.

Time passed.

The more he drank, the more he wanted to drink. Every glass seemed to bring new discoveries of drunken perception. So, this was why everyone had been acting so weird. Alcohol built up courage, altered your perceptions, and relaxed you.

But no matter how much he drank, everything stayed the same for him. Sure, he got more relaxed and comfortable with himself, sort of like everyone else around him, but his demeanor never changed. He was still disconnected from them.

All he wanted to do was put his head down on the table and rest. He skipped over the urge to vomit or talk to random strangers incoherently. A popular behavior at this state of alcohol consumption, from what he'd seen. Instead, he had skyrocketed right to the pass out stage.

He didn't care about appearances or paying attention to his surroundings. Though, he did manage to wonder just what that guy was staring at over there. Invading his personal space, instead of minding his own business. In fact, he had half a mind to yell out and give him a piece of his mind, until he stumbled. Or rather, they both stumbled, because it was just his reflection in a mirror.

The great and powerful Ash, risen from his own ashes, hadn't recognized his own face staring back at him in the distance. How appropriate.

He ran a hand over his face and head, and saw his reflection do the same. It was a little odd, not having all that hair and the long beard. The Moses look wasn't as popular as it once was, so he had opted for clean shaven and bald.

He went to place his head on the table and fell straight to the floor instead, which was even better and more comfortable. It didn't matter. Nothing mattered anymore.

WHEN ASH AWOKE, HE WAS SPRAWLED OUT ON THE FLOOR, COVERED in the smell of wine and beer. A big hulking shape of a man was conveniently manhandling him back upright. There was an unmistakable smell of rotten that made him want to vomit.

Despite being almost a full six feet tall, this thing was still carrying him like a child. It had to be eight feet itself, easily. Lumbering about with a massive bulk of super steroid-like—Frankenstein. A Frankenstein monster was dragging him through a bar.

This had to be another one of his crazy dreams. Where else would he find a green pallored, dazed automaton, with mindless eyes, but no bolts in the neck that he could see? At least somebody had put clothes on it, though he half expected purple pants instead of the stretch jeans and barely fitting green shirt.

There was a pounding and stabbing pain at the back of his head, that he'd initially thought was just Frankenstein stomping around. Then he heard some screaming and commotion, but he couldn't get a good look, because Frankenstein was blatantly ignoring any attempts he made to stand on his own legs and walk. Still disoriented, trying to figure out if people had hangovers in dreams, and wondering what would happen if he tangled up Frankenstein's legs somehow, Ash was distracted even further.

Somehow, he had taken flight, being hurled some forty feet through the air, as everything slowed to a crawl. Time out.

He was covering some serious distance, trying to right himself to see where he was going. But at the same time, the alcohol told him it was all just a very vivid and realistic dream, that made him float slowly forward.

He caught the image of his own reflection again, right before it shattered, raining broken glass all around him. His body careened heavily off a wall, to fall to the floor, with some bottles, liquids, and other fine accoutrements as company.

Everything returned to normal speed. Time in.

The pain he felt told him that everything was, in fact, real. A quick check reported back no broken bones, though his body did just want to lie there in shock and bleed a little. He needed to pull himself together before Frankenstein came over to check on him.

He must have been behind a bar, because he looked up in time to see two girls hop over it to join him. One of them was a blonde with blue eyes and the other had brown eyes with wavy brown hair. They were both wearing the same all black outfits. With long sleeve shirts and pants. Either could have been in a fashion magazine.

Each one had a knife in her hand. Both sets of pretty eyes, with matching murderous looks, that danced gleefully like little candle flames.

Ash began to panic.

He ran out of room and had nowhere to back up. So, he tried climbing over the bar with his back to his two hosts, but nothing was working. His slow-moving brain and slow-moving body just didn't have the whole coordination thing going.

This was it then. Payback for all the people he'd killed.

Everything went red.

THE NEXT THING HE KNEW, HE WAS STANDING OVER HIS WOULD-BE assailants. Both of them were crumpled to the ground. He leaned in over one of the girls (a blonde, where the other was brunette), opened his mouth, and bit into her neck.

That first drop that touched his tongue, sent a great thrill that ran from the top of his head to the tips of his toes. It was the most delicious drink ever. Far better than the wine or the beer.

Every fiber of his being drank her in like a sponge. It was her blood, now coursing through his veins, and it was exhilarating. Had he ever really been alive before this moment?

When she was dry, he bit into the front of her throat, crushing it to a pulp. Then he snapped her spine.

He moved to the brunette and drank her in like a starving victim of famine. When she ran dry, he snapped her neck, so that her head hung down her back, with vacant eyes staring behind her. He forgot about her.

His light brown eyes had a reddish tint to them, that receded back to normal in a mirror. Sharp canines had protruded from his upper and lower teeth, and these too were even now returning to normal. He licked some errant blood from his lips and turned, to have to suddenly brace himself up against the bar.

A dull fire had begun to course through him, burning through his haze, and bringing clarity to his thoughts. It made him pant and break out into a cold sweat, and the alcohol invigorated right out of his system. The pain brought him to his knees.

His mind's eye changed from apathy, to rage and indignation. His cold darkness, to the white-hot fires of the sun.

Ash screamed from the core of his being.

A nova exploded.

CHAPTER 6
BAR FIGHT

"Sometimes I marvel at the things you are allowed to get away with," said a pretty woman with wavy dark curls and light brown eyes. She wore an all-black outfit with matching boots, and had a way about her that suggested she had been drinking heavily.

"Should I not inform our Queen of your debauchery then?" another woman responded. This one wore the same outfit but had blonde hair, and green eyes the color of emeralds, that sparkled from across the room. There was a collar around her neck with a chain dangling from the front of it.

"You impertinent cow! How dare you?"

"Tonight, I dare, and more," said the blonde, turning her back and walking away.

The brown eyed woman grabbed the chain and pulled on it hard to bring the blonde to heel. "This disrespect will end right here and now," she said.

Ash watched the display in silence. Not quite sure how he got there. The last thing he remembered was feeling very sleepy after drinking too much.

The blonde slave girl turned out to be a troublemaker. She managed to whirl her slave chain overhead, master in tow, and slam that brunette's face into a wall. Her captor must have let go because the chain was then further used as a weapon, catching at least two people in the face to full effect.

Something slammed into Ash that knocked him into a nearby wall. It was the smell that gave away his attacker. It was Frankenstein from his dream. There couldn't be two hulking behemoths running around that smelled that bad. At least he hoped not. The one that backed away to purvey its handiwork looked exactly how he remembered.

Shaking off the stupor the impact had lulled him into, his eyes were fast enough to register milk-white skin, and eyes the color of green emeralds, in a blur of motion.

"After her!" yelled a woman's voice.

It looked like the master had gotten back into the flow of things again, having pulled her face out of the sheet rock. True to form, the minions began to coalesce into a fighting force that was now aimed after the escapee.

This was the part where Ash decided to get noticed in a positive light, contrary to his latest dance with Frankenstein. It was his turn to be a blur of motion and cause some damage.

He fancied it a sort of dominos game, as he slammed head-first, into the front of the bad guy conga line that had developed. Not pretty, but effective. It would buy slave girl some time to get away. The resulting, getting swarmed over and beat, was something he hadn't quite thought out.

Swiftly drowning in a sea of bodies, it wouldn't be long before the weight of their numbers crushed the air from his lungs.

"The within, without," he said with the authority of command. The words carried the demand that could not be refused. Snapping his fingers, a moment later sent out the concussive force of a grenade. Bodies went flying into walls, furniture, and each other.

Facedown and totally vulnerable, Ash could make out the sounds of a few of his would-be assailants getting themselves together and reorienting to their surroundings. Accompanied by groaning and the moving of what must be broken furniture.

There was nothing that he could do.

First there was the sound of approaching footfalls, then a severe shooting pain ripped a scream of agony from his lips. The pressure of weight and the accompanying shock that radiated through his body, told him his left arm was broken.

The source of his torment flipped him over. The first kick to his face brought his awareness to focus briefly, so that he was able to make out what his attacker looked like. The second kick to his face broke his nose and made him wonder how long he would be able to last.

Cruel, hateful eyes of a spoiled child sat in a scarred-up face, that reminded Ash of a wild dog. Devoid of anything short of self-hate, and readily able to share that hate with anything weak enough to have the lower hand.

"Come here," the man said, and proceeded to drag Ash's body. He had turned his back and thought there was nothing to worry about. He was correct in that assumption.

Grabbing a fistful of hair, Ash smashed the man's face into a nearby wall, so hard that he heard bones break and felt the life seep from him. When another person took hold of him, to aid their comrade-in-arms, the blond man's eyes were gouged out, killing him.

Ash took the limp body and slammed it into another. This one a woman. Sending both clear across the room.

He took a seat next to a mirror to fix his broken nose, which healed instantly. His body was repairing itself at an alarming rate. Even his arm was good as new.

He got back to his feet and ran towards the steps, after the slave girl, but stopped dead in his tracks.

Frankenstein had found him again. It took a grab at air, where Ash had just been standing. It wasn't very forthcoming with what it wanted, so Ash nailed it. Slamming his fist against its face as hard as he could. There was a loud crack, and the great towering mass jerked, went limp, and crumpled to the floor.

The slave girl had smashed one of the windows open with a bar stool, and was now working her way onto the metal grating. She stopped briefly when she saw him approach. Her face wary. For his part, he was absolutely star struck. The shape of her face with its high cheekbones, gold hair the color of the sun itself, and her green eyes, like a tropical paradise.

"Behind you!" she yelled.

Ash shook himself out of his reverie, and spun around just in time to see Frankenstein running right for him. As nimble as a cat, Ash slipped around the behemoth and assumed the tactic it had planned for him; putting everything he had into shoving the creature along the path it had chosen.

He let out a loud yell and summoned up whatever strength he could muster. The creature went through an unbroken window, through the metal grating behind it, onto the street, and into a waiting parked car.

Crashing into the tan sedan got the alarm started, but Ash wasn't done yet. He set to work pummeling Frankenstein. When it finally stopped putting up a fight, he hit it two more times for good measure, and decided to get moving in case it still got up.

Separating himself from his opponent, he scanned the area to get his bearings. The woman was already gone.

It was early enough in the morning, that the sun had yet to peek over the horizon. The town was still asleep in this part of Monticello, New York. He figured the glimpse of motion caught four blocks down, probably marked where he needed to be. It had to be them.

He sprinted the distance and saw a lone straggler climbing up a fire escape. The buildings in this neighborhood were small by New York City standards, where he was from. This one, maybe ten stories max, with an exterior the color of brick. The metal ladder was still locked in its safety position, far above the ground, but he made the grab for it and started climbing.

When he reached the top, he had just enough time to glimpse what was going on a couple of rooftops over, before somebody grabbed him and lifted him right off the ladder. It was a smiling woman. This one blonde with hazel eyes, and a small mole under one of them. They were face to face, with his body dangling off the rooftop.

"What have we here, a little birdie?" she said.

"What?" he asked and was promptly released.

Time slowed.

～

HE WONDERED IF HE'D SURVIVE LONG ENOUGH TO HEAL THE damage, or just outright die.

～

TIME RESUMED.

The twit hadn't tossed him clear of the fire escape, because his left leg banged into metal, turning his body headfirst. His shin hurt a great deal, and he hoped it wasn't broken. He tried to shut the pain out and focus.

Quickly, he grabbed about two landings down, and voila, no red splotch on the pavement. Just pain and anger, and the inevitable jarring of muscle, sinew, and tendon.

A very useful memory was kind enough to surface that almost made the whole thing worth it. Ash willed it and found that he could float upwards like a kite on a gentle breeze.

Once up top, a combination of floating and running--rooftop to rooftop--and he had landed exactly where he wanted to be.

Quietly, he snuck up behind a familiar silhouette.

He didn't speak. He didn't posture. Nothing. He grabbed her ponytail from behind with both hands.

A curt "Hello," was followed by a spinning-hurl, and an equally curt "Goodbye," and his quarry screamed down the side of the building.

She wasn't the one he was there to save. He'd already spotted his fair damsel off in the distance of a neighboring rooftop.

A mob of attackers kept pressing towards her, but they weren't making any headway. Every so often one member would get too close, get hurt by the damsel, and have to pull back. No matter how brutal she was, sooner or later she'd run out of endurance and be at their mercy.

That was one outcome.

He had always been partial to heroes stepping in to save the day. With that thought in mind, he ran straight at the mob from behind, and leapt high into the air. Turning so that he'd face the bad guys, with his back to the damsel.

"I'm here to help you," he told the damsel upon landing, without taking his eyes off the opposition.

She didn't respond, but he didn't need her to. He grabbed a nearby thug by the face, smashed the back of his skull into the face of another and kicked some other fool in the nuts.

"We're both going to die now," she said. "You should have stayed away."

There were an awful lot of them, and they were stronger by far than they had any right to be. It would only take a single lucky shot to hurt her.

"I don't have time for this," he announced. A quick wave of his hand summoned a temporary invisible barrier.

Then he turned, scooped the woman up in his arms, and jumped off the roof.

CHAPTER 7
THE QUEEN

Technology was the hub that tied humanity together and created a global community where you could find out what your neighbor; a half world away, was up to. The information traveled very fast and kept everyone somewhat accountable to everyone else, despite the solidarity of countrymen. Things just weren't what they used to be.

Secrets were easier to keep back in the past. Everyone knew how to mind their own business and respected the sanctity of other people's problems. At least to the extent that distant countries knew better than to meddle in foreign affairs.

Yes, those days were gone, but there were still remnants. Mere dust compared to what once was. All you had to do was know where to look. Some unknown longitude, and an unknown latitude. Off the coast of secret waters.

There was nothing out of the ordinary about the sands. Waves caressed the shores and inhabitants tended the crops, fished at sea, and saw to any number of tropical island duties. On the surface.

You had to take a closer look. In your mind's eye, a time of secret societies with agendas, intrigue, and politics. How would such a thing be today?

A very deep look and you would realize hidden catacombs beneath this lush paradise, with its exotic flowers, and rich ocean breeze. Secret caves filled with a secret society, lost to the world, but still very much alive. Look beneath the surface to see the truth:

THE QUEEN PACED HER THRONE ROOM, PULLING HER THOUGHTS together. All the pieces were in place and the game was progressing quite satisfactorily.

She was cold and calculating. She would sacrifice and destroy every piece on the board to achieve her aims. There would be no tolerance for anyone veering off the path she had set in motion.

So many years of careful planning and timeless dedication had already gone into her ultimate destiny. With the finish line nearly in sight, her power base was about to be etched in stone and multiplied beyond comprehension. This was the home stretch.

Calm, cool, and collected. Composure, poise, and elegance. Command, power, and finality. Devastating, determined, and absolute. She continued to embody these attributes and more and they would serve her well, no matter what. Focus. Breath deep. Collect yourself.

Her self-affirmations complete, the Queen sat on her throne and assumed the character that all her subjects feared and admired. She possessed a relaxed, almost carefree demeanor with eyes of ice, that would kill you where you stand, lay, or sit. Without regret or hesitation. Hers were the eyes of death.

"Bring in the next offender," she ordered.

There was no emotion. Her voice was as cold as her eyes. Her words were law, absolute and without question, on punishment to be determined by the self-same Queen. No matter the decree, it would be carried out. Period.

The summary of incident droned on. There was something about this one she didn't like. Those damn shifty eyes made her ill, and she had already decided the sentence on that alone, before the testimony. It was just a formality, after all. The poor soul was dead the moment he had looked at her with those damnable eyes. He should have kept them to the ground. Now his head would roll on it.

"Execute him," she ordered, cutting the orator off in mid-sentence.

The snapping of her fingers brought the two guards, who summarily chained the victim up and beheaded him with a large axe; amidst the usual protestations, pleading and inane blather.

The Queen rolled her shale-colored eyes in boredom and called for the next victim. This one would be allowed to live because he was quite pretty. Something about murder or some such.

"Absolved," she ordered, and waved her hand dismissively for a third victim to enter.

Disloyalty to the throne was the next charge. Unforgivable and punishable by impalement through the chest with a spear, so ordered by the Queen.

And so, the morning droned on in monotony, with just enough momentum to kindle her appetite for breakfast. The morning meal, as with all meals, was naturally held in her private chambers. She held the same feigned interest for her food, as she had for this morning's proceeds—half-heartedly playing with a young strapping youth. He must have been about sixteen or so, and she drained the life out of him in a handful of minutes. She rang her hand bell, to signal that the corpse was to be collected.

Absently blotting at splotches of blood from the morning meal, she made way to the study to deal with the day's political paperwork. More tedium, ad nauseam, that she really couldn't even remember when it was done. One minute it started, and one minute it was over, with everything else in-between absent.

By the end, it took almost all her effort to remove the servants in a cordial fashion, so depleted was her patience for the drudgery of government. When she was completely alone again, she again took up pacing, lost in thoughts that once again assumed the forefront of consideration.

How much longer did she have to wait? Everything was coming into focus. The years of planning were beginning to bear fruits that would soon ripen. She could almost taste her great victory, and it was positively driving her mad with desire.

Chanovalle Remseldorne, Queen of the Realm, wanted what was rightfully hers. Right this instant and without further hindrance. Why did she have to wait a moment longer? What was the delay?

The fury built inside her and swelled; greater and greater, until she could contain it no longer. Everything went red as she reached critical mass and screamed out.

As loud and long as she could, until she ran out of breath and her throat threatened to lose its voice. Then she took out her fury on the room, upending furniture and smashing anything with glass. Beautifully mirrored armoires, hope chests, vanity mirrors, a desk with gold inlay, a collection of little glass globes with artwork inside, even the fine paintings on the walls; everything was smashed and torn asunder until nothing survived the onslaught. Nothing survived. Nothing.

As her temper cooled, Chanovalle saw that she was almost as disheveled as whatever was left of the room. A broken remnant of a mirror showed long black curls in disarray atop her head. Her pointy fangs had elongated in response to her outburst; a typical vampire reaction. But most alarmingly, further inspection revealed an errant breast that had gone astray of a low-cut bodice.

Naturally, her beauty allowed a certain amount of leeway as to what look she could pull off, but she doubted that even she could assume this one (her ripped and torn blue silk dress was not serviceable in the least). Cold hard eyes that did not fit her stunning looks, flared the last vestige of a now-subsided anger.

Looking around one last time to survey her handiwork, the Queen finessed her look as best she could, made for the door, and smiled. A softer set of obsidian-like, piercing cold eyes, met the genuine look of satisfaction that danced on her face.

It was good to vent occasionally, to relieve the stress. It allowed a release that could not be found in mere opulence. As Queen though, she was afforded whatever luxury she dared, and when she returned to this room tomorrow, there would be new furniture to replace what she had destroyed.

The servants would just assume that she had not liked the décor. No one would know that she had lost her cool, so to speak, as no one knew the nature of her current plan. Nor could they and be allowed to live.

Queen Chanovalle headed to her bed chambers. The outburst had taken its toll and she wanted a nap. Her plotting would resume in the morning when she was fresh. After all, she already had The Child of Destiny in her possession. The rest was just a matter of time.

CHAPTER 8

A BIRD IN THE HAND

"What do you mean she is gone?!? Where did she go? She did not just disappear!" yelled Azure, simultaneously punching Zirus in the chest.

How could they let this happen? Didn't they understand? Azure took a deep breath and tried to compose herself.

"Find her. Track her. Do whatever it takes. Whatever! Whatever it is that you must do to have the Queen's prized slave in front of me. Alive and in one piece," she punctuated her frustrations on Zirus's chest once more. "All are dismissed and on the hunt. Now!"

Azure made it a point to glare at her sister Margerie, before she went off to join the others. She had delegated responsibility of the slave to her sister, so any errors ultimately fell on her own shoulders. The sheer magnitude of it all floored her and had her sicking up.

Azure arranged her brown curly hair tied atop her head, as she emptied the contents of her stomach. She took a deep breath and let the night's breeze clear her thoughts. She had to stay calm and think things through. Anger was not the solution.

Calm and thoughtful. Relaxed and focused. Calm.

All accounts corroborated that the slave had been thrown off the building by its would-be rescuer. A last effort at final defiance.

The problem was that there was no sign of them. Even as far as the dogs were concerned, there was nothing.

The Queen would have a fit and everyone would die. There were no excuses.

Find the slave and live. That was the axiom she had handed out with the implied "and keep looking until you do" and that was what she held onto herself.

Azure had wandered into a laundromat, according to the signs. It smelled of soap and clothing and it was warmer than outside. Here, she was able to clean herself up and acquire an outfit to disguise her appearance. The woman who donated to her cause was simply rendered unconscious, instead of killed. No time for even the simple pleasures.

She was in the field on a mission and had to conduct herself as such. Azure had ultimately blamed her own lax attitude for the present predicament, and was fast on the road to making amends.

The business was the hunt. Each piece of it. Down to the naked woman lying before her.

Azure had stripped the victim completely and donned every article. This one was blonde and tan-skinned from over-exposure to the sun, where Azure had hair of night and sky-blue eyes; with very pale skin, shy of the sun.

Quite different, but Azure had judged correctly, in that they possessed a similar frame. How fortuitous. With this streak of luck, she would have the Queen's slave back in her custody in no time at all.

"Let's see you pull your little disappearing act this time," she told the naked body.

FREDDY WALKED INTO THE KITCHEN, ABSENTLY RUBBING AT HIS belly. Bending over, he peeked through the little window in the oven door. It looked like Martha was making meatloaf again. He didn't mind. She made the best meatloaf he ever tasted. He smiled as he stood up, satisfied that tonight was going so well.

She'd gone to the store. Probably to get some potatoes, to mash them up to go with the meatloaf. She would put garlic in both. It was one of his favorite dishes.

Maybe she'd let him have a beer tonight too. That would be great.

Making his way into the living room; Freddy sat in his favorite chair, turned the fifty-inch LCD television on, and began flipping through the channels until he found something of interest:

BILL PARSONS: "IN WORLD NEWS TODAY, PEACE TALKS RESUME, AS United Nations delegates continue with negotiations, in connection with the growing crisis in Western Africa. Thomas Shear has more on the story. Thomas?"

Thomas Shear: "Thanks, Bill. I'm here in Paris, France, where once again the United Nations is trying to make a difference in this world that we live in. This time members are addressing representatives in the various West African countries, that are being affected by civil unrest, in connection with diamond mines in Sierra Leone. Without going too much into detail at the moment, it is the hope of the United Nations that through these talks, an agreement can be reached to resolve things peacefully. I had the opportunity to briefly speak to Executive Representative Alexander Edwards, of the United Nations Peace Building Commission, moments ago."

Alexander Edwards, U.N. Representative (PBC): "Any time that you are faced with a historical tragedy such as this one (where innocent civilians have lost life and limb), I think that it is imperative to step in and lend a hand if you can. To make sure that something like this never happens again.

"I think I speak on behalf of my fellow United Nations members, when I say that we're not going to rest until the war and chaos stops. We are doing everything that we can, to put an end to these horrible— horrible things. And it is our hope, that future generations will be able to look upon these things, as a lesson to be learned, rather than a continued part of their lives. Thank you."

Thomas Shear: "There you have it, Bill. Of course, Mr. Edwards is referring to efforts by the UN PBC to put an end to the atrocities (that you've probably already heard of), perpetrated by the aggressive factions in that region.

"An area whose notoriety precedes it. Where innocent civilians—those lucky enough to survive—have had their arms chopped off with machetes. Places like Sierra Leone, Burundi, Guinea-Bissau, and Central African Republic; also known as CAR. Just to give you an idea of why these talks are so important. Back to you, Bill."

Bill Parsons: "Thank you, Tom. Please stay tuned, as we hope to keep you updated on the situation as it develops. And now, the weather, with Weather Anchor Melanie Anders. Melanie?"

Melanie Anders: "Thank you, Bill. It looks like we're going to be in for some unusual weather, as a tropical front seems to have moved into the area, to mix in with the colder winds that are here already. What this means for you at home, is that we're in for a wind advisory; with winds up to fifty miles per hour. Please stay tuned later this evening for an update."

"Did she go back through the gate?" asked Initiate Pepper.

"Yeah, she prolly went through the gate," chimed in Captain Zephyr. "That would explain how we lost her scent and everything."

"So, a slave breaks free," added Major Gordon. "Lets all hell loose. All because she is homesick? I don't buy it."

"Neither do I," agreed Azure. After scouring the immediate area in a fruitless endeavor, she had called together a meeting with her top people. Including her, that made ten altogether. Maybe cooler heads would prevail, where her own blind indignation had not. "Based on what happened," she continued. "It was a definite break for freedom, hands down. There is no way she went back after all that."

"So, where did she go, then?" asked Initiate Fann, shrugging her shoulders.

"Not around here, or we would smell her," said the Major.

"On this, we agree," offered Magistrate Margaret, still humbled by an earlier private speech, where Azure had put her in her place for losing the slave in the first place.

"So, she just disappeared without a trace, then?" asked Specialist Vixl with a smile.

"Your point?" asked Initiate Lenna.

"Yes, what is your point, exactly?" Initiate Pepper asked.

"My point is," exclaimed Specialist Vixl. "That I do not understand what we are doing right now. We know nothing! We have—nothing! I don't know how you can all be so calm about all this."

"We are calm, Specialist Vixl," said Major Gordon, tapping a finger on a nearby table. "Because we have no choice. Precisely why, we are going to find the slave."

"There is always the alternative," Azure offered, with a note of disgust in her voice. She was referring to the inevitable death sentence from the Queen. The increased tension in the room told her that everyone knew exactly what she was talking about. "No? Not up for that, huh? Then let us continue and stop wasting time.

"The question is this: You are a slave. You get free. Where do you go?"

"Far from here," said Initiate Fanna. "If it were me, I would go to the city. It is the closest place to go to have a good time."

"And best of all," added Initiate Lenna, walking up to stand beside Fanna. "There are so many people, you would be a needle in a haystack."

"Great," blurted out Specialist Vixl, folding his arms across his chest.

Everyone waited in silence for her decision. Azure had the final word. "I think it's our best move," she said. "Let's assign some tasks. Major Gordon?"

"Thank you, Commander," said Major Gordon, raising his voice confidently, now that he had a plan to create. "The way I see it," he began. "we should focus on Manhattan. It is the city's hub. Frankly, I do not think she will be able to resist it. We should coordinate our efforts with that in mind.

"I have a map here," he said, and spread it out on the floor in front of him, so that everyone could see it. "I think we can easily patrol on foot and in a couple of vehicles. We can commandeer them either here, or on the site."

"I'm opting for a vehicle for what is left of my team, since there are only two of us," said Captain Zephyr quickly.

"Done," Azure agreed. She acknowledged the Captain's nod of respect with one of her own and waited for Major Gordon to continue his speech.

"We will set up our squads, so that all key areas are constantly patrolled and monitored, with random factors thrown in. Brace yourselves people. We are digging in on this one. Morning and night." He ran his hand over his good eye before continuing. "We will refine it in route and be ready to go on site. Comments?"

"Profile?" asked Specialist Vixl.

"Low," responded Azure. "We do not want her to see us coming and run off somewhere else." She paused for effect and then she said, "If that happens, we are all as good as dead."

"Remember people," offered Major Gordon, while picking the map up off the floor, "how you patrol is up to your team leader. That is going to be everyone here. Whichever one of you spots her, call for backup, and then handle the situation appropriately. Bear in mind, our Commander probably will not look favorably on someone who lets the slave get away, a second time. Comments?"

"I wish we could kill her," sulked Vixl, still with folded arms, leaning up against a nearby wall.

"No matter what you think you know about the incident," warned Azure. "whether you were there or not—I myself was not—I do not want any slacking. No under estimation. No posturing. Save it for another time.

"Search and retrieve, people. Nothing else. Do I make myself clear?"

"Yes, Commander!" everyone shouted in unison.

∾

I CAN'T BELIEVE IT ACTUALLY WORKED, HE THOUGHT. THEY BOTH made it. For the first time, Ash felt like he was on the winning side.

"I still do not understand," said his female guest. She sat cross-legged on his living room floor, staring down at it. Maybe she was in shock. It wasn't every day that you won your freedom.

"What don't you understand?" asked Ash, looking at the top of her head. He had opted to stay standing.

"What happened?"

"Are you talking about a step-by-step instant replay, or the fact that I saved you?"

"I know that you saved me, but I do not understand how," she told the floor.

This was not how he had pictured the aftermath of his daring rescue, at all. Maybe a hug would have been in order. At least a thank you. Everybody got at least that much, didn't they?

If the place were bigger than a studio, he would have stormed off into another room. As it was, he had half a mind to just walk out and leave her alone. Maybe when he came back, she'd stop acting so weird.

"We got away. Isn't that all that matters?" he asked.

"We should both be dead," she said.

"But we're not," he said. "You'd think you'd be happier about that, instead of being all mopey."

"Mopey? What does that mean?"

"Down in the dumps. It's like sad, I guess. Not exactly the way you're supposed to act when you get away from the bad guys."

She paused for a moment. This time she was looking at Ash when she said, "Thank you for your help. Now, where are we and what do you want from me?"

Ash's heart sank. Did she want to leave already?

"You are welcome," he said. "I still don't know anything about you, or what was going on back there. Why don't we start with that?"

She got up and walked around examining the little space, as if he didn't say anything. It was a studio apartment. All the amenities were there. Small kitchen, bathroom with shower, and living space. The cupboards and closets were empty and so was the refrigerator, because of his unusual diet. It was all painted white because he hadn't gotten around to adding any color, and there was a minimal amount of furniture.

It didn't take her too long to turn back to face him.

"My name is Kayala," she said, by way of introduction. "I come from a foreign land you will not find on any of your maps. I am not sure how I came to be in your lands, as many things are secret to me." She broke eye contact and began fiddling with the collar around her neck before continuing.

"I am what you would probably consider a slave, but I am treated more like a pet. When I came here, I decided I would be free, once I saw that there was someplace else to go.

"The reason everyone was after me is because I belong to the Queen. I am her pet. And to lose me, will probably cause some people to die," she paused and took a deep breath. Closing her eyes. Then she said, "I am very tired and would sleep if that is acceptable."

"Yes, of course. Please. The bed's over there in the corner," he said, indicating the wall behind her with a nod of his head. "Let me see if I can find some clean sheets."

He didn't really need sleep himself, at this point, so he just posted up at a wall, around a corner from the bed area. He didn't tell her she was the only person he'd ever had over to visit. The closest thing he'd ever had to a friend.

KAYALA AWOKE TO FIND THAT HER DREAM WAS A REALITY. SHE HAD finally escaped her captors and was free to follow her own whims. It was a step in the right direction.

She lay comfortably in a bed. Not caged and chained to the wall as usual.

The only remnants of her old life were the collar around her neck; attached to a loose chain, and the leather army uniform that she wore. She'd be rid of them the first chance she got.

Her unknown benefactor was beyond her sight, keeping watch. He was the other side of what she knew. Compelled to help others instead of torturing them for pleasure.

It was good to be able to let her guard down. It made her comfortable enough to fall back to sleep.

Everything was going to work out great. She was home free.

A DARK TUNNEL IN THE DEPTHS OF THE WORLD...

Water beating everything down at night in a storm. Hard overwhelming rain. All the endless water...

Burning. Scorching. The sun burns through everything, turning it all to cinders—to ash...

So cold and wet. Freezing. So cold it burns—all the ice and snow...

Winds of gale-force destroy everything and break the world...

A lone bird shudders...

Another dream. He could tell, because it was not the first time he had seen this one. He must have fallen asleep after all. Only, it was supposed to stop here. This time there was more to it.

The view went back to the bird, which was strangely calm now. Was it the calm before the storm?

The view pulled back to reveal the bird perched atop a tree branch.

The branch snaps and falls to the ground. The bird, perched the whole time, like it was glued to the spot. On the ground, a shadow covers the bird, and the view pulls back to reveal a young girl.

Freckles. Blonde hair. Emerald eyes. Kayala?

How'd she get into his dream? Why? Am—

He remembered a long time ago. How long, he was not sure, but it was happening again. He was happening again.

—CLANG— STEEL ON STEEL. —CLANG—

The familiar sounds of battle. Shouting. Screaming. Orders.

The familiar smells of battle. Fear. Sweat. Death.

Loss mingled with victory. The battlefield.

Where will he end up? On which side of the rope?

THE OPPONENT IS FIERCE AND WELL TRAINED. WE FIGHT AND I SEEM TO win, but I was deceived. He had been toying with me.

He gets stronger and feral, and my own skills are put to a test of new measure. It is all I can do to fend him off.

The ground begins to shake, or I am weakening. I do not know.

The rocks open, and we continue our fight in a cavern. I feel everything seeping from me. My strength falters. My knees buckle. A big shake throws me at my opponent, or I hurl myself at him. I cannot discern the truth in the chaos.

The feral one bites me as I stab wildly with my sword and knife. I am lost... but the walls come down around us and I survive. To die? Not yet. I crawl out of a cave.

The feral one lies decapitated where we struggled. I think a rock fell on him or I hit him with one. Maybe both.

I am weak. I feel that I must be dying.

The world slips out from under me...and puts me on my horse. He carries me to safety, away from death.

The world slips out from under me.

HE AWOKE TO FIND HIMSELF PRONE ON THE GROUND. ON THE FLOOR of his current domicile. He was guarding Kayala, and they were safe. He had been dreaming.

He couldn't tell how long he had been out of it, but it was long enough for her to have left. Kayala was gone.

Some protector, he thought, as he stood up, making a last-ditch effort to look out the window. The street was empty, except for the gloss of a soft rain that fell from the sky. The sun shone through the clouds as much as it could, giving the appearance of evening, to the afternoon. Random cars were parked along the sidewalk as usual, in accordance with the parking sign on the block. The green metal, reminiscent of a flower stem, with the white and red at the top, the bud.

She was in his mind's eye. The emerald eyes with the fierce glow of determination. The golden hair, that was a beam of raw sunlight, spun into silk. The inviting curve of her hips. The athletic womanly musculature, that called out to him whenever she so much as shifted her weight.

The damsel in distress, with undercurrents of the knight. It was intoxicating.

Ash resumed his seat on the floor, against the wall where he had originally placed himself, and sighed. His eyes studying the material of his black sneakers, as if they held the secrets to the universe, and might reveal them at any second. It was either that or start crying.

"You are caught in the grip of madness, by a lone woman my friend." The silence of the room was the only answer.

CHAPTER 9
AZURE SKIES

S he sat atop one of a small collection of big rocks; laid out behind an outcropping of buildings, somewhere in New York City. Nothing mattered to her, as much as the little piece of mind that she was able to gather, away from the stresses that engulfed her entire existence.

Everything was set up and properly engaged. Her resources were broken up into small contingents, and those were further broken down into scouts, that were now scouring this city and the surrounding territories. The slave could not have gotten far, and Azure was going to find her, wherever she might be.

But these things did nothing to quell the frustration she felt, at not having found the Child of Destiny. There had been no positive reports. No leads. It was as if the slave had disappeared off the face of the world.

She could not call for reinforcements from home, because that would send out the message of a mistake on her part. That left her with what she had on hand. And what did that amount to?

Some approximately fifty soldiers at her command, with seven of them Initiated. Either good or bad, depending on how you looked at it. The liability of it being that, of course the Initiated would only be capable of venturing forth in the hours that the sun was set. They were, like herself, imbued with the nature of the Queen herself. As was the reward for worthiness to the Royal Highness.

Never allowed to bask in the light of the sun's rays forever more—but oh, so sweet that last part. Forever. And it was very real and very magical, that promise, aside even from the other gifts that came with it. Nothing in existence was guaranteed, but if you were cautious enough and did not bumble your way into stupidity—mainly as long as you kept yourself out of appreciable harm—then you would never die. Never grow old. Never know disease or illness. Who needed the sun, when the lack of it gave such gifts?

Worthiness imbued you with great speed, and strength, and increased senses. Along with enhanced reflexes, and enhanced durability. She had stumbled upon some of the popular books here in New York. They had touched on these very things, despite the erroneous material that was inevitable in such 'flights of fancy.'

Vampires are real, she thought to herself. And I'm one of them.

Her Queen had, in her great majesty, bestowed upon Azure these gifts of immortality and great power. They made her a creature beyond the ken of mortals. For that, she was eternally grateful.

Even so, she was far from omnipotent, and her great ruler was still as powerful in relation to her, as ever she was to a human. The Queen could still easily snuff out even Azure's existence, should the whim take her.

Maybe that was what truly caused these pangs of fear in her heart. It was one thing to lose your life, that in and of itself had no hold over her. But it was quite another to lose, in the blink of an eye, the promise of an eternal existence. Sooner snuff out the flames of the Gods eternal and pay no heed, so far removed from mortals was she and her kind.

No, Azure. Get a grip over yourself. You are doing the best that you can, and everything is going to work out. Do not give into melancholy thoughts. Hold true to your purpose and your resolve.

It seemed only yesterday she was permitted to speak to the Great Queen Chanovalle, undisputed ruler of the realm, entire. A privilege she received more than most, as Commander of the army, but she still cherished it with all her heart, whenever such a thing came about. And on that day, she had been received in the Queen's quarters, of all things. Something that had only happened once before. It was a momentous occasion that she would never forget.

SHE WAS JUST RETURNING FROM PUTTING THE TROOPS THROUGH their regular combat drills when Captain Vanzer came up, saluted, and relayed the message that she was to be received by the Queen in her personal quarters.

How unusual, she thought, and almost became worried, until she rationalized that everything was likely just fine. If she had in some way offended the Queen, then she would have simply been shackled and tried. If she was to gain some prestigious honor, that would be done on a grander scale than a meeting in the royal quarters. What could it be?

Ordinarily, she would have taken her time after the evening's training, but now she made sure she was clean and presentable, without her usual luxury of soaking in the bath. A quick scrub and a change into something presentable was sufficient. She opted for a simple black silk top, with black silk bottoms that covered both legs separately. She never wore clothing that constricted her movements and made her feel vulnerable. She didn't have any dresses or skirts in her wardrobe at all. She chose simple black sandals for her feet, the kind that went no further than the ankle.

Her hair she left natural. Her shoulder-length brown curls, hanging down to air dry, as she made her way through the hallway. She thought absently about how things in this part of the castle were typical of any such dwelling. High ceilings of at least twenty feet. The whole structure was made of stone bricks, with tapestries hanging on the walls depicting battles and mythological scenes of the Gods. As well as historical battles and legends. Red carpet rugs throughout, to enhance whatever warmth was created by fireplaces within, for cold nights when the stone cooled oh so fast.

Occasionally, she ran into one of her soldiers and returned a salute, or offered a polite nod, or word of greeting for what might pass for royalty in another setting. Here, everyone was obviously beneath the Queen, but there was of course some level of hierarchy amongst the denizens of the castle, depending on their station and their level of importance to the realm. As it happened, there were very few individuals who could even consider themselves Azure's equal, which was saying much, as she herself only answered to the Queen. Those individuals were usually not to be found within these walls, unless a Gathering of the High Ones was convened. They tended to have their own sub-kingdoms to run in other parts of the land, so the Queen didn't have to be everywhere at once, though she still was the sole administer of justice.

Eventually, Azure came to the royal quarters located some two floors below ground level, with the usual guards at the outer double doors. She noted that Captain Vanzer was present before he saluted her.

"Attention" he bellowed, causing the guards to assume the rigid stance.

"As you were," she said, returning his salute. She noted in passing that everything seemed to be acceptable. All the members of the Queen's guard were appropriately attired and neat, with the buckles and straps of their black leather uniforms appropriately fastened. The shine and gloss to whatever metal that showed, including what she could see of the shields at their backs, seemed adequate. The eyes of the four soldiers stayed locked forward as they should be. The Captain of course, was under no such constraint, as he had her leave.

When she passed through the double doors, there was another contingent of four soldiers guarding another set of identical heavy wooden double doors, at the end of a long corridor about the width of four men. She heard Captain Vanzer give the "At ease," command, even as this next set was brought to attention by the senior ranking member.

"As you were," she said, returning the second salute as well, as she continued down the hall. Beyond these doors there would be another single door, at the end of a two-man width corridor, but no guard. That single guardian would be found inside the Queen's apartments, precisely as Azure had arranged, being solely responsible for the Queen's security. At this end there was no door handle or otherwise apparent means of entry. The door could only be opened from within.

Three knocks and it was opened by another guard. A young one whose name she did not know. He had no scars and lacked the seasoned look to his eyes that she attributed to experience. Dirty blonde hair and blue eyes. Almost androgynous in his appearance. Too pretty.

"Wait outside," she ordered.

He didn't hesitate in the slightest, waiting only for her to enter the room herself before he took his leave, as she was expected, and everyone knew the Commander of the Army on sight.

"Yes sir," he said and closed the door behind him.

Azure locked the door before she made her way to the next one, some fifty feet away, that lead to the Queen's private quarters. She took a deep breath and exhaled as she made ready for whatever awaited her on the other side. There were no guards or locks at this point, but she knocked on the door regardless.

"Enter," came the royal voice.

"Your majesty," Azure said as she lowered her head in respect, with the door still in hand, half opened. Azure kept her eyes on the floor.

"Ah, Commander Azure. I've been expecting you. Please come in," said the Queen.

Only after being welcomed, did she take her gaze off the floor and close the door, taking steps to stand before the Queen. She noted in passing that the Queen was in a purple gown that was probably very expensive, covering her arms to her wrists, and almost concealing the purple shoes she wore on her feet. The royal crown sat atop her head in its gold splendor, with her hair the color of night, appropriately styled, as she sat resting on an exact replica of the throne that she had in the Grand Hall. She gave off the usual air of command, with her piercing dark gray eyes imbued with an immense power and hardness, though she herself seemed at ease on the surface.

"How can I be of assistance, my Queen?" she asked.

"Please, have a seat," was the response. The Queen gestured to a nearby chair off to her right.

Azure did as she was told, and the Queen slid off the throne and came to sit in a chair opposite her in an unusually intimate display. Sitting like this, she thought the Queen was probably about her same size but reminded herself that such things were irrelevant as indicators of true strength. They were both vampires, true. But the Queen was far older, and thus far more powerful.

The next moments will tell me if I have done something wrong or if I am still in her good graces, Azure thought.

"I have a task for you, that I think you are going to enjoy," said the Queen. "It is multi-faceted and something that I think is worthy of your talents. I am going to go over the basic parts, here with you now, and then we will get very specific at a later time."

Good graces, Azure thought, trying not to look visibly relieved.

"I need you to take a small contingent of men with you through the Shimmering Gate for a reconnaissance of sorts, to investigate certain coordinates that I have in mind. It is a bit of a pet project. A hobby, if you will. That is the main component. The next piece is a bit eccentric, on my part," the Queen paused for effect and then continued, as Azure nodded in agreement.

"I want you to take my slave Kayala with you," she said matter-of-factly.

"Your personal slave, Highness? "Azure asked, somewhat shocked. She almost did not believe her ears. "The prized one?"

"That is the one, exactly. Call it a whim," said the Queen. She smiled.

"I would be honored, your Majesty," said Azure.

She leaned over almost conspiratorially, and came very close to Azure's ear, almost in a whisper. "But there is, of course, a certain way that I want to go about it," she said.

"Yes?" asked Azure, somewhat nervous and confused. In all her memory, her Queen had never been this intimate.

"I want it done secretly. I do not want anyone to know that you have left until you are gone, and I certainly do not want anyone to suspect that Kayala is with you. In fact, when I make it known that you have gone, I still want the appearance that my slave is here, as normal. Further, I want you to assign someone other than yourself to watch over her while you are on the other side. I do not want Kayala to be seen as important while she is there."

The Queen sat back in her chair once more, before continuing. "I trust that you have someone in mind?" she asked.

"Yes—Yes, I do, Highness," replied Azure, still somewhat shocked. "Captain Margerie."

"Your sister? Yes. She will do nicely," said the Queen, shaking her head in agreement. "You have my leave, Commander."

Dismissed, Azure got up from her seat, lowered her head respectfully, and made for the door.

"One last thing, Commander," said the Queen.

Azure turned her entire body to face where the Queen still sat, at that unusually intimate place.

"While you are away, I want my guards doubled. And I want them on high alert," she ordered. "That is all"

"As you wish," responded Azure. She made for the door, and bowed her head before leaving, with the respectful "Majesty."

THAT WAS OVER TWO WEEKS AGO. THAT LEFT THREE WEEKS TO FIND Kayala. Maybe four.

Not for the first time, Azure caught herself wondering if the whole thing was a test. Did it even matter? The result would be the same, if she couldn't turn this thing around. Death for failure.

Azure rubbed her hands together briskly and slid off the rock. It was getting cold. She picked a direction and started walking so that she could warm up a bit. Hopefully, her army was having some luck.

After a week of searching for Kayala, Ash realized he probably wasn't going to see her again. "Idiot."

She was wearing a leash and collar, the first time he saw her, for crying out loud. Why bother with his boring ass, when she could be running around enjoying her newfound freedom?

He had a dream about her last night. It had seemed so real. Made him think she was his destiny.

His brain was so dumb sometimes.

Naturally, there had been other women, but this one was different. This one confused him the most.

On the one hand, there was a 'hunger' where he wanted to hold Kayala in his arms, like he had on the rooftop. On the other hand, there was a different 'hunger.' The one where he couldn't stop feeding on people.

Up until now, he'd been able to stop gambling with women's lives. No. That wasn't the truth. While he'd stayed away from women that he wanted to be intimate with, he hadn't been able to stop killing, when he got too hungry.

He wanted friends. He wanted a girlfriend. What was wrong with that?

It was hard to think straight when he was so lonely.

Maybe she was better off without him.

A few days later, Ash started looking into his past again. It was the only way he could distract his thoughts from Kayala. Despite technically having no clue what he was doing or where to start, like all super sleuths before him, he took a guess and ended up in the library.

Shelves upon shelves of books, collectively sat on a bookcase. Many of these bookcases, lined the floors of the library, creating corridors and passages of knowledge.

He went through it all. Even fiction, as there were often grains of truth in legends and folklore. He perused anything that caught his attention, hoping to stumble onto his needle in a haystack.

Later still, Ash journeyed all over the city, researching every location that came to mind. Newspaper stands, bookstores, college libraries, museums, and art exhibits.

Eventually, he ventured into an old bookstore that showed potential, in a book entitled 'Theocracy, Runes, & Stories'. The book alone might be meaningless, but over the course of his research, he had uncovered other texts that corroborated the same information. They pointed to a place called Castle Hill, Delaware.

A couple of tour pamphlets, some food and water, some maps and such, and he was on his motorcycle headed for a bit of a scavenger hunt. The fresh air, the wind, and the open road blurring past invigorated his spirit. He was a lone adventurer out on the road of mystery. Clad in a helmet, goggles, leather jacket and gloves, with jeans and leather boots. He soared on his metal steed towards justice, and truth, and all things good and hearty. Just like a Knight of the Roundtable on a quest.

Out on the open road of the I-95 South, there wasn't much to do, other than look at the sky and the trees racing by. His thoughts naturally went back over what had happened in his life. Was he a vampire? Something vampire-like? Worse?

Books he'd read so far (mainly fantasy fiction), mentioned a blood lust, fatal allergy to sunlight, and super-human strength. He preferred the night a bit, but the sun didn't bother him at all. Holy ground, another staple in the stories on vampire weaknesses, didn't bother him either.

When there was a full moon, he didn't change into anything or feel the need to howl, so he guessed werewolf was off the list as well. He still killed people. What did that?

Something water didn't hurt. Or holy water, for that matter. Or silver, or gold, or garlic. Something that didn't have any of the weaknesses he had read about at all, really.

And what about his memories? What if when they finally returned, he turned into a totally different person?

It didn't take long to reach Delaware. Three hours or so.

Everything was peaceful and quiet, without the hustle and bustle that he had become accustomed to in the city. If there were any tall buildings, they were someplace else. Here, there were a lot of trees, nature, and quiet.

He pulled off the main highway, into a rest stop to stretch his legs and give his body a respite from the long ride. It was around two in the morning, so it was easy to get a spot right near the front, where the main food court was. He didn't pay attention to the other patrons inside, except for a glance to see if any of them looked interesting. They didn't.

Everyone he saw, was determined to dress and cut their hair as if they were stuck in the 1980's. Here were people that not only weren't concerned about staying current in their sense of fashion, but they were actually almost on the verge of a thirty-year fashion deficit.

After a quick scouting of the area and acquiring a hotel room, he was ready for a more hands-on approach. Climbing a mountain top.

'To discover the treasure within, only a journey to heaven would suffice,' or so the story went. An old Army and Navy surplus store provided the trinkets he needed. Then, all he needed was sunrise. It was still too dark outside to do anything quite so dangerous, so he headed over to his room.

Off a little distance from the motel he was staying in, was a mountain range. He didn't know the name of the mountain he sought, except that it should be the tallest in height, in what his map said was a place called Iron Castle Hill Park.

Ash took off his clothes down to his briefs and t-shirt and laid down to get some sleep. Stretching and yawning, he dozed off, before he even realized tiredness had seeped into his limbs.

A LONE CLOUD FLOATS IN THE SKY. A RAY OF THE SUN BLOTS everything out with glare. When it recedes, the sky is full of clouds. All of them join one another to form a great fog that covers the entire earth, to completely block out the sun. Soon it is the only thing there is.

The mist solidifies and becomes rock. There is a tremor as the land twists and turns and roils. Breaking into fragments and pieces floating in the water. The sun returns.

One fragment stands out from afar. A bird swoops down at incredible speed, until a mountain range comes into view. The bird flies closer still to land atop one of the mountains. Perched atop the peak, it surveys the land around it and is compelled to sing beautiful music. The bird's song causes greenery to erupt from the surroundings until a lush forest lies fully formed.

The bird flies away. When it looks back, it sees the mountains surrounded by its handiwork and smiles.

CHAPTER 10
SOLDIERS

"A re you happy now?" asked Initiate Fann, clearly irritated, as she threw her hands up in frustration. She was leaning up against the side of their gray vehicle, while Dap hobbled about on the sidewalk.

"That I shot him in the chest for shooting me in my leg?" asked Sergeant Dap, still limping. "Yes, as a matter of fact I am. I feel much better."

"Idiot," called out Specialist Leon, from the backseat of the car.

"To hell with you," said Sergeant Dap. "How the hell was I supposed to know I'd get shot?"

"Look at the neighborhood, Dap," replied Initiate Fann. "It is not exactly a rich neighborhood."

"Yeah, but I thought only the police could have guns. How was I supposed to know?"

"How was I supposed to know," mimicked Specialist Leon, with a little squeaky voice.

"You going to just stand there and bleed all night?" asked Specialist Herin, from the front passenger seat. "In case you forgot, we have got stuff to do."

"He's right," agreed Initiate Fann. "Get your bleeding ass in the car, Dap. That is an order."

"Yes, sir. I am moving as fast as I can."

They drove around the neighborhood, despite their bleeding comrade, who sat in the back seat with two more soldiers; Specialists Pinker and Leon. Specialist Herin sat at shotgun in the front, with Initiate Fann driving. They were all from another world called Pandoria, where Sergeant Dap's injury was considered a scratch at best. In their world human beings healed better and faster than they did here in New York, where they were now.

Their entire squadron had broken up into teams to find their Queen's favorite pet slave girl. The search had been narrowed down to New York City by those in charge, but it was still a big place, with an enormous population. The odds were against them, but that did not matter. They were professionals.

"I still cannot believe you did that," said Initiate Fann, stopping the car at a red light.

"Who me?" asked Sergeant Dap. "I only did it for everybody else's entertainment."

"I bet that is what you tell all the girls," teased Specialist Leon.

"She knows she loved it," said Sergeant Dap.

"Why is that, exactly?" asked Initiate Fann.

"You got a meal out of it, did you not?" he asked.

"Oh yeah," she agreed. "I almost forgot about that. Thanks, Dap."

"All this time, he was just trying to get in her good graces," said Specialist Herin. "And here we thought you were just a rank amateur."

"There is a method to my madness, Specialist," said Sergeant Dap. "There is a method."

"I don't know what we would do without you, Yorlo," said Specialist Kuln, spread out on the sidewalk, looking up at the sunlight.

"Walk?" asked Sergeant Yorlo, bent over the flat tire. They had run over something sharp, and out of the five of them, he was the only one who knew what to do to fix it.

"Not me," said Sergeant Kah, shaking his head.

"How so?" asked Sergeant Atam. He was apparently capable of multitasking. Checking out every single woman that passed by, but still listening in on the conversation.

"If it were up to me, I'd just grab another car," replied Sergeant Kah, from his seat on the curb.

"That is precisely why you are not in charge, Kah," said the Specialist. "If it were up to you, we would be dodging the authorities and looking for the slave at the same time."

"At least it would be exciting," said Sergeant Kah, fiddling with his shoelaces.

Their banter went on back and forth until Sergeant Yorlo got the car up and running again. Nobody really seemed to mind because it was daytime, something they didn't see much of back home. So, it was a special treat that helped alleviate the monotony of their shared task.

"I get the impression that men have to prove themselves way more than the women do," Sergeant Atam was saying.

"I agree," said Specialist Kuln. It was his turn at the wheel.

"And the women know it," agreed Sergeant Kah.

"There's no denying it," said Sergeant Yorlo. He had won the right to sit in the front with the Specialist this time around, for fixing the tire.

"Look at Initiate Pepper," continued Sergeant Atam, still managing to ogle every woman he saw through the back window. "Talk about a total disaster on legs. How did she get initiated?"

"I hope we find her soon. I have not had a woman in forever," said Sergeant Kah.

"Who, Initiate Pepper?" asked the Specialist, turning onto the next street.

"No, the slave, Specialist," replied Sergeant Kah.

"I'd kill you myself if you touched her, Kah," the Specialist warned. "That would get us killed just as much as not finding her."

"No, not her," Sergeant Kah laughed. "I'm not suicidal. Of course not. I only meant, so we could be done already and have some fun."

"With women we can actually touch," added Sergeant Yorlo.

"Yeah," exclaimed Sergeant Kah.

"In that case, I agree with you," said Specialist Kuln.

"Me too," Sergeant Atam agreed.

"WE LIVE WHAT, THREE TIMES LONGER THAN THE PEOPLE HERE?" asked Specialist Vixl, from the back seat of the black Ford Explorer.

"Something like that," agreed Specialist Menses, seated next to him. He was still marveling at the beautiful day outside.

"But it is not the same as living forever," said Specialist Vixl.

"No, really?" asked Specialist Orlondo.

"You don't say," Sergeant Zirus chimed in.

"Hey fellas, somebody call the Queen, quick," said Specialist Ester. He had turned from the front passenger seat, so that he could look at everybody in the back. "I think we got our next Initiate candidate right here. Whatta ya say?"

"I'd vote for him," agreed Specialist Orlondo.

"It's too bad we're not a democracy, huh Ester?" asked Sergeant Zirus.

"We tried, buddy," Specialist Ester said, with mock sympathy.

"Thanks Guys," said Specialist Vixl with a smile on his face. "Oh, by the way, Ester," he continued. "You do realize you have a girl's name, do you not?"

"What are you carrying on about now, Vixl?" asked Ester, turning back around so he could see his face again.

"Out here, Ester is a girl's name" said Specialist Vixl.

"Your point?" asked Specialist Ester. All the humor had gone out of his face, but Vixl pretended not to notice.

"I was merely pointing out," continued Specialist Vixl, "that you'd probably have a better shot at initiation than poor little old me, because you're one step closer to being a woman."

"Oh, I see," Specialist Ester said, nodding his head in agreement. And then he made a quick grab for Specialist Vixl's neck.

"Somebody can't take a joke," laughed Specialist Vixl, easily fending off the assault.

~

"IS THIS REALLY NECESSARY?" ASKED SPECIALIST KARN, FROM THE front passenger seat of the Volvo.

"Yes," replied Specialist Azn.

"What are you going to do with him?" asked Specialist Pimmo, from the back seat.

"Have not decided yet," said Specialist Azn.

Leaning forward to reach the driver's ear, but still loud enough for everybody to hear him, Sergeant Nelfo said, "I know you are going to kill him."

"Maybe," said Specialist Azn, rolling his eyes.

"I wish Initiate Kimmy was here," sighed Specialist Karn.

"And why is that, exactly?" asked Specialist Azn, raising his voice, in irritation.

"Because you are going to get us in trouble," admitted Specialist Karn.

"Knock it off, Azn!" yelled Specialist Pimmo. "Contrary to your own belief system, not everyone is afraid of you. And the only one you even outrank here is Nelfo."

"Your point?" asked Specialist Azn.

"My point is that you are not fooling anybody," continued Specialist Pimmo. "The guy you threw in the trunk is not the only one that knows. Everybody in here knows the accident back there was entirely your fault. We all know you cannot drive worth a damn."

"So, what if it was?" Specialist Azn asked, shrugging his shoulders. "I got us another one."

"Yeah, we know," agreed Specialist Pimmo. "The same one you crashed into."

"And?"

"And it is no wonder we are not fighting any police right now."

"You are over dramatic," said Specialist Azn.

"Me?!?" yelled Specialist Pimmo, punching the dashboard. "First, you crashed into another car because you drive like a blind old lady. Then, you took the driver out of the car that you crashed into and threw him in the trunk of his own car. Then, you stole the car and made us all accessories to a very public automobile theft. Am I missing anything?"

"See what I mean?" asked Specialist Azn. "Over dramatic."

"ID, REPORT IN," SAID INITIATE LENNA, INTO HER PORTABLE CELL phone.

"What else would I do?" asked Specialist Id. "I mean, I picked up your call, did I not?"

"Just do it, Id," she pleaded

"Everything's quiet here," he said. "I actually spotted a few girls that fit the profile, but it was not her. The eye color was off."

"Where are you now?" she asked.

"Walking across 57th Street, heading west."

"Roger that. I'll check back with you in two hours."

"That's a copy," he said, and then hung up.

Lenna dialed the next number on her phone, waiting for Rojen to pick up.

"Talk to me," said the Specialist.

"How's your night going?" she asked.

"No news, is good news."

"I take it, that means you have not found anything either?"

"That is correct."

"Where are you at?" she asked.

"I'm on 42nd Street, heading east."

"That's a copy. I will check back in a few."

"Night, love," he said, and then hung up.

Lenna dialed the number for Kip.

He picked up on the first ring and said "No. I haven't seen her."

"How did you know what I was going to ask you?" asked Initiate Lenna.

"I'm psychic," said Specialist Kip.

"Oh? So, what's my next question, then?"

"Headed west on 34th Street."

"Call you later," she said, disconnecting on her end. She dialed the last number and waited for the other end to stop ringing. When it did, she said "Sergeant."

"Initiate," replied the man on the other end.

"I'm assuming you haven't found her?" she asked.

"You assume correctly."

"And you are?"

"Walking east along 23rd Street, Initiate. Is there anything else?"

"That is it. Thanks."

"Roger that," he said before hanging up.

Lenna was walking across 14th Street herself, trying to figure out when she was going to eat. With all the people out and about, it would be a cinch to grab one and suck it dry. All the drunk people came out from the clubs and bars later in the evening, so that might be the easiest time.

PEPPER KICKED THE BOUNCER IN THE GROIN. HE THOUGHT HE WAS all big and strong with all those muscles, but he was only human. He should count his lucky stars that she did not kill him right here and now, except that would have endangered the mission. Also, as the Initiate, she was setting the example for the others.

"Come on, let's go!" she screamed out. "We haven't got all day!"

Ernden and Farl were holding their own against six burly guys in the bar. She wasn't sure if the group worked here, or if they were just regular people out to have a good time. Bo and Donve were back-to-back, fighting off about twice that amount. She decided to lend them a hand, figuring the smaller group could wait.

If it was up to her, she'd have stayed on the sidelines, but then her four subordinates would have probably told how she started the bar fight. It hadn't even been her fault, really. Some guy grabbed her butt, and then she slapped him so hard, she was almost afraid she'd killed him.

Apparently, the guy was here with some friends, and they saw that she was with four of her own people, and the brawl started. Men were not supposed to fight women here, generally speaking, so they did the next best thing. Fighting her companions. The whole thing had her struggling with a fit of the giggles, because she was by far the strongest one around, which made it ludicrous to ignore her.

She made it a point to get a few hits in anyway, when she finally stopped laughing. By then the whole place was in an uproar. Back on Pandoria, she could have ended something like this in a couple seconds flat.

All she'd had to do was bear her fangs and growl and everything would have stopped immediately. Here though, it would have blown their cover and gotten her in trouble instead.

After knocking two men out, she decided to change her tactics. She slammed one of the four men, into the remaining previous group of six. The one with Ernden and Farl. This freed them up to help Bo and Donve, against their greater number of opponents.

"Come on fellas, let's put it on 'em!" she shouted. When each of them looked at her, trying to see what she meant, she made it a point to use the hand signal for non-lethal force. Though part of her wished she would have just walked off to the bathroom and left them to do whatever. As fun as it was, without any killing, she just didn't see the point of being here all night.

~

"Why exactly is it that we're out here again?" asked Specialist Cimron, throwing his hands out.

"And where's the car?" added Specialist Needles.

"We're not taking the car today. I've got something else planned," said Captain Ellis.

"Like?" asked Sergeant Jindle, rubbing at his face.

"Just a bit farther, and I'll show you," said the Captain.

After they walked two avenues and four blocks, they saw his bright idea.

"Bicycles?" asked Specialist Needles. "What do we need bicycles for?"

"Yeah, we're down at— What's this place called again?" asked Sergeant Jindle.

"South Street Seaport," answered Specialist Cimron.

"Yeah," Sergeant Jindle agreed. "This area's perfect for walking. Whatta we need bicycles for?"

"I was thinking that we'd do something healthy today," said the Captain.

"Healthy?" asked Specialist Needles, with a note of disgust.

"Oh, ye of little faith," Captain Ellis said, shaking his head. "Trust me."

Fortunately, the Captain found a credit card, that the bicycle rental service accepted as collateral for the four bikes. He'd stolen the card from a wealthy-looking man on Park Avenue. It was a warm day with the sun high in the sky. Perfect for a nice bike ride.

He'd had it up to the top of his head with all the seriousness of the whole thing. They were looking for a needle in a haystack, as if it mattered where they looked, at those odds. He'd rather have fun before he died.

The men complained and carried on like little old ladies walking upstairs, the whole ride up north. They may have even hated it. But when they finally got up to Central Park, and realized they were going to be riding inside of it, they changed their tune.

"Why didn't you just tell us we were coming up here before?" asked Specialist Cimron, huffing and puffing out of breath.

"Yeah, why?" agreed Sergeant Jindle.

"I thought you'd appreciate it more this way," replied Captain Ellis.

"I will share with you, however," he continued, "that I plan to remain inside the park for the entire time that we're here."

"Really?" asked Specialist Needles. He too was huffing and puffing from the exertion. Only Jindle and the Captain seemed unaffected.

"If there's no disagreement," replied the Captain, with a smile.

"So, all our time on this assignment is going to be spent in the park?" asked Sergeant Jindle.

"Except when we're getting food," said Captain Ellis.

"Cool!" exclaimed Sergeant Jindle.

CAPTAIN PRATLE SAT IN THE BARNES AND NOBLE BOOKSTORE AND perused the magazines stacked on the table. They were all full of clothing for women and tips on life from their perspective. He just liked looking at the pictures. Life was so different here.

Take the roles of men and women, for example. The exact opposite of Pandoria, where women were afforded infinitely more respect than men. None of that really mattered because he was just passing through, but all those pictures had got him thinking.

He took two aspirin pills with some water, in a bottle he got from a vendor before he came inside. It was probably just one of the stress headaches he got from time to time. Just because he looked all cool, calm, and collected on the surface, didn't mean that all the craziness wasn't affecting him.

It wasn't fair that the mistakes of others had all but put his head on the chopping block. In a perfect world, he'd be in the audience laughing as the fools were killed in the Queen's arena.

Pratle closed his eyes and rubbed his hands over them.

Calm down, he thought. Relax. All he could do was already being done.

He took a leisurely stroll through the aisles of books, every now and then, picking one up that looked interesting. There was a nice assortment of journals that he looked through to pass the time. He looked at a pile of board games and puzzle books. Every so often a pretty woman would come into view, and he looked at those too.

Eventually, he tired of it and took the escalator back up to street level. 86th Street was a pretty busy place that had more than a few things he might be interested in. Walking aimlessly, he came upon a store called Cold Stone that sold ice-cream.

That'll hit the spot nicely, he thought, and went inside.

MAJOR GORDON WAS NOT A HAPPY CAMPER. IT WAS TRUE THAT HE was mildly entertained in his undercover costume, but the task ahead was very close to making him downright mad. He knew it would not do, because anger always made a person careless and sloppy, but those thoughts did nothing to cool his simmering emotions.

He was already doing the best he could under the circumstances, with his usual inventiveness. But the police vehicle he had appropriated could only do so much. No one would bother him or Caymon as he cruised around in the patrol car. No one would question his authority at all, with the police uniform he wore. He seemed to have full control of the situation, but it was a lie and he knew it.

Pretending to be a member of the police was not going to help him find the slave any faster. He could not truly infiltrate their ranks because there was always the chance that someone would know the one he was parading around as, and blow his cover. From the moment the idea came to him, it seemed like the best way to keep Caymon hidden from the authorities and nosy passersbys. They did not allow wolves in the city, whether they were domesticated or not.

The only real benefit, aside from increased stealth, was that he could pretend to be just like the man he had made a meal of, earlier in the evening. He now had the credentials necessary to have a canine on patrol with him. Something that could be invaluable in a place like this. All he had to do was keep to the shadows, so no one realized his friend was not a German shepherd.

He wondered how the rest of his men were doing. It was not time to check in with them for another two hours still. He had set the three of them up in their own patrol car, so they could at least feel special for a little bit. He figured it would take the edge off of all the pointless searching.

In the end, as far as he was concerned, if the fates willed it, they would find the girl. If not, there was not a thing any of them would be able to do about it.

"Just too many damn people in this city," he told Caymon, scratching him behind his ears.

~

"Well at least you're alive," said Magistrate Margaret.

"That is true," agreed Specialist Fonch.

"I guess," said Captain Nemma, from the driver's seat. "I just wish I would have done better, is all."

"Look, Nemma," offered Magistrate Margaret. "I do not know that I'd have done any better myself. Once you threw him off the roof, it was perfectly acceptable to figure he would just die."

"I would have too," agreed Specialist Fonch. He was laid out across the entire back seat, and except for his commentary, he seemed to be sleeping.

"We need to find someplace to sleep," ordered the Magistrate. "The sun will be up in an hour."

"Roger that, Magistrate," Captain Nemma said, and she sped up the vehicle.

So far, their travels had been uneventful. Azure had put her on a little side mission to check for ritual site possibilities. Initially they were all supposed to be checking out the points simultaneously to save time, but with the recent events of this runaway slave business, things had changed.

Margaret blamed herself, but there wasn't really anything she could do about it, other than focus on her job. If anyone would have even hinted that the slave was that strong, she would have laughed in their face. The woman was positively superhuman, especially considering she wasn't even Initiated, like Margaret. A regular person put through the wall like she had been, would have probably had their face crushed.

Well, it was in everyone else's hands now.

Their little trio was just coming back from Riverhead, Long Island. Shortly after dusk, they would be on their way to Randall's Island, a spot in the Bronx Zoo that Fonch had pinpointed, and another place called Roosevelt Island. None of the locations had any meaning, as far as she could tell, but the Queen had plotted it all out through some calculations and they were supposed to check it all out in person.

Supposedly, the gold coin she held in her pocket would glow when they found what they were looking for, instead of the nothing it had done so far. Fonch, who was educated in local tech and geography, said it had no mechanical components. He said it had to be magical.

Maybe if she found what the Queen was looking for, she would not get killed for losing the slave.

"Fat chance," she said aloud.

"What?" asked Captain Nemma, taking her eyes off the road to look at Margaret.

"It is nothing. Just thinking," Margaret said, biting her lower lip.

CHAPTER 11
KAYALA

L eaning over the edge of a small mountainside of steps, on an
island in the street, she felt the press of the hot sun against
her exposed skin. Long hours spent in the night had made
her especially vulnerable to its power, but she was thankful, none-
theless. It represented another facet of her freedom.

The same as the giant television screens, playing out the images
before her, on the sides of huge buildings. Or hot tar. Or the sun's glare
reflecting off the unending flow of four-wheeled vehicles with people
in them. Single-minded in their pursuit of some unknown destination.

The others, walking the street like a hoard of giant insects, milling
about with their hive mentality, streaming along indefinitely and innu-
merable. The only break in the incessant movement, at the dictate of a
light apparatus, designed to coordinate the two, as they swarmed about.

Perched as she was, with her bird's eye view, she saw the madness
of it all. The never-ending press of bodies, as separate from them up
here, as she appeared to be one of them, when she inevitably walked
amongst them once more.

She wore loose-fitting blue jeans, cuffed at the bottom because they
were too long. A brown short sleeved t-shirt that said, 'Care Bears

Rule!' in neon pink. Black feather-light Chinese slippers for her feet. And a medium-sized green canvas bag placed on a step beside her, for her other belongings.

Not hard to come by at all. Almost fate.

KAYALA HAD BEEN STROLLING ALONG IN THE EARLY MORNING HOURS, with the sun barely creeping over the horizon, wondering what her next move was going to be. Walking by a small food store called 7 Eleven, just as a woman around her own age exited, to walk in front of her in the same direction. The woman was too engrossed in her food to pay Kayala any mind.

Short of outright theft, she did not have the currency for food, clothing, or shelter, which were her main priorities. Also, it was bad enough she still had the collar and chain on, let alone the soldier's outfit that most people did not wear. It was an opportunity too perfect to pass up.

In no time at all, she was soon sporting her current outfit, the green bag on her back emptied of its books, and two hundred and fifty dollars in her pocket. True, her benefactor was a little bit taller and a bit disproportioned, but for all intents and purposes, a most opportune moment.

From there, it was relatively easy. The bus driver had let her on despite her lack of change, taking her to the Staten Island Ferry, which lead her to Manhattan. According to the tourist guide in the food store, that was the place that had the most attractions (She had gone back to buy some food for herself, before setting off on the long journey). She had also correctly reasoned it as the best place to have her collar removed.

Once on Manhattan from the boat, it was a simple matter to purchase a MetroCard and use it to travel the city via the subway system. She was able to rid herself of the collar around her neck, thanks to a locksmith.

"Woah, your boyfriend's sure into some really kinky stuff, huh?" he had asked, with a smile on his face.

"Yes," she had said, after a brief hesitation. "Can you get it off?"

"Piece of cake, sweetheart. Just gimmie a sec."

Just like that, and she was truly free. At his urging, she had actually been able to sell the collar in the jewelry district for a thousand dollars.

"This whole thing is solid platinum," said the man behind the counter. He was an older gentleman with salt and pepper hair. He had a long beard and wore a very small circular hat that only covered the back of his head.

"What will you give me for it?" she had asked, in a hurry to finally be rid of it. It was even easier to obtain than her first sum of money, and four times the amount. At the time, she was also still blissfully unaware of the value of a dollar. In hindsight, she should have asked for more. The chain, she kept in her bag as a weapon for emergencies.

And that is how she ended up in Times Square.

FROM HER CURRENT VANTAGE POINT SHE COULD SEE TWO STREETS, one on either side of her street island. The right one was completely devoid of cars, while the left had no such restrictions. She opted for the thrill of walking to the right, until the cars took over, forcing her back onto the sidewalk. Eventually, she saw a building that took up an entire sidewalk by itself, off to the left. It was odd that such a thing could escape the conformity that dictated multiple such structures per block, and Kayala wandered inside.

It was vast. Enclosed and cut off from sunlight, but with artificial lights. With white floors, walls, and ceilings. Glass structures with all manner of items for purchase immediately drew her eye, to behold painted dyes for the face, scented oils, and other creature comforts.

People milled about here as well, but in a diminished capacity, which may have simply been because there was limited space. Just when she was suitably impressed with the sheer variety and quantity of wares, she found metallic steps that moved her to upper levels, doubling—no tripling—more! Kayala began to wonder if there was anything that wasn't for sale in this place.

It was here, at a jewelry counter, that she found out how badly she had been taken advantage of when she sold her collar, by way of comparing similar items. No matter. She was just glad to be rid of it.

All in all, a most educational experience, that finally taught her the value of the twelve hundred dollars she had on her person. A paltry sum in such an arena, to be sure, but not unmanageable. She noticed that much like food purchases, the prices fluctuated even amongst similar items, depending on the name as much as the style.

Of course, there were so many people. It was so big with so much to see. So much so, that she soon became exhausted and wanted to leave.

Outside, thanks to the directions of a friendly woman, Kayala set out looking for food at once. All her browsing had finally depleted the last of her energy reserves. Lightheaded and faint, she soon found herself inside another building, this one made of a lot of glass. Inside, her sensitive nose caught a whiff of something that immediately sent her stomach to rumbling. She expectantly headed farther in, all but ignoring the new wonder.

The innards of this structure were infinitely different from the place she had just been. From where she stood, she could see the other levels and the metal stairs leading to some of them. At the other place, she had easily gotten lost by all the twists and turns, and different compartments. Here everything, though mostly glass, was organized in square walkways, one atop the other, in a simplicity so friendly that finding her way was assured. She could not tell how high the ceiling was. A hundred meters?

"Excuse me. Do you know where I can get some food?" she asked a man that seemed like he might work there. He wore a uniform and hat that set him apart from the other people.

"Take those two escalators there, down to the bottom floor there, and head to the back," he said, pointing out where he meant.

"Thank you very much," she said, rushing off.

He nodded and said, "No problem."

In the back, she found about ten different food stores, each with many different options. For the sake of expediency, she headed for the shortest line, so that she ended up with a tuna fish sandwich and the largest cup of water they had for sale, with ice inside to keep it cold.

The space was set up so that the food stores formed a perimeter around an open space, filled with tables and chairs for patrons. A welcome convenience, that was hindered by the sheer number of people inside it, which was greater than the seating arrangement allowed for. It was so packed that she had half-considered sitting on the floor, when fortune smiled on her, and a man near her vacated his chair.

Relief washed over her gently, as she relished the small victory, and wolfed down her food. When she was done with the sandwich, she purchased another. This one she ate at a slow relaxed pace, taking in the beauty of the place and watching other people eat. By the time she was back outside, she had finished the melted ice in her cup.

A short distance across the street, was a little island of a park amidst the traffic of nearby cars. It was a gated area with little trees, flowers, and small plants. Scattered about were a few tables and chairs for leisure. A sign said it was called Herald Square. Kayala found an empty seat in a corner and decided to relax.

The greenery was a welcomed addition to her surroundings, that had been sorely missed in all her time spent indoors. Even amid the chaos of the city, it became a sanctuary from the unfeeling structures and alien world around her. If she did not look up, things were hidden from view well enough where she sat, that she could imagine herself someplace safe.

It was a place where the only thing required of her was to smell the fresh air provided by nature's gentle creatures. To bask in the serenity they offered and take in their welcome fragrance. Where she could be proud of herself.

When she had her fill, Kayala continued south down 6th Avenue. When she hit 14th Street on that Avenue, she turned east because it looked more interesting that way. Before long, she came to a large park that someone told her was called Union Square. She did not bother wondering what made it a square for more than a few seconds. The last square she had been at had been more of a small triangle.

There was a very large sidewalk with a series of short steps, another large space to walk, more steps, and another space, and steps leading to a park beyond that. Everyone seemed to like sitting on all the steps past the first set as if they were chairs, even though she spotted places to sit inside the park.

Three young women were sitting next to one another and seemed to really be enjoying their conversation.

"Sorry to bother you," she said. "But, can you tell me what is so special about these steps?"

"What do you mean?" asked the one in the middle. Her hair was very short and pink, red, and brown. Her eyes were brown as well. The other two women, like bookends, looked to her like she was their leader.

"Well," she continued. "There is so many people on them. I thought there might be a reason I did not understand."

"No reason," the woman replied, shaking her head. "They all just wanna be cool like us." At that, her companions started giggling and one of them chimed in "Yea!"

"Oh, okay. Thanks," said Kayala.

"No problem," said the leader.

Kayala left the trio to talk amongst themselves and headed over to where the park was. She did not see the point of sitting on stone steps, with the fresh greenery calling to her, in easy reach. Part of that feeling most likely had to do with too many years spent indoors.

As a slave, she had only been able to appreciate nature hurriedly and in passing, only en route to a destination. She had never had the privilege of being outdoors for leisure. Running around the track was supposed to fulfill that need and take care of her fitness at the same time. The relaxation element only existed during her time in the bath, when she was left alone, or when she was locked away for punishment or sleep.

She found her mind wandering back to him again, as it seemed to be doing of late. She pushed him out of her thoughts. Leaving the one named Ash may have been a rash decision, in hindsight, but it was her decision to make. She needed to be on her own to learn self-sufficiency. Not tied to another master.

The wood she sat on stretched a great distance in either direction, broken up into sections for multiple people to seat themselves. There was another one that mirrored it, opposite where she sat, and others like it throughout the area. People walked freely along the path between. Trees swayed in the gentle breeze behind the seats, amid grass that was on the ground. Some people even laid on this grass, but she had seen dogs idling on it already and did not trust it to be a clean area.

Even though Kayala had only recently escaped the rule of her Queen, she was not a complete fool on her own. She knew there were rules that the people of her new home followed. She knew that a whim contradictory to the general rules here would be punished, if discovered by what they called 'The Police' or 'Cops', who were their militia.

Her real problem was money. It complicated things beyond her means right now. Like everyone else around here, she needed food and clothing, and shelter. Unlike everyone else, she could not wrap her mind around going from the amount she had now, to replenishing it when the time came. Short of just taking it.

Right now, she had a set of clothing that helped her to blend in. She did not have any food, water, or shelter in her possession. She did, however, have something like twelve hundred dollars to her name, but it wasn't a great enough amount. It only meant that she would be able to eat for a couple of weeks. For anything beyond that she would need a far greater sum, which was not likely to be carried around by anyone. She had studied how much money people used and what the prices of most general items were. Enough to know that she needed a constant influx of money to function properly.

Food stores. She forgot what they were called, but she had seen big ones that had boxes full of money. She would have to go to one of those to get some food the next time she was hungry. If the metal boxes had enough money in them, she could take it from one of those places.

If each one held two to three hundred dollars, and there were five of them, she could acquire up to fifteen hundred dollars in addition to what she already possessed. Which was still not enough money to get herself a living space. Though, it would be enough for her to eat for a third of a year.

That would at least put her mind at rest on that score. If she did that a total of three times, she would not have to worry about feeding herself for an entire year. All she needed to do was get another set of clothes for a disguise and steal the money from three different locations.

After that was taken care of, she would have to figure out a way to have her own space. How was she going to do that?

The most drastic plan she came up with was to just kill someone outside of their home and take possession of their belongings. Their food, shelter, and everything else. She did not want to do something that sinister if she could help it. Far better to do what she was already doing, which was living in the big park.

They called it Central Park, and her reconnaissance proved that it was far greater than she had originally thought. Easily fifty blocks long and three blocks wide. She could hide in a place like that forever, without ever being captured. It was packed with trees and grass, and flowers and bushes, and it was almost like a great nation of a park, composed of smaller parks inside of it. Unfortunately, it was all still out in the open, which would not do when it got cold.

Kayala knew that Ash fancied her. If she thought back, she had smelled his desire from the moment she ran past him that night at the bar. He was a beautiful man, and she fancied him as well, but she was not ready to enslave herself to another master. The culture was also completely alien to her at the time that she had been with him. So, she had left to find her own way.

She was so tired. She could barely keep her eyes open. If she sat here and closed her eyes for some rest, no one would bother her. She had seen others do it in the past. When she had enough rest, she would get back to thinking about her options and her new life.

~

SHE HAD FINALLY DONE IT. AFTER WEEKS OF CRYING, BEGGING, pleading, and pulling out all the stops, Inalia had managed to reschedule a new test for Trigonometry. Thank God. Mr. Fincher had lost this round and she was about to win the war. He hadn't counted on Inalia going over his head to the Dean, but then he really hadn't left her much choice.

"I'm sorry Inalia, there's nothing I can do. It's out of my hands," he had told her, with a solemn look in his eyes. And he had the nerve to give her the old responsibility speech again. As if she could control the trains. Smug bastard. At least until the Dean got a hold of him, anyway. That Dean Connelly was a real ball buster.

Rumor had it that she was the first female Dean at Bronx High School of Science, and she was no pushover. Whatever she wanted done, got done. No if, ands, or buts; where Annie Connelly was concerned. Period.

Inalia couldn't even begin to express her gratitude at having Ms. Connelly in her corner. Without her help, Inalia would be finished, finni-toe, and all those other sayings.

She had managed to just squeak by on a grade of sixty-five in his class last year, which let her move on to being a Junior instead of getting Super Sophomore status (which was what it was called when you got held back a grade). At the time, she hadn't cared because she passed, and that was all she thought mattered. That was before she had a heart to heart with her friend Jenny.

Apparently, in order to get into a good college, you had to have good grades in all your classes. Jenny had told Inalia that the low grade would probably jeopardize her ability to get into Yale with her. They were planning on going together and had planned the whole thing out since they first became friends, back when she was ten years old.

They both thought everything through and asked all their friends if there was anything that would help, or if Inalia would be stuck going to a community college. As far as everyone was concerned, she was pretty much dead in the water, but maybe if she went to see the dean, maybe she'd be able to help out. That was the consensus.

She never really knew what Dean Connelly could have said to her Social Studies teacher, but whatever it was, it worked. The next thing she knew, her final grade was changed to an eighty. From talking to the dean, it seemed like maybe she also thought that Mr. Fincher had been too hard on Inalia throughout the semester. Whoever said there were no such things as miracles was wrong.

Things were finally starting to take a turn for the better. From here on out everything was going to be fantastic. It was a new era filled with the promise of greatness.

A celebration was called for. And what better way to celebrate than to head over to the local Stone Cold? That would definitely hit the spot, and it was the perfect reward for a job well done. Tada!

It actually took a couple of extra stops on the train; a detour of sorts, to reach it, but since it was for a good cause it was worth it. She could taste it now:

A banana split with strawberry, vanilla, and chocolate; rainbow sprinkles, strawberry syrup, whipped cream, and a single cherry to top it all off. Sheer perfection. It was going to be monumental.

IT WASN'T LONG BEFORE INALIA WAS ON LINE WAITING TO MAKE HER purchase. Two more people to go and it was banana split time. All she had to do was check her saliva flow. Her taste buds were on overdrive and had her drooling like a maniac. Just a few moments more of composure, and then the moment of truth—

"What are you doing here?" asked a man from just behind her.

"Excuse me?" Inalia asked, as she turned to see who it was.

"I said, what are you doing here?"

"Am I supposed to know you from somewhere?"

The guy behind her was easily thirty years old with very sharp features and a look that amounted to a sneer. He might be a teacher or something, but school was out, so why was he getting on her case?

"Quit being coy. You're coming with me," and then he grabbed her arm and started pulling her out of the store.

"Hey, let go of me. What the hell do you think you're doing?"

"You can drop the act. That little disguise might work on someone else, but I'm not buying it," he stated matter-of-factly.

"Disguise? What the fuck are you talking about you whack job? Let me go right now or I'll scream for the cops," she said. She tried to get her arm free of his vice-like grip.

"Oh?" was all he said before he pulled back and punched Inalia in the face.

Caught off guard and completely unawares, the last thing she saw was a quick movement, followed by a sharp pain. Everything faded to black, as she floated away to someplace she had never been. Like a cloud on the breeze in the sky.

"MARTHA, SOMEONE'S AT THE DOOR!" YELLED FREDDY.

"What are you telling me for?" Martha yelled back.

"Come on, honey! Can you get the door? I'm watching the news!"

When he heard her footsteps pass by, he knew that she was getting the door and he raised the volume on his fifty-inch LCD television:

JANICE MONAHAN: "GOOD EVENING, I'M JANICE MONAHAN. BILL Parsons has the night off. Our top story tonight:

Peace talks continue as United Nations delegates take a stand for injustice abroad. Thomas Shear has more details."

Thomas Shear: "Thank you, Melanie. I'm here in Paris, France, at the United Nations Summit meeting that's got all the world on the edge of its seat. Praying that something can be done about the terror going on in Sierra Leone and other neighboring African countries. Such as Burundi, Guinea-Bissau, and Central African Republic, also known as CAR. Right now, talks are continuing right behind the very doors I'm standing in front of, that may hold the fate of hundreds of thousands in the balance.

"This reporter was fortunate enough to speak with a key member of these talks."

Alexander Edwards, U.N. Representative (PBC): "Any time that you are faced with a historical tragedy such as this one, where innocent civilians have lost life and limb, I think that it is imperative to step in and lend a hand if you can, to make sure that something like this never happens again. I think I speak on behalf of my fellow United Nations members when I say that we're not going to rest until the war and chaos stops. We are doing everything that we can, to put an end to these horrible—horrible things. And it is our hope that future generations will be able to look upon these things as a lesson to be learned, rather than a continued part of their lives. Thank you."

Thomas Shear: "When asked what his feelings might be if something like this happened here in the U.S., he had this to say."

Alexander Edwards, U.N. Representative (PBC): "Well as we all know, nothing like this could happen back home in America. Perish the thought. Part of the reason I'm able to even do something like this, is because of the value system we hold back home and in most of the world. And knowing that those values are keeping my daughter safe at home right now. I love you, Inalia."

Thomas Shear: "Mr. Edwards went on to say that the talks seem to be going well and members are hoping to see an equitable solution shortly."

Janice Monahan: "Thank you, Thomas. And now, the weather."

Melanie Anders: "Thank you, Janice. As I said earlier, it looks like some of those tropical storm winds should be entering the Metro area as early as the next two days. An advisory is in effect, and authorities are recommending that those of you that will be in that area when the storm hits; tape up your windows, get some bottled water and canned goods, and have spare batteries at hand for your flashlights. With the possibility of fifty mile per hour winds and stronger gusts, there's no telling what kind of damage to expect."

Janice Monahan: "And, which storm is this again, Melanie?"

Melanie Anders: "Well, as it turns out, we don't actually have a name for this one, Janice. Most tropical storms are cyclical, so that they come up around certain times of the year. This one's not one of those. It just sort of popped up out of nowhere."

Janice Monahan: "And do you think that's more of a reason to be careful?"

Melanie Anders: "Definitely. You should never underestimate any of these storms, but we are keeping an eye on things on the weather radar. Please stay tuned, and we'll keep you up to the minute at home."

Janice Monahan: "Thank you, Melanie."

Melanie Anders: "Janice."

CHAPTER 12
ALYSSA RUNNING DEER

Alyssa Running Deer ran through Central Park as she often did on nights like this. The wind was in her face and the trees seemed to stream by effortlessly, with the wet grass caressing her feet. She felt invigorated and truly alive, leaping over a small rock, to land on pavement, with her nails clicking ever so softly, as she slowed to a walk. The full moon was out in all its glory, calling out to her, but she controlled the impulse to howl. No sense in terrifying anyone unduly, if she could help it. The night was young, and there would be time to speak to sister moon later.

There was no one in the immediate vicinity, as far as she could tell. It was a shame she couldn't see in full color like this, but it was a small price to pay, considering she really shouldn't be able to see this well at night in the first place. Ordinarily.

Fortunately, she was anything but normal, with four clawed paws, sharp teeth, and the white fur coat to prove it. One might almost mistake her for a Husky breed with perhaps a bit of German Shepherd thrown in for good measure, with some Saint Bernard for size. Instead of the predator that she was.

There would be no master picking up her leavings or fetching her food. Nor would she be fetching anything either. And a trip to the dog run? No dog would come within four square blocks of her, master, or no master. The thing might as well be closed for renovations, until she decided to leave.

It was all idle fancy, really. Dog run. Ha! Hilarious. Why run in a small square when she had the entire field of this great park at her disposal?

Alyssa continued the route of her patrol, bounding north, in a swift sprint. Listening for odd sounds. Sniffing for strange scents. Using her keen eyesight to spot the unusual.

She fancied herself a superhero on nights like this. A vigilante, really. She'd foiled many an attempt to satiate unsavory appetites. She knew that she couldn't save or protect everybody, but she liked to do her part. It was also a great way to stay in shape and keep her reflexes intact. In direct contrast to normal city life.

She was jogging around with no distinct thought in her head, tongue lolling out of her mouth, when she heard something off in the distance. A woman's voice.

"Please. Leave me alone," said the voice.

Alyssa stifled a growl and bared her teeth in anger. This might be a problem.

"I don't want any trouble," pleaded the voice.

Which way? She sniffed the air, and tried to find the source, darting off to her left.

"Somebody helps me!" the woman screamed out.

Alyssa flew across the underbrush, at a full sprint. She'd figured out the woman's location and locked onto her scent. Obviously, she was not alone. She smelled of fear, and there was a man with her. No. Men. Four of them. Almost there. Help was on the way.

It seemed she'd get the chance to sing out to sister moon after all. Not quite close enough to intervene, she stopped dead in her tracks and let the call out. Her melodious song went out before her for all to hear.

It said Beware! A true hunter is about!

Any second, she would be upon them. Just through that outcropping of trees up ahead. Alyssa sailed over a small bush and came right in front, with her back to the woman, baring her fangs as her growl escaped her throat. She thought she smelled the woman's fear subside almost immediately, as soon as she realized this strange animal had come to save her.

They had sought to encircle the woman like a pack, two at her front, and two at her flank. Alyssa had heard their easy footsteps approaching—and heard them still, as they had become cautious at her appearance. The woman only knew of the two she could see, by her reaction. She was completely unaware of the others behind her.

"Woah. Is that your dog, lady?" asked the one on the right. He had light colored hair; maybe blonde, and light eyes. He wore a leather jacket, jeans, and white sneakers. He was in his late teens or early twenties.

"That's a big dog," said his companion. He was African American with dark skin and hair, cut close to his scalp. This one wore a ski jacket with feathers inside of it, with jeans and white sneakers as well. The same age, but a little smarter than his friend. He took a few steps back.

She knew what her enemies saw. She'd seen herself in mirrors plenty of times, as she practiced for maximum scariness. It was like seeing the biggest Saint Bernard you'd ever seen, but aerodynamic and savage, with a body, every square inch, made for killing. Teeth bared. Ears back. Tail down. Snow white fur, making you feel that she might be a ghost, come from the world of the dead, to rip your soul from its mortal coil.

Alyssa let her rump lightly bump the woman behind her. Pushing her back slightly, with a firm nudge, as she continued to growl ahead. This would convey the message that she was there as a protector. The men had stopped their forward advance and stayed where they were. Smart. Either that or they were hoping their friends might catch her unawares from the other side.

She guided the woman back and to the left, and then turned to face the other way, to show that she was fully aware of the others trying to sneak in closer.

"Holy shit," said one of that set, hidden in shadow. "It saw us," he whispered. He needn't have bothered, with her ears, she fancied she could hear a pin drop in the grass. They were trying to keep to the nearby trees, so she hadn't caught a look at them just yet. No worries. They knew that she was aware of them now, and that was the important part.

The trick to being a werewolf, if there was one, was moderation whenever it could be achieved. An overly savage attack held the possibility of changing these young miscreants into one of her type, which was a gift they were far from earning on a good day. She also had newspapers, and other forms of public opinion to consider as well. The last thing she wanted was the police to be patrolling the park, looking for her specifically.

Wolves didn't do things the way dogs did. A dog, for example might try to bite someone on the arm or butt, or maybe on the leg. A wolf? A direct attack, or a feint, with the sole intent of a strike for the jugular and death. A disemboweling, perhaps. But all of it with a very final end in mind.

This called for the proper application of a gentler aggression than these boys deserved. With just enough purchase to make sure they disappeared immediately. She decided to choose the closest one. It was the most effective and expedient means of resolution, after all.

Alyssa was off like a rocket, and had her teeth bitten into the man with the leather jacket, like a knife through butter. He tasted of jean material, skin, muscle, tendon, fat, and blood. Too much flavor. She must have chomped down harder than she thought.

Wolves have stronger jaws than a regular dog, and werewolves have ten times that. Lucky for him, she was old enough so that when the taste of blood hit her mouth (and the smell of it mixed with his fear, hit her nose), she was able to fight the urge to rip the appendage clear off. Werewolves like bones and chew toys too.

The fellow hit the floor like a sack of potatoes. Screaming.

She held onto him, eyeing his friends menacingly. Her message? You are food.

The pair in the shadows were the first to run. The remaining attacker followed suit.

A few moments later, she released the leg. Tuning out her prey's meaningless complaints.

Alyssa whined at the woman and let her tongue hang, in her best 'I come in peace,' impression, then turned and grabbed the woman's jacket sleeve. She hardly had a chance to flinch, before being pulled along like a child might. A very strong child, tugging to show her which way they should go. No one followed, and it wasn't long before they left the would-be assailants far behind in the night.

She was a young thing of late teens or early twenties, that had wandered out and found herself in the wrong place at the wrong time. Like most of the young, probably figuring that nothing bad was going to happen if she took a brief walk through the park. It wasn't even midnight yet, after all. Still too early for anything mean to find her, or so she thought.

She was an attractive woman, maybe Puerto Rican, with dark hair that she'd wrapped up on top of her head, and dark eyes, set into a pretty face. Maybe around five foot two, in her dark jeans and dark down coat, and dark patent leather shoes. The stench of fear, fell away from her just like the disaster she had averted. She would live to see another day, hopefully somehow wiser than she'd been recently. Maybe even start a family one day.

She walked the woman to an opening, so she could exit the park at west fifty-ninth street, where she might be able to take a train, or go to the cops, or whatever she needed to do. Someplace where there were people around and she'd have a better chance at staying safe. When they got there, she whined and pushed with her muzzle, indicating that the woman should go on alone. The city proper wasn't the place for a werewolf to go roaming around, on the best of nights.

At the opening, the woman got down on her knees and held Alyssa by her head and neck in a hug. She may have even been crying slightly.

"I don't know if you can understand me," she said, "but thank you so much." When she finally stood up, Alyssa thought she heard her sniffle, as she wiped at her face with her arm. "I owe you," she said.

It was the never forget you look that Alyssa had seen several times. That look that said that one day fate would come into play, and the mouse would do a favor for the lion. Utter nonsense, to be sure, but not unappreciated. A mouse helping a real lion? Indeed.

"Good-bye," said the woman, and then she turned and walked away. If she had turned around for a last parting look, Alyssa didn't know. She was already running back into the park, hidden from the view of prying eyes.

She decided to double back and was relieved to find that only a smear of blood remained of the pack of young men. They probably imagined that she would come back and eat them, if they decided to stay in the park and wait for an ambulance. Staying out of sight, she followed the scent of the injured one, to see where they'd gotten off to. She wanted to make sure they were out of her park, before she went home for the night.

On the way, she happened to pass the new dwelling that had been set up by a young woman. It was a tent hidden in some bushes and trees. A great job at camouflage, really. She'd never have known it was there if it weren't for her nose. There was no chance that anyone else, not similarly gifted, would stumble onto it either. For their sakes at least. This woman didn't smell like prey. Not at all.

There was a dangerous undercurrent to her scent that made Alyssa wary. It smelled more like the dwelling of a jungle cat than something frail and human. Whether she had a gun, or a knife, or whatever other instrument of violence (though that alone wouldn't have made Alyssa so cautious), instinct told Alyssa that therein lay something that might hurt her. This woman could take care of herself and had no need of whatever protection Alyssa had to offer. Of that she was certain.

Once it was clear that the troublemakers had left her stomping grounds, she made her way to where she had stashed her clothes. Following the terrain, and the landmarks in the skyline overhead, it was a simple matter to find the eighties in the middle of the park. Sniffing the air for the distinct perfume of the little treat she had left herself in a small cage, allowed her to zero in on where she had hidden the rabbit. It was still safe and sound, though utterly terrified at her approach. When she pressed down on the mechanism that opened the door, it flew out of the thing as if it were a bird. She gave it a fair head start of a count of ten before she ran after it.

Before long she was munching on the tender flesh of a quarter pound of raw rabbit. A nice full moon treat, that she savored like the fine morsel that it was. Positively exquisite.

After she washed her muzzle and front paws in a nearby pond, Alyssa began the change. It was slightly difficult, because the moon wanted her to turn into a werewolf, not change out of one, but it was just a minor technicality.

Five minutes later, she was back to her old human self. With her Native American features in stark contrast to her snow-white hair and eyebrows, with piercing gray eyes to boot, as usual. Standing to her full height of five foot ten, she took her time dressing, to wrinkle her clothes as little as possible. Just because she was a little on the wild side sometimes was no excuse to walk around looking disheveled.

Replica moccasin boots, with a brown leather skirt down to her ankles, topped off with a white cotton turtleneck, and suede leather jacket. Native American style, with the strips of leather running down it at the appropriate points. She knew that she looked somewhere in her mid-twenties with prematurely white hair, when in fact she was closer to two hundred, having been born at the start of the Industrial Revolution, here in America. Her Sioux and Cherokee ancestry was as plain as her complexion or the nose on her face.

She let her waist-length straight hair hide inside her jacket, rather than tie it up tonight, as she bent over to pick up her leather backpack. She threw the empty cage that still smelled like rabbit, as far across the park as she could, which was pretty far. While perhaps not as deadly in human form, she was still not prey.

Alyssa was stronger than any man, with eyes and ears super sharp, if dulled down when compared to her other form. She could easily run a marathon at a sustained fast pace, with reflexes beyond most humans. She healed any wound not infected with silver very fast. She

was never sick with virus or cold, never grew old or mentally enfee-
bled, and was thin and muscular with ample hips and bosom. All with a
very pretty face to boot, if she didn't mind her own say so.

She tossed the backpack across her shoulders, placed her sunglasses
on her face to hide her eyes, and slipped over the wall of the park at
east eighty-sixth street as silent as a mouse. Her nose immediately told
her no one was in the vicinity, of which she was grateful. She didn't like
slinking around when she wasn't working if she could help it, prefer-
ring to keep her job and personal life as separate as possible. It helped
if people perceived you as a klutz or worse in your everyday life, when
you were a master thief by trade.

Jewels, gold, and safe deposit boxes. None of it was safe when
Alyssa Running Deer was on the prowl for riches. In truth, not a bank
vault existed that she couldn't get into if she had half a mind to, but
that wasn't what she was about. For her, it was about the elegance of
the caper. It wasn't about bulldozing your way through it all, but
rather, secreting your prize away as if it disappeared of its own accord.
Sowing the seeds of doubt in the establishment's ability to protect
itself, perhaps from thieving employees on the take or something
worse. And of course, getting richer in the process. That was the best
part. There was nothing in the world like spending other people's
money.

Oh, but how could she do such a thing? You might ask. It was easy
to rationalize it, really. What about all the land that the white man had
stolen from her people over the years and things like that? That was
what she might tell someone if she ever got caught. The truth was she
enjoyed the rush of taking things right out from under someone's nose,
especially any someone that was trying too hard to keep it. Family
heirlooms. Sacred mementos. Priceless works of art. The more
precious it was the more she was inclined to take it. Because she
wanted it. Because it would show everyone that nothing was truly safe.
Because she could.

What was the alternative? Read about how Little Red Riding Hood
continues to outsmart that poor wolf after all these years. How long
would she be able to do that? A day?

Soon she was in her building at ninety-sixth street and West End Avenue, safe and sound from all the cares of the world. It was time to call it quits, at least for some shuteye. Yes, werewolves sleep.

"Good evening, Ms. Running Deer," said Jeffrey the Doorman, as he opened the lobby door for her. He was wearing his usual red doorman's outfit, with the gold trim. The kind that she imagined every doorman there ever was probably had in their closet. It was like he was a movie usher, but with a hat. Jeffrey was sixty years old, with the white hair and wrinkles to prove it. His blue eyes were gentle and caring. His diminutive size, at about five and a half feet, was more reassuring than anything else. It was like somebody's father inviting you into their home for some milk and cookies.

He'd been a doorman for fifteen years of his life. Another five and he was probably going to retire. She'd miss him when the time came, to the full extent that their level of acquaintance would allow. So far, she'd only lived in the building for about a year herself. She told everyone she was in banking. He thought she was some hotshot financial wiz.

"Working hard tonight, Jeffrey?" she asked.

"All the time."

"That's good."

"Got any tips for me? You know, I'm retiring soon."

"So you continue to tell me. Don't worry, Jeffrey, the minute something heats up, you'll be the first to know." She smiled.

"That's good to know. Keep me posted."

"Will do. Have a good night," she said, pressing the button for the elevator.

"Good night to you too, ma'am."

She stifled a yawn, as the electric doors closed. Just plain old Alyssa, riding the elevator up to her apartment on the sixth floor. Totally unaware that someone was waiting for her until she all but stepped on him.

"What can I do for you?" she asked, annoyed at the doorman. He knew better than to let visitors up without her permission. Unless it was a neighbor's guest. But at this hour? Not likely.

It was a short little Asian man, sitting Indian style directly in front of her door. His hair looked like it hadn't been combed in weeks. He must have been meditating or sleeping, because he snapped out of whatever it was, to look up at her.

"Hello," he said, in perfect English.

"You're in front of my door," she said. "Why is that?"

"I wish to speak with you."

"About?" She crossed her arms over her chest. With the full moon out, she was just as likely to rip his face clean off, as much as stand here and talk. You might say, it brought out the animal in her. And right now, that part of her didn't like having her space invaded.

"You're not human," he said.

Alyssa took a quick whiff to see what kind of impression she could get of him, but as far as her nose was concerned, he didn't exist. She could smell the fibers of the clothing he wore, but he had no scent of his own.

"Neither are you." A low growl had slipped out of her throat. "If you think I'm not human, you might also think that it's in your best interest to get away from the front of my door."

"I mean you no—"

"Now!"

He stood up to his full height, which must have been around five feet, and walked back to where the elevator was down the hall, with Alyssa hot on his heels. When he turned around, he was looking up into her gray eyes with the same calm he had exhibited at her door. His posture and everything about him spoke of serenity. But that was no excuse to go disrespecting her privacy like this.

"Take this elevator downstairs," she ordered. "Go into the lobby. Walk out the front door in the lobby and exit the building. If I ever see you up here again without my permission, I'm going to kill you. Do you understand?"

"Yes."

"Good," she pressed the elevator button for emphasis, calling it up, and turned around back to her apartment.

"I'm sorry I upset you, but I just want to talk," he called out.

Alyssa ignored him. She didn't care what he wanted or why he had come. It was a very simple equation. He had two options. One: leave like she told him, and live. Two: stay and die. That was it, and it didn't involve any discussion.

She was going to go inside her apartment, put some tea on the stove, and probably be asleep within the hour. If he was anywhere in either her hallway or the lobby of her building when she left in the morning, he was a dead man.

CHAPTER 13
JINX

When Inalia came to, she did not like what she saw. As strong as those feelings were, she liked how she felt even less. As bad as that was, everything went decidedly downhill once her memory woke up (apparently there had been a delay).

Her aching jaw told her that little guy had punched her hard enough to knock her unconscious. While she was out, he tied her up and she was probably in the guy's closet at home. Now it was just a matter of time before she found out if he was gonna rape, eat, or kill her, or all three. Just have to sit back and relax and find out in due time. NOT!

Inalia struggled as hard as she could against the ropes that bound her. There was a way to get out of here and she was going to find it. Just keep struggling. And trying. And she would find herself lucky her captor had never been a Boy Scout and that her left leg was coming loose. YES!

A little more squirming and determination and it was home free city. Leg free. Both legs free. Both arms free. Nothing more but walking home from wherever this place was. She'd love to see the look on that little guy's face...when he was sitting in a chair, staring directly at her, as she walked out of the closet. Not quite what she had in mind.

"Sorry, little one. Not that easy. But you should know better," and then he was almost on her, quick as a wink.

But Inalia was ready for him this time and no sooner had he grabbed at her, then she was where he had been, with chair in hand. And when Inalia clubbed him with that chair, it was his turn to hit the ground.

When he did, she clubbed him with the chair another two times for good measure, and made for the door leading out of the tiny bedroom. Naturally, she hadn't expected the three guys standing in the hallway outside that door and she was generally surprised all over again.

Accomplices? What the hell is going on, Inalia thought, making a mad dash down the opposite direction of the hallway, stifling a scream.

Inalia was on the track team in high school and she was fast as hell. She left those guys wide-eyed and choking on her dust. They'd better hope there was no way out this way. Everything was a blur. She was in a house. Everything was narrow.

Please don't let them catch me.

But luck was still on Inalia's side as she dashed down the flight of stairs that came to view.

Please don't let them catch me.

All she had to do was stay focused, just like on the track, and she'd be home free.

Please don't let them catch me.

She repeated the mantra. Not daring to turn around, for fear that someone might be about to grab her, if she slowed even a hair.

There! That one had to be the way out. The door with lots of locks on it.

Inalia tore through the locks as fast as she had run, to reveal... Trees! Wonderful trees. Sweet success!

"Excuse me."

Inalia turned just in time to get hit in her face again. She was unconscious before she hit the ground.

"Just where do you think you're going?" asked the woman.

SOMETHING DISTURBS HER REVERIE.

She screams with every fiber of her being, as consciousness is thrust upon her and she is ripped away from the arms of mother earth. Her furious body immersed in a deep red liquid heat.

She pulls down to the rocky bottom and thrusts with her legs. Her will. Her entire being. To freedom.

Pulling. Kicking. Propelling her up through a small opening that will lead to...

The surface. Where she lies gasping for breath. The fire in her lungs subsides. She shivers. Scorching red liquid pools around her body.

When she is ready, she walks through the mountain entrance.

ONCE OUTSIDE, THE FRESH AIR BROUGHT A GNAWING HUNGER UP from the depths of her very empty stomach. It was not possible, at this point, to know when she had last fed. Nor did it matter. It was simply her time to eat a very big meal. But where?

Originally, she had chosen these grounds because they were teeming with life. All manner of beast had roamed and provided very nice hunting. Time, as with many things, had changed that.

She set about scouting the much-changed landscape immediately. It was a little rough at first, for as famished as she was, and lethargic as a result, the full potential of her abilities could not be realized. Her senses were obscured by a haze.

She hardly noticed the trees and plants around her, and was barely conscious of the grass underfoot. The light of the sun was no more than a dream to her.

Fortunately, it wasn't too long before she stumbled upon a farm. It was full of horses, cows, chickens, and the usual creatures one might expect to find at such a place. There was even a barn.

When it seemed that no one was around, she began to stalk a victim. She pounced on an unsuspecting cow so soft, quiet, and fast, that it looked as though the thing had fallen of its own volition.

No sooner had the cow's body fallen to the floor, then she began draining its life force. Slowly at first, but faster and with a stronger pull that increased as her hunger came to life. Soon she was ravenously devouring its life. Gorging herself. Until it ran out.

She killed two more cows that way, before she was able to reign in her appetite and regain her composure. She was not at full strength, but it was enough.

To her nose, things were broken up into levels of life and death, that amounted to the reflected strength of one's essence. She could also discern the subtle undercurrents on herself that reeked of cow. After she slaked her thirst with the waters of a nearby lake, the stench of her victims was easily washed away, when she dove into those same waters.

After she had bathed, she took a respite at the water's edge and studied her reflection. It was as if she hadn't aged a day. The same bald head. The same fiery red eyes. The same Jinx.

Something had disturbed her long slumber. Something important.

Unfortunately, in such a restful state, she had not been able to discern what it was. That left her at a huge disadvantage and with nothing but speculation.

At the water's edge, she stretched and yawned, lazily lying on the ground. The night sky was before her, with its many stars twinkling out their welcome. They were some of the few things that were older than her. Along with Mother Earth, of course. Taking a deep breath, she studied the majesty of it all, humbling herself to the power of these miracles.

A long time ago, so far that she should not be able to remember, she had been mortal once. Human. Possessed of all the human frailties. Aging, disease, weakness. She had been destined for a short-lived existence, with little or no meaning. Or that was what she was led to believe.

Once she was named Mirabelle Elsie Sue Ivner, daughter of Morgun Ivner and Shavolia Ivner. Her eyes and hair had been the simplest brown back then, with her pale skin, and sickly constitution. She was always sick as a youth. Always being tended to by the kind ministrations of her mother, and her father, when he was available and not off gathering food or supplies.

She had hated being a burden, and more than once thought they'd be better off if she just up and disappeared. Perhaps dying by one of her fevers, as she was quite prone to get them.

Always a hindrance. Always the newborn babe. Helpless, no matter how much the woman she became. Still, both her parents took care of her and smiled their loving smiles, and never said a harsh word towards her, their only child.

Though they weren't rich by any means, they always managed to have enough so that she never went hungry. She suspected that they had at times not fed themselves. Secreting away the pain of their hunger. Protecting her tender spirit.

Then the plague came. A terrible disease that wiped out the village of Fenren, and its neighboring territories, of which her family was a part. She saw, for the very first time, the irony of a role reversal.

The disease had wrapped itself around the tender hearts of her parents, while she, the forever sick, was untouched. It fell to her to take care of them now, and she did not falter in those duties. She did for them no less than she had been gifted her entire life. But no matter how hard she tried, or how much of her tender spirit she offered to their ailing hearts, it was not enough.

A few fleeting months passed, before she had survived them. Children should not have to bury their parents.

Mirabelle Elsie Sue Ivner, as they had named her, got together all her worldly possessions and burned that little farm to the ground, and the plague with it. She would have to fend for herself now. So, she turned her back on her early life, with tears streaming down her face like small rivers.

Years passed like the wind and she soon found herself the member of a cult, paying homage to some god called Mistenyar, Goddess of Magic. They provided her clothing, shelter, and food, in exchange for her duties of preparing rites, learning their history, and praying to Mistenyar as one of the faithful.

Every day was the same, until the day that a High Acolyte had called upon her to participate in a secret ceremony. She had thanked him profusely for the honor and gone willingly, of course. He escorted her up an endless flight of stairs leading to a cave, impossibly high in the mountains. There he instructed her to wait in prayer, to receive her guidance from Mistenyar.

She spent what must have been hours, prostrated on the ground before the mouth of the cave, waiting for the unknown. It seemed that she might fall asleep right there on the rock face. Unexpectedly, an alien voice rumbled through her head.

"My faithful servant," the voice said.

She was instantly awake, no longer giving way to unconsciousness. Had she imagined it?

"It is I, Mistenyar," the voice continued. "You have been chosen for a great honor, if you are willing to accept. As much as you are suited for it, I will not thrust it upon you. I am a merciful Goddess."

Mirabelle Elsie Sue Ivner began the litany, "Great Mistenyar, above and beyond—"

"Hold!" said the voice in her head, cutting her off. "I know that you are faithful. This demonstration is not necessary to me. Please be at ease and make yourself comfortable." Images, placed in her mind by the Goddess, showed her that she should sit comfortably and cease her posture of prayer.

Faithful servant that she was, she obeyed immediately. Cautiously.

"It is my will to elevate you to a place beyond your fellows, in my esteem. From this moment forth, you will be my right-hand of the faithful. Far beyond anything you could possibly imagine. Imbued with powers beyond your comprehension. You will be the executor of my will. My wrath. My shield. My benevolent hand. The extension of my will, as personally dictated by myself. Carrying out my mandate personally, by my authority, as me." Images assaulted Mirabelle Elsie Sue Ivner's mind as confirmation.

In her mind's eye, she saw herself destroying whole communities, protecting innocents against unimaginable assaults, changing the face of history by her own hand, all at the behest of her magnificent Goddess Mistenyar. As the right-hand of the Goddess, she would no longer be frail and weak, no longer be at the tender mercies of anything ever again.

"I accept, Mistenyar," she said, in response.

"Be sure of this," came the voice. "Once you do this, you cannot return to how you are now."

"I understand. And I accept," said Mirabelle Elsie Sue Ivner.

"Step forth, into the cave, and follow the passage. Do not fear me. Of all those in existence, you have the least to fear," said the voice.

It was true. All of it. Mirabelle Elsie Sue Ivner disappeared from the face of the earth that night, during her eighteenth year, and in her place stood Jinx, much the same way as she was now. Though she did not call herself Jinx back then.

She saw Mistenyar with her own eyes, scared trembling creature that she was, in the presence of such majesty. She had never seen a dragon in person before. The paintings and images of the cult were a poor substitute.

Mistenyar was a huge creature. Easily some five stories high. Scales of silver and white. Blue reptilian eyes, but with a great wisdom behind them, and an intelligence unrivaled by man. Yet somehow gentle in those moments.

A creature with claws able to shred through solid rock like a dried tree leaf. With movements at least as fast and graceful as a mountain lion, and wings like a giant bat. Nothing was safe from her judgment. All these attributes Mistenyar possessed. Far beyond anything in nature. Making her an undisputed master of all, save perhaps others of her kind. Virtually indestructible

Mistenyar the dragon said she came in peace, and so it was. But if it had been otherwise, what could a mere girl do in objection? Scream? Cry? Hurl out obscenities? She was the breeze against the mountain, as the strongest threat she could offer. She knew these things just by looking upon the great creature before her, and she chose to trust.

Mistenyar used terrible magic that permeated every cell of Jinx's existence that night. It lasted an eternity. She writhed in agony, with an undertone of bliss. It was the best way to describe it, short of experiencing it yourself.

It was as if everything in her was super charged beyond capacity, and then the amount was double, and triple, and quadruple. Higher and higher, with more and more energy. Each time making her think that she could hold no more, as thresholds were reached and shattered.

Her mind. Her body. Her spirit. Her sense of self and who she was. All of it stretched impossibly thin, but not like a spider web of silk, or even a steel cable. It was spider web constructed of diamond. Everything, down to the makeup of her cells, felt indestructible.

When it was over, she sat on the ground, much like she did now, but in awe, instead of the rediscovery she relished this night. She was faster and stronger than almost anything. She could see and hear, even now in complete darkness, as if the sun still shone. She could fly like a bird, even though she had no wings. Her skin was as tough as the strongest hide. She had no need of clothing, or shoes, or anything at all to protect her from the elements. Extremes of heat and cold, meant nothing to her. She could communicate with her mind, much like her creator, with anything she could see. She had also been imbued with many magical potentialities, etched into her very spirit, so that she did not need complex spells to work them.

Everything had been like Mistenyar had told her, excepting certain knowledge that was hers, as part of her promotion. Mistenyar was not truly a Goddess, but placed herself in such a position as a right of power. Jinx was no longer to hold her in such worship.

"Think of yourself as my messenger," Mistenyar had told her, some hundreds upon hundreds of years ago.

No longer being the simpleton, she had understood the nature of things almost instinctively. The frail, young girl would have not been able to comprehend what was going on. The new and improved version simply nodded in agreement without the slightest lack of under-standing.

"So be it," she had answered her new master.

Gone were her dull brown hair and eyes, her frail pale skin, and bony limbs. In their place? Jinx's skin had a rich tan color, as if she lived in a tropical climate. Her skinny body was replaced with a more robust one with muscle and vitality. Her hair and eyebrows were completely gone, as was all the hair of her body, including her eyelashes. Her eyes were red. Not amber, or some other hue, but a rich red the same color of rose petals. Even her nails had changed, capable of cutting through most skin with ease, so sharp and strong were they.

She didn't know it at the time, but the dragon had also imbued her with a long life. Disease. Famine. Age. Natural disaster. All these things and worse came and went, but she stood unaffected always. She had been constructed to be the perfect liaison for her master and she was. Performing her tasks with diligence and ease.

She interceded on behalf of Mistenyar in any way the dragon wished. Whether it be to turn the tide of an entire war, to reroute flood waters, evade natural disasters, and anything and everything. Even protecting the physical welfare of her benefactor. Whatever was required, she did without hesitation, always. Until the day that every-thing changed.

That day that her mistress left to go into a deep sleep somewhere even secret to Jinx. Mistenyar said she needed to sleep to replenish her energies and that such a thing was common for dragons. She said that she didn't know how long it would last and that Jinx was free of her charge. That she was free to pursue her own destiny now. That if, by chance, the dragon did wake in her lifetime, that they would be reunited, but as peers. No longer would their association be that of master and student.

Feeling somewhat dejected and abandoned, Jinx went forth to do as her one-time master had instructed, roaming the world on her own. It was during this time that she became known as the Lady Death and had her own throng of worshipers doing her bidding, much as Mistenyar had before her. Jinx's ways took a more sinister bent, which was different from the dragon. It was a reflection of her anger, at being cast aside. First by her parents through nature, and then through Mistenyar later. Any power that opposed her, was vanquished accordingly.

With time she changed and moved on to other places, leaving her followers to worship an empty altar, until such a time as a brave one among them might venture forth and discover it abandoned. She did not care. Her interests had changed as she matured. Alone once more, she took the name she carried now, and moved easily through the world of man.

Soon she possessed her own messenger to convey her will, and guard her, and act in much the same way as she had conducted herself for Mistenyar, whose whereabouts she was totally unaware of. As in slumber, the dragon's raw energies, went to such a low level as to be undetectable by even one such as her.

After a time, she too went into a slumber, though she didn't know if it was necessary, as much as she had become bored with her environment and the world around her. What better time to sleep? Dreaming during her slumber, as the years passed by. Completely undisturbed.

Eventually, she awoke once more, with the world changed and fresh. Mother Earth was full of new energy and mysteries. At the forefront of her attention were the mysterious energies she had picked up. Familiar, but different.

No sooner had she awoken, disoriented as she was, then they simply disappeared. It was a bright beacon of powerful energy, akin to what she herself might possess, if not greater. Then it simply ceased to exist.

Was it another dragon? Would her friend and mentor Mistenyar be waking soon as well? She didn't know.

Jinx changed her seated position into a low crouch. She smelled the night air, taking in the scents of deer, insects, trees, flowers, grass, and mold. She listened as far as her hearing would take her, picking up an unusual hum that she was unfamiliar with, apart from the natural sounds she expected. She leaned forward onto the balls of her feet, her breath quickening. Her blood started a low simmer, as she absently licked the sharp fang of her upper right canine tooth. Her lip curled ever so slightly.

In a blur of motion, she went from complete stillness, to complete motion; tearing through the earth as her legs pounded it mercilessly. Running at half speed, the wind caressing her naked flesh. She pushed herself to one hundred percent, to see what she was truly capable of.

It was doubtful that she was not the fastest thing in existence. A lone adolescent boar, only aware of her after she was long gone, with swirling leaves, and broken mushrooms floating in her wake; the only proof of her passage. The pack of deer she had smelled ran away from her, and she ran ahead of them as if they were all standing still.

Without pause she ran until she came to a cliff, where she took a deep breath and dove into the cold waters some fifty feet below. Deep. Until she hit the underwater floor, and coasted along the bottom, caressing it ever so gently with her body, before she made for the surface of the water. At the top, she treaded with her arms and legs, leisurely taking in the beauty of the night's full moon.

Some things never change.

When she had her fill of it, she willed herself into the sky and took flight, like a water bird. She did not possess the great wings of her maker, but had been gifted with the ability to soar with the winds, regardless. She immediately made for the clouds with a far greater speed than she remembered. It seemed her abilities had grown, even in her slumber.

Fantastic. This was going to be fun.

She let out a great peal of laughter and hurled herself through a patch of the watery mist. It was great to be alive.

"Your Highness, you are awake," came a familiar voice into her mind. She was somewhat disappointed that it was not her maker, Mistenyar, but pleased to find out that she was not alone. The one who called himself Twister was still with her.

"Yes, my faithful one. I have returned," she slowed her movements so that she but hovered in the air, before continuing the telepathic communication. "How long have I been asleep?" she asked.

"About four hundred years, give or take," said Twister. "Please allow me to bring you up to date."

Jinx paused to let it fully sink in. Four hundred years. Could it have been so long?

"Yes. As always, I would appreciate your assistance in this matter. Do you know where to find me?"

"Of course, Highness. I have not forgotten. It will take me three days to arrive, unless you require me sooner."

"That is fine. I've been asleep for four hundred years, Twister. Another three days isn't going to kill me."

His laughter. And then, "I am on my way."

The communication ended, leaving Jinx back to her own thoughts. So much time had passed. Almost as much as half her entire existence. Why had she slept so long? What happened to Mistenyar and the other immortals of the earth? Were they all still asleep, as she had been only moments before?

Not to worry. Twister would know. It was likely that if they all slept, they would soon wake, as she had. Perhaps not now. But soon. How would she be received then, no longer the agent of her master? Would they set out to test her mettle, or respect her autonomy?

Jinx willed herself back home and disappeared. She did not fly. She did not even move. One moment she was in the sky, and the next moment she wasn't. It was instantaneous. It was magic.

CHAPTER 14
SWITCHED

After much thought, Kayala found herself back at Ash's home. She felt guilty for leaving after he helped rescue her, but the situation had been demeaning. She did not want his pity for a slave. She wanted a meeting of equals. Going off on her own had been the only way to establish her independence.

Finding Ash's place was not difficult at all. The challenge was getting into the building in the first place. It was a small building located in a place called Staten Island. Taking the boat that would ferry her across the water and retracing her steps had been straight forward.

The size of the building resulted in few occupants, forcing Kayala to wait. Eventually, walking into the building as someone happened to leave. She half-hoped it would be Ash, as it might be a little less uncomfortable. Maybe she could have followed him for a bit and pretended to have accidentally bumped into him.

Fate seemed to have other ideas, and it looked like the more direct approach was required. The heavy-set man who lumbered out of the building bore no resemblance to Ash at all, but the man was willing to let her into the building without protest.

She walked up the three flights of stairs, got up her nerve, and knocked on the door with false confidence. It was all she could do not to let her imagination run wild with possibilities. What if she was a burden? What if he was with another woman?

It didn't help that he wasn't answering the door. Though, he could probably tell it was her and could just as easily be ignoring her.

"Hello." She told the door. "Are you home? It's umm...me. Hello?"

There was no answer and there were no sounds coming from inside. In a futile attempt, she tried the doorknob and found the door to be unlocked. How odd. Odd, but lucky. It was good that she did not have to force it, which would have only added to the awkwardness.

Inside everything looked as she remembered, though her sleeping area had been cleaned up. Ash was not home but she decided to stay and wait for him to return. It would give her some solace from the outside world while she waited.

Kayala locked the door. It was a far cry from how she had been accustomed to living. His apartment was more than welcome. Offering her a greater piece of mind than she had known in the past weeks, out on her own.

She chose an open space where she could sit cross-legged, setting the small bundle of her belongings on the floor. Her hands, she rested on the red material of her sweatpants, running them lightly across the fabric. She absently played with her tan workman boots, fussing with the laces.

From time to time, she would rock her body back and forth or change the positioning of her legs. Also, she took to whistling a catchy tune she had heard in a store and playing with her hair.

Shaking her head and humming the same tune, while leaning back with her palms on the floor, shaking her foot to the beat, she came to realize that she was extremely nervous. Why else would she be straining to listen as hard as she could for the merest footfall? Or, so pointedly ignoring the window, and her desire to stand staring out of it to the street below. Slowly soaking in her sweat, with her warm coat still wrapped around her, waiting for his final judgment.

Kayala began to cry.

It was an odd sensation and she didn't know what to make of it. She touched her hand to her wet face in disbelief. One moment she was fine, and the next, she was so defeated. But why now? She couldn't see the reason for it, but that did not stop the tears from streaming down her face.

She stripped the shoes and socks off her feet, and removed her coat, throwing the items into a corner of the room. Then she headed to the bathroom where she proceeded to splash her face at the sink. A reddened face stared back with green eyes, and disheveled yellow hair, in the mirror.

What a mess.

In her anxiety she had forgotten to eat. A foolish mistake. Kayala searched the place for food. She found raviolis in one of Ash's cupboards, pulled the little metal handle atop it, and ate out of the can with a spoon she found in a kitchen drawer.

Much better.

She stripped off the remainder of her clothing, and slipped into a warm bath, using the oils she had acquired surreptitiously in her travels. The soothing waters washed away the tension. Relaxing her uneasy spirit.

Before long she was staring at the backs of her eyelids, with her thoughts running around loosely like wild horses in open fields of lush greenery.

SHE HAD TAKEN TO SLEEPING IN CENTRAL PARK, INSIDE A TENT that she appropriated from a sporting goods store. The location was camouflaged so that even in daylight hours, hidden within bushes and surrounding trees, it was very hard for someone to spot her little domicile. Sure, she could easily be killed in her sleep, but it was the best she could do.

She roamed the City of New York and hunted and salvaged. Always exploring the area outside of the great park in the daylight hours and returning back inside, to locate her tent and hide the items she had found. She made it a point to enter the park in the sixties before heading farther north where she lived in the upper hundreds. The better to throw off the trail of any would-be pursuit.

It was an empty existence with the sole purpose of keeping her alive. Everything she acquired was misbegotten. She was the social outcast here, as much as she had ever been in bondage. And worse, she could not see her way clear to better advantage, without drastic measures.

When she had first started out, enthralled with the power of her new freedom, she wanted to run wild on her own. Great, where she would have been as nothing in captivity. Her enthusiasm and boundless energy seemed more than enough to accomplish anything her heart desired.

But along the way, she began to see what type of person she would have to be. What it would take to go from absolutely nothing to something of great respect. She found that she did not have the stomach for it.

"Ignorant... Stupid... Slave girl," she berated herself under her breath.

Would that she were like her lifelong captors. Full of a selfishness that destroyed everything in favor of the one. Always! A world where the cold-blooded killer had everything on a whim, where the size of the predator determined achievement. As everyone was a hunter, and failure meant death.

She could not bring herself to burden this world with that philosophy. No matter, that here, it was an easy way to have what you wanted, as even the strongest of them—the meanest they had to offer, was nothing to her.

But that wasn't the woman that she was, and unfortunately in her freedom, and in life, she had to be true to herself no matter what. That was how she came to accept her fate.

Though she was loath to admit it, she needed help.

It was time to swallow her pride and ask Ash for help.

PRESENTLY, SHE SETTLED ON HIS COUCH AND WATCHED SOME television to distract herself while waiting. When she had her fill, she stripped off the dark blue towel wrapped around her middle, to bare skin, to stretch out on his bed. She found a slight comfort in how the bed smelled like him, more than anywhere else in the apartment. It wasn't long before she was fast asleep.

BACK HOME, THE QUEEN HAD NO IDEA WHAT WAS GOING ON WITH her search party. All she knew, was that they were due to return with a report of the reconnaissance mission. Soon, all the planning and hard work would finally bear fruit. Just a taste, to be sure, but after so very long without. To finally see the proof of her faith. The very manifestation of her resolve. Given shape.

Well it was about damn time! She was no simple fool to be cast aside. Her will was not a pipe dream. Not some untenable wish. Her aims were real with far-reaching realizations of a scope and power unimaginable to almost anything.

Chanovalle's sights were not set on something as trivial as self-promotion. Not so mediocre. The very potential of this event. This occurrence. Might change her comprehension of reality itself.

Part of the burden of achieving her goal lay in burying it in half-truths and obscurity, when what she really wanted was to shout her genius from the highest mountain top. Lest some mindless fool steal all her glory out from under her at the moment of truth. Far better to hold it all in and risk insanity.

As Queen, she had at her disposal certain powers, by right of law. The very thing she, herself created. And in so doing, if she were unable to use these tools to full effect, ruthlessly directing things to reach her aims, then Chanovalle Remseldorne was a fool. An impossibility, confirmed by those same laws.

Imagine calling the Queen a fool and being allowed to live. She half imagined she might call a conference together declaring herself such a one to see what took place. Saw herself, killing each and every one that did not come to her defense instantaneously.

She was no fool. Mad genius perhaps. Maybe even a little eccentric. Even this was to her advantage, as a form of subterfuge she wielded to keep her enemies on their toes. Though she did not know who they might be exactly, it was inevitable that she had individuals set against her. Causing her to use all manner of feint and parry in her strategies.

Like the one she had used in getting rid of the Child of Destiny. A brilliantly masterful stroke, if she dared say so herself. Countering the conspiracy she felt brewing here in her own castle, by sending the very instrument of the manifestation of all she had been working on these long years, far, far away. How would they be able to kill her pet then? When they did not even know her whereabouts? Impossible. Impossibly brilliant, on her part, yet again.

She had sent Kayala with her reconnaissance group, as a veritable honor guard, to the docile world that existed through the Shimmering Gate. To a concentration of a human race that had not the spine or the inclination, let alone the ability, to harm a single hair on anyone's pretty little head. Safely tucked away from any predators bold enough to accidentally destroy the Queens' plans. Accidentally, because other than herself, no one in the entire realm knew anything about Kayala's role as the Child of Destiny. Another stroke of brilliance.

Just imagine it. As if she could let such a one live. So why even create the temptation, by spreading the knowledge that she coveted above all, that of the true value of the girl, Kayala. The one that was destined to imbue her with unspeakable magical power. Such that it was, beyond even what she already possessed, as an immortal vampire. Only to propel her even farther away from the human cattle she tread underfoot like little ants, and bring her to her true ultimate goal.

Wherein she would be able to return to her home world, which was even superior to this beautiful realm of Pandoria that she ruled. The place she had been cast out of by magic gone awry, during a battle between the two dominant factions of her true home. Both of them, races of noble vampire, with humans as nothing more than food.

She would return and assume her rightful place as ruler of that realm as well. Mistress of two worlds instead of one, and many more to follow.

With Kayala fulfilling her key role. All the waiting. All the planning. All the work.

Soon it would all matter. All of it.

"JUST WHERE DO YOU THINK YOU'RE GOING?" SHE ASKED THE unconscious girl at her feet. An answer, of course, was of no consequence, as the slave's role was predestined, and placed once more in Azure's capable charge. Fate, it seemed, had smiled upon her.

The surprise of it had left her speechless, as the very thing she had been hunting these past three days had all but came out to greet her. It took no time at all for Azure to regain her composure and subdue her quarry. Years of battle training and command instinctively came to the fore, to seize control once more.

Apparently, the slave had been fleeing her would-be captors, which had allowed Azure to catch her off guard. The three of them were even now stumbling towards her, in the dark of night.

"Where is your Captain?" she asked, as the three men saluted.

"He must be in the house, Commander," said the shortest of the three. "We didn't get a chance to check on him, since the slave had gotten free."

"You go find him yourself, while you other two bring her back inside," she said.

It didn't matter to Azure what these others were called. They were already dead; they just did not know it yet. Someone had to take responsibility for this mess, and after this last failing, it was going to be these three. Pratle would live if the slave hadn't killed him, as a reward for finding her in the first place.

Once inside the house, Azure made sure the front door was secure. Now that she was here to set it all right, everything would run like clockwork.

Captain Pratle made his way downstairs into the living area where

Azure sat, inspecting the damage he had suffered. That it was but a scratch, was enough shame, but with the escape added, it was good he did not meet her eyes.

"This time you'll do it right, or not at all," she told him. It was through her mercy that he yet lived, and she would brook no more stupidity. Any further failure would see his head on a pike.

She tossed the sticky paper she had acquired, at his feet. "Wrap her up with this."

"How was it that you came by this domicile?" she asked the shortest of the three soldiers.

"We killed the people who were inside and threw the bodies downstairs, Commander," he said.

"Show me."

As ordered, he showed her the whereabouts of their victims and even escorted her down the stairs. Azure paced around the underground room a bit and then started her way up the stairs, turning briefly halfway.

"You know what? I have an idea. Stay here for a moment. I'm going to send the others down to help you with my next task," then she turned and continued her ascent. "You two," she ordered, "take that silver tape from the Captain and bind the bodies downstairs. I want this to look like a botched kidnapping."

"Yes, Commander," they said in unison, and proceeded down the steps.

Azure closed and locked the door when they had passed. They might assume she wanted private words with the Captain, which she did.

"I have a vehicle I procured, outside. I want that stowed into it immediately," she indicated the slave with her eyes. "Then I want this place burned to the ground," this she whispered so as not to alert the others. "The men do not leave this place. Am I clear, Captain?"

"Loud and clear, Commander," answered Pratle, with eyes still averted to the ground.

"Good. I'll wait for you in the car." Azure had already checked to make sure there was no escape from the lower room. It would be a simple matter to rid herself of the nuisance within.

Later, if the lapse in her guardianship of the slave came up, she would blame it on the bumbling trio. Her Queen would respect her dispatch of justice and probably berate her on poor training or some such. With the slave back in the Queen's yoke, there would be no harm, no foul.

The emblem outside the car said Ford. It was silver and had four doors. She opened a door and sat in the front passenger seat, strapping the seatbelt into place. She felt a bit of tension leave her shoulders and leaned back in the seat. One of the first things she would do when she got home was to get a back rub.

When Pratle finally came back, the house was ablaze with smoke building inside. She waited a few minutes to savor the moment, and then instructed him to start the car and drive off. Her bad luck streak had finally come to an end.

INALIA REGAINED CONSCIOUSNESS AND WISHED SHE HADN'T. IT WAS like she had been sucked into one of those horror movies that gave her nightmares. Her arms were tied behind her at the wrists, ankles tied together, and her mouth was taped shut. Unable to move or speak, she was just grateful she could see. Knowing you were lying down in the backseat of a moving car was slightly better than being left to your imagination.

I'm so dead, she thought, struggling not to cry. She tried desperately to distract herself. Now was not the time to lose it.

Looking out the window showed nothing but the night sky, and she couldn't see her abductors at all. There were two of them and they were taking her somewhere else. Three people in total, if she included herself. That's all she had fact-wise.

Everything was cut and dry at this point. Inalia was confident she was being sold into slavery overseas. All blonde hair and green eyes, like she was. Probably all exotic and stuff to those people over there.

The ones that would add her to their harem. Maybe she wasn't going to die after all.

She closed her eyes again, fighting the great wave of despair that threatened to overwhelm her. It was all she could do not to cry like a little girl.

So much for college. Or life.

THE THREE OF THEM DROVE AROUND FOR AN ETERNITY IN SILENCE. Eventually, the car came to a complete stop and the driver got out. After a while, the back door was opened by her head, and she was uncomfortably man-handled, and slung over someone's shoulder. It was a man. Probably the driver. He had dark black hair and a black leather jacket.

The ground was made of tar, and she thought she saw a motel sign for a second. The door to their room swung open and she was tossed down onto a bed.

Hopefully they would take the gag off and untie her, but if not, at least let her know what was going on. Either it was going to be slavery or they were going to kill her right here in the hotel room. That's where they always killed people in the horror movies.

Not knowing was so hard. She couldn't even explain it in her head. All she could do was feel it.

Crying until the salt of her tears formed a desert on her face, that mirrored the desert inside, of her hopes and dreams. All those little voices that told her everything was going to be alright, gone.

The uncontrollable shaking. Wanting to scream until her vocal cords snapped, but still scream and never stop, with broken strings flapping around, destroyed and useless in her throat. Begging the world for just one more chance. PLEASE! Because she would do anything. ANYTHING!

CHAPTER 15
INNOCENCE LOST

T he surrounding territory was flat. There was no other word for it. In the big city there had been tall magnificent buildings everywhere you looked, dwarfing everything else around them. Here, everything was a little shack by comparison. Where people had been compressed into that small space like ants, out here everything was all but deserted. A few roads framed by trees and wildlife. A few shops and pit stops, sprinkled around. Nothing more.

The temperature had dropped as well, causing him to close the snaps of his jacket and flip up the collar. His breath came out misty, warmer than the air outside. Just like he was smoking a cigarette, a favorite pastime of the locals.

Pratle was a soldier, first and foremost, but he wasn't without feelings. With the slave girl tied up over his shoulder like she was, it had been all he could do not to slam her down on the ground and have his way with her. If it weren't for the Commander being there, he would have spread her legs right there, outside next to the car. She just smelled so good. But the Commander was there, and she would have killed him right there on the same spot.

So naturally, all worked up like he was, the first thing he did when he was ordered out of the little room, was try to score some action. He walked across the highway to what looked like a place for food. It was opened and had a couple of people inside, so he went in to check it out.

He was already dressed in an outfit that a local would wear, having acquired it from a man he'd beat unconscious. Leather jacket, plaid white and gray shirt, black jeans, white socks, dark leather shoes. He thought it went well with his dark eyes and hair, and the sharp features of his face.

He bit his lip, standing in the entryway. He needed something low-key. Something the Commander wouldn't notice. She was already upset about the slave situation as it was. The last thing he wanted was to bring more heat his way.

He took a seat by the front window and waited. From here, he could see the motel across the road, and come running if it looked like the Commander was looking for him. She was in a mood though, so that was unlikely.

A little old lady put a list of options he could eat on the table and offered him a cup of coffee. Her name tag said Flo.

"Do you want milk with that?" she asked, pulling out a little notepad.

"Yes."

"Do you know what you want?"

"Not yet."

"Okay. I'll be right back with your coffee."

Pratle perused the list in the meantime.

She had the heavy steps and labored breathing, that made it clear that walking was an effort. She placed a cup of coffee down on the table and a glass of water.

"Can I have breakfast, or do I have to order dinner?" he asked, when she was done.

"Yeah, you can have breakfast, if you want," she said.

"I'll have the number five," he began. "Two eggs, two pancakes, and bacon."

"Okay," she said.

"Can I have sausage with that as well?"

"Sausage? Sure. Anything else?"

"And ham. I'll pay extra for some ham too."

"Ham? Okay. That it?"

"I'd like a large glass of orange juice as well."

"Okay. Coming right up, sir."

"Thank you," he said, and proceeded to take a sip of his coffee. "Where's the bathroom?" he asked when she passed by a minute later.

"Go straight back, turn right, and take the steps down. Can't miss it," said Flo.

"Thanks." Pratle got up from the booth he was in and went off in search of the bathroom. Straight back. Turn right. Take the steps down. And there was the bathroom with the little man painted on it. Next to it was the bathroom for women. They liked to separate the two out here, which he found amusing.

Inside he used a urinal, washed his hands, fixed his hair in the mirror, and was back in his seat lickity-split, about five minutes before Flo arrived with his food.

"You know what?" he asked her. "I just realized I forgot something."

She had pulled out her notepad again. "Go ahead," she said.

"Can I get a vanilla shake too?"

"Alrighty. One vanilla shake."

"Thank you so much," he said, as politely as he knew how.

"You're welcome," she replied, before walking off to take another customer's order at the counter.

Pratle took his time eating his food. It was really good, and he enjoyed it a great deal. The sun was starting to show over the horizon, judging by the reddish hue. It looked like they were staying in the motel for the night after all, due to the Commander's skin condition. Great. He could use the freedom.

It won't be long before people start coming into this place for breakfast, he thought.

Flo brought his vanilla shake when he was about halfway done with his meal. He thanked her and went back to eating. It came with toast with butter on it, and he used that to sop up the broken egg yolk that had leaked onto his plate. Up until then he had only had a sip of his shake to make sure that it was good, which it was.

When Pratle was done with his meal he drank the shake until it was all gone, slurping up every last drop. Then he finished what was left of his coffee.

"Will that be all?" asked Flo, when she noticed that he was done, about five minutes later.

"I'd like some more coffee, please," said Pratle.

"Okay," she said. And off she went.

Pratle made it a point to nurse his coffee so that it lasted as long as possible, and then when he was done he got a refill and nursed that as well. It wasn't long before the breakfast crowd started streaming in, just like he had expected. He was pleased to see that younger women came in, nowhere near as old as old Flo.

It made him smile.

He hailed Flo and asked her for the check. When she came back with it, he made sure to leave her with a handsome tip. He gave her ten dollars for herself. He would have tipped her more, but he didn't want to attract any more attention than he already had.

Looking around, he figured out a plan quick enough. He walked over to the ladies room, down the flight of stairs and knocked on the door. There was no answer, so he went in, but left the door unlocked. The first one to come inside would be his.

Luckily, he didn't have to wait long. Some lady walked in and was completely shocked when she saw him sitting on the toilet. In one smooth motion, he grabbed her and locked the door, putting his hand over her mouth before she had a chance to scream out.

"You know what I want," he told her from behind. "Now take your clothes off."

When she didn't seem to listen right, he turned her around and punched her face with everything he had. As she was now stunned and pacified, he got to work stripping just enough to get the job done. When she resisted again, he threw another punch to her face. He tried not to break her nose, but probably broke her jaw. She was sobbing, but still ended up getting punched again when she continued to resist.

Finally, she got the message and there were no more punches. Just other kinds of fun.

When he was done with her, he cleaned himself off, and walked out of the restaurant entirely. He wasn't worried about anyone chasing after him any time soon. People didn't pay attention enough for that to happen.

At some point he had drowned her in the toilet, then slit her wrists with his knife to make it look like a suicide. By the time they realized she had drowned, they wouldn't even try looking for him. He left the knife and placed it in the dead woman's hand. With the door locked from the inside, everything would look official.

He had other knives. It was fine. Ideally, he'd have let her live to play with some more, but there was no time. Commander Azure already had steam coming out of her ears, so he had to be careful. No sense ending up like those three flunkies he'd reduced to dust. She wasn't to be fooled with. Not that one. He'd seen the end result of those that had tried. Tried and died. And all that before the Queen had Initiated her.

The Initiates had abilities far beyond anything someone like him would be able to deal with. Best to keep a low profile and do whatever she wanted. Pratle hadn't gotten this far by being belligerent. Never when his life was on the line.

He walked across the highway to the other side where the motel was, looking back casually over his shoulder, to make sure no one was watching him. Time to take care of those chores the Commander had lined up for him.

ONCE PRATLE HAD TOSSED THE SLAVE DOWN ON THE BED, HE turned and left as ordered. Azure locked the door and went to the bathroom inside the room. She wasn't worried about the slave going anywhere, all tied up like a stuffed pig. She relieved herself, and on second thought, came out and ripped the tape off the slave's mouth before returning to the smaller room for a bath.

"You realize screaming will be punished," she stated to the room, then she closed the bathroom door.

The slave knew the rules well enough over the years. She was treasured, but not required to be necessarily pristine. Her virtue had to be intact and she could not be maimed. The Queen would take any such thing as a personal affront. Certain minor torture and discomforts were permissible sometimes. It depended on how cautious or creative you were.

As long as everything was back to normal, Azure's head would stay attached. Also, the slave wasn't aware of the Queen's mandate, other than knowing she was her personal property. She was aware that Azure was the Queen's right hand, as well, and was likely afforded special treatment as befitted her station.

As expected, when she returned to the other room, newly clean and rejuvenated, the slave was still lying on the bed. She did turn to face Azure though, as she came out of the bathroom, wrapped in a white towel. She looked like she had something to say. Azure arched an eyebrow.

"What are you going to do with me?" asked the slave.

"Return you to the Queen, of course," Azure replied. She didn't understand the point of such a stupid question. It was beyond obvious. She began to turn her back on the slave, so she could replace her clothing.

"What do you mean return?" was the next question.

"What are you going on about, Kayala? Did I hit your head that hard? Now isn't the time to try my patience." If she was trying to get a rise out of her it wouldn't work.

"Look, I don't know what your problem is. You people are the ones who kidnapped me," replied the slave, raising her voice. "And I don't know who you think you are or what the fuck your problem is!" she yelled. "That you can't just answer my God damn question," she had managed to stand and was crying at the same time; still tied up. "Instead of asking me some psycho-babble bullshit and acting like you know me, when you don't even know me. You don't know my name, and you don't know shit!" She screamed at the top of her lungs. Overcome with rage, her hands had gotten free and found themselves around her captor's neck.

Azure was at a loss for words, and not just because she was being choked, but because this was unconscionable. What lunacy was this? Kayala never acted like this. But as sure as she had eyes, it was her.

The trick was not to smash her into the television. Azure proceeded to bang her opponents elbows with balled up fists, then ducked down and kicked out, tripping legs and sending the slave to the floor. In her anger, Kayala had ignored that her legs were still taped together, and that was her undoing.

Azure's towel had come undone, but it didn't faze her. She was more than comfortable in her own skin, and the thing would only hinder her movements. She had crouched low in preparation for the next assault, but it never came. Seeing her opponent lying there impotent, she stood up to her full height in disbelief.

The Kayala she knew, though a slave, was a competent fighter and tough as a horse. In all the time she had been around, no one had ever seen her cry over a little fall. She wasn't artful, but she was a fierce brawler, that everyone took seriously. Nothing at all like the scared little girl here.

Oh, that fate would be so cruel as this? Madness beyond measure. This couldn't be happening. Could the brief stay in this world have addled her brain so?

Then she caught it. Something she had overlooked in all her excitement. The scent was off! It wasn't her!

Azure sat on the floor. What was she going to do now? Her nose didn't lie.

All this time she was so sure. Then, in the time it took to dress, an illusion was stripped away, and she had been marked a complete failure.

Azure's head would be on a pike so fast, she might as well kill herself here and save her honor.

"Who in demon's name are you?" she asked the imposter.

⁓

IT WAS WARM INSIDE EVEN THOUGH SHE WASN'T COVERED WITH A blanket. Someone had thoughtfully turned up the thermostat so that it was almost hot. Other than that, it was the typical motel room that you might see in the movies. Cheap full-sized bed. White walls. Small little table next to the bed. A desk up against another wall. A TV put close to the other wall, near the door. Left alone in the room, she had taken it all in, appreciating all its dullness as best she could. Waiting for the verdict. Waiting to find out what they were planning to do with her. Until she snapped.

A switch went off inside her, that she didn't even know she had. One minute she was her normal self, and the next, she had totally lost it. Somehow her hands were free, and she was going to knock that woman's blue eyes right out of her fool head, like a couple of marbles. And after that she'd rip every hair of her black evil hair right off her head, till she looked like a rag doll.

She failed almost as soon as the thought was in her head, and then everything just changed. All her anger went away.

So, this was what it was like to have a breakdown. She felt so powerless. So helpless. Even when she had all but lost her reason, trying so hard to be free, she had been swatted away like a little girl.

What had she ever done to deserve this? How bad, at this point in her life, could she possibly have been? These thoughts and feelings assaulted the core of her being, to drown out all hope and resistance, in a flood of tears.

The impact when she fell, had ripped the breath from her and then she collected the air, just so the dam could break. The tears began to flow freely and Inalia cried and blubbered, in the sorrow of her great defeat.

She had turned her back to her jailer and curled up into a fetal position on the floor, waiting to get beat. At the sound of the woman's voice, her body involuntarily jerked. She turned shyly, to see if it was a trick.

"This does not seem to add up at all," said the woman, in a disbelief that paralleled Inalia's own feelings. "This is not how we act. This is not how we are reared. It's almost as if you've turned into one of the sheep."

Inalia was grabbed roughly, pulled up, and slapped in her face so hard that she momentarily stopped crying. Spots floated in her eyes and she almost forgot where she was.

"What did you do that for?" she asked in shock. Her left hand had come to her rescue too late and was holding her face. She sobbed, and wet tears continued to steam down it. Then she was abruptly released in response to her question, falling to the floor again.

"But you haven't turned into one of them at all. You are one of them," said the woman, turning her back on Inalia, as if she no longer mattered.

"I don't understand you," Inalia mumbled. "Please don't hit me again, but I still don't know what you're talking about."

"You are not the one I'm looking for," the woman told her. "In as much as you look exactly like her, you are not the one."

"So that means you're going to let me go?" asked Inalia. She felt a hint of hope peek outside.

"No, I cannot."

"But why not? You just said I'm not the one you're looking for," Inalia sniffled.

The woman turned to look down at Inalia's shocked and confused face. "I'm going to tell you a few things that you need to know." She sat down next to Inalia as if confiding in a dear friend. "Listen and understand," she told her. "Or, you will die."

And the finality of those last words, along with the other things Azure mentioned, stamped out the embers of any hope Inalia might have had left. The spirit inside of her curled up into a ball and braced for the impact of its inevitable destruction.

Gone. It was all slipping through her fingers. Each word she heard leeched more out of her, imprisoning and constricting, but draining away as well. It was so different to finally hear what was in store for her, instead of what her wild imagination told her might happen.

～

AZURE FOUND HERSELF VULNERABLE IN A WAY SHE WOULD GIVE NO voice to, though her thoughts were sick with the illness of it. Worse still, to let it out.

It was a conspiracy. A great roiling thing that teetered on the edge of her own destruction. A rabid beast, that she alone fought to control.

Kayala was gone and it was too late to get her back. That was a fact that would have killed Azure instantly once she returned home. Such was the impetuous Queen Chanovalle, in her anger.

The conclusion was sure, but not inevitable, as it turned out. For Azure had somehow discovered Inalia; an exact duplicate of Kayala in appearance, if not in spirit. She did not think like Kayala or act like Kayala, simply because she was someone else entirely. But did the Queen even care?

How close was the Queen to her favorite pet? What did she know of the true person underneath? Probably no more than Azure knew of most of her soldiers.

Therefore, Inalia was perfectly suitable, as much as you could ever hope to replace the superficial physical trappings of a thing. She was not a person. She was a toy for the amusement of the master, and she would be treated and viewed as such. It was just a matter of bringing this one in line and making sure she was covered in the same oils and fragrances, to cover up the deceitful smell of her.

It would fall to Azure to teach this Inalia the tricks and mannerisms of her predecessor. She had the little time afforded in their journey and perhaps intermittent exercise runs down the line. It should be enough to pull the ruse together. It had to be.

As to how sure Azure was of the outcome? She was confident enough to bet her life on it. Everyone would believe this creature to be Kayla, temporarily lost slave to the Queen of Pandoria. Anyone that doubted that would be killed.

CHAPTER 16
OLD FRIENDS

By the time Ash had climbed up and found an entrance into the mountain, the sun was almost about as high in the sky as it was going to get, and so was he. Looking down from the top of the world, he wondered how long someone would scream before hitting the bottom. All you'd need was a strong gust of wind pulling you off the mountain to get started.

Thankfully, he had anchored himself down by ropes, so that plummeting down the mountain wasn't a real concern.

He eyed the opening with other concerns. Even with his newfound abilities, God only knew what lay beyond. He'd already met opponents far superior to what he expected. At a place as ominous as this, it was easy for his imagination to run wild.

Working up his nerve, he pulled a flashlight out of his bag. The batteries were fresh. He even had an extra flashlight stowed away. Placing the bag on his back, he stepped into the unknown.

There were many twists and turns in a labyrinth of tunnels. Forty-five minutes passed before he found anything promising. A set of stairs.

Traveling down the winding flight, brought him to a doorway awash in the light of torches a short distance beyond, in another part of the maze. It was bright enough, at this point that he wouldn't need the flashlight, so he shut it off. Making sure to carefully stuff it back in his bag. The little flames danced on the walls, to a shared song. So captivating and almost hypnotic was their show, that Ash almost walked right into the little Asian guy standing around the corner.

He was tiny for a man, at no more than five feet. Standing somewhere below Ash's shoulder. He wore his dark hair haphazard and wore unremarkable clothing. He looked like the archetype for the average Asian tourist. All he was missing was a camera.

They stood and stared at one another for a more than awkward amount of time, with the little fellow not saying a word. Ash broke the silence.

"Hello?" he said. More a question than a greeting.

"Hello," came the response. And then there was another awkward silence.

"What is this place?" he asked. But there was no response. "You light all these?" The little man just stared at him until Ash became uncomfortable.

Figuring the little guy might not really know English, Ash started to walk around him.

"I am not permitted to let you pass," said the Asian fellow, in perfect English. He had raised his left arm, pressing his hand against a wall, to block the path ahead.

"So, you do understand English," said Ash, somewhat annoyed. He took two steps back to an acceptable talking distance. "So, umm, what is this place? Again. And why exactly are you getting in my way?"

"I cannot tell you," was the response. The little arm never strayed from the wall, continuing to bar the way. The awkward silence had returned as well, with the same intrusive staring of a moment ago.

Ash looked the fellow up and down, trying to impress upon him the silliness of the situation. He was a small man of five feet, max. While Ash, on the other hand, was about six feet tall. There weren't any bulging muscles. In fact, the little guy was puny, with the shoulders of a little boy.

"Are you going to get out of my way?" he asked in irritation. Ash was looking back the way he had come, but there was no question who his words were for.

"No."

"Fair enough," he said, and then Ash was a blur of motion.

He had simply ducked very low under that little arm and walked past as if it wasn't there. As fast as he was, the little Asian guy still grabbed the bag on Ash's back and pulled it. Ash slid out of the pack and prepared for the inevitable fight.

The two of them began to dance. It was the dance of combat.

The Asian fellow flowed in and out of complex maneuvers honed through years of practice. Simple moves developed into more serious expressions, tending to leave Ash overwhelmed.

Incorporated into the dance were elements to further each man's goal. Ash struggled to move forward along the path, while his adversary attempted to hinder his progress and even reverse it.

Unable to out finesse his opponent, Ash rushed at him, scooping him up into his arms, ending up in a modified football tackle. The duo fell in a jumble of limbs.

When he stood up, he saw that he had made it into another room. The tunnel had opened into a big cavern and it was here that both men fought in earnest. No longer confined, the two could cut loose and really show what they were made of. Now their battle truly began.

As little as he was, his skills were spectacular. That Asian face—probably Chinese, he thought in passing—it was moving all over the place, as the little guy jumped and whirled around. Unhindered, in a vast space with probably five or more stories of clearance, his acrobatic prowess was quite impressive.

Ash changed tactics. Up until now he had been defensive. Now he switched to all-out attack.

Initially, it seemed to do the trick, as the little guy was taken by surprise, but that disappeared and he was able to stay just beyond Ash's reach, blocking just before a successful hit. This was it then. It was time to go for broke and take off the kid gloves. Ash pummeled away with strikes as fast as he could muster.

A punch was blocked and followed up by an elbow, followed by another punch and a kick. A dodge turned into a grab, which flowed into a throw and then evasion to avoid a counterstrike. Something bubbled up from a repressed memory and gave Ash an idea, as his head slid by a strike that could have knocked him unconscious.

Once again, he got in close and followed up with a series of attacks, but in a different sequence. This time, when his fist was blocked just shy of connecting, he opened his hand and let out an energy that originated from inside, and shot out of his open palm, into his opponent's chest.

His adversary was thrown back as if hit by a car. Slamming into a wall that knocked him unconscious.

Ash intuitively looked over his shoulder. It was the last thing he would have expected in a million years. Still crouched low to the ground, he stood to his full height waiting for the delusion to pass. Instead, whatever he thought he saw began to move towards him.

From all the way down at the other end of the cavern it looked like a woman. She was completely naked. She walked with an easy grace and self-assurance that reminded Ash of royalty. All his senses told him that she was in fact, very real.

Ash had started walking to meet her near the middle of the cavern. The closer she got, the more he could see and the better she looked. At around five feet (about the size of his Asian dance partner), she had an athletic build like a gymnast. She had no hair at all. Not even eyebrows, or eyelashes. Her pupils were dark red with a like-colored iris, with the "white part" a lighter red.

She spoke first. "Are you the one that awakened me?"

"I'm not sure," he said. "I doubt it. Who are you again?"

"Call me Jinx," she said. A smirk touched her face and disappeared. "Did you do that?"

"What? The little guy? I guess so." Momentarily lost in thought, he was completely taken by surprise when she grabbed him. He half thought she was going to kiss him, but that was pure fantasy. What she did do, however, was throw him clear across the room.

"Get out of here, or die," she said.

"Thanks for the warning," he said, from where he'd hit the ground.

She was too far away to do anything, and he was getting awfully tired of people telling him what to do. Ash checked to make sure nothing was sprained or broken, then started walking along the wall, away from yet another person trying to kick the crap out of him.

Glancing in her direction, he was fortunate enough to see what amounted to a boulder flying in the air, on a trajectory with exactly where he happened to be standing. With a silent thank you to the universe, Ash sprinted and leapt forward, with barely enough time to avoid being crushed.

"What the hell is wrong with you?!?' he screamed. Why was everyone always trying to kill him?

She threw another boulder.

This time when the boulder came, Ash had more than enough time to outrun the attack. He jumped towards the wall at an angle, pushed off with both feet, and threw himself towards the hot girl with the hot temper. When he landed, he hit the ground running. Somehow, she had still managed to swat a rock at him. He thought he was done for sure.

Unbelievably, even to himself, he managed to flip over it, rolling across and over the top. Clear of the obstacle, he landed, slammed into the girl and grabbed hold of her wrists in an attempt to subdue her. That was how the second battle of the day started.

It was an awkward and unsettling fight. She was naked and breathtaking, but she was also dangerous. If he let his guard down, she'd kill him. The only thing saving him right now was his speed.

Her strength was beyond imagination, but she was crude. Where the little Asian guy's fighting had been a thing of beauty and grace, this woman was a clumsy brute. A few times she lunged out with her nails and missed, only to hit a rock wall where Ash had been standing. She would spray gravel in the air each time. There was no telling how severe he'd be ripped apart if she ever connected.

She tried to bite and claw and destroy him with every fiber. All the while, he was worried that Mr. Kung-fu would wake up and help her out. He'd be dead for sure if that happened.

Distracted by his thoughts, Ash realized those claws were headed for him way too late, and he was suddenly done for. The horror of it compelled a self-defense mechanism into being, and he instinctively warded off the blow. But it was with his mind.

Again, a concussive force rushed outwards from deep inside. This time it emanated outward more powerfully and shot her clear across the room, like a home run hit at a baseball game.

JINX FOUND HERSELF SUDDENLY AIRBORNE, BUT NOT OF HER OWN will. He must have done it. The coy one who hides his true self. This power of now and before, it was clear to her. It was the magic of old.

She had willed herself to slow down when she first realized what had happened to her. Control was regained before she crashed into the top of her mountain lair. Hovering above, she paused to look at him. There was no evidence of the power he had wielded against her, that had disabled her guardian, or that had awakened her weeks ago. It was bottled inside somehow.

She had the ability to sense the relative power of all those she came into contact with. All except him. That is what had puzzled her when she sensed him in the lair. He was insignificant, blazed to greatness, and then went back to insignificant again. She had engineered their battle to test him, so she could be certain. At the end, there he was assuredly dead, and she realized she had misjudged him. It had saddened her to waste such a physical specimen (she found him attractive), but she had gambled on him and he had lost. And then, impossibly, he turned the tables on her.

"The test is done, and you have passed," she said, as she floated down to land about five lengths from the man. "We can talk peacefully."

"Do you maybe want to put on some clothes?" he asked. "I'm not complaining at all, in any way actually. But you are distracting me."

Jinx willed a flowing white mist around her that coalesced into a long white t-shirt, that came down past her knees. On second thought, she changed the color to black, then crossed her legs and hovered three feet from the ground.

The man continued to stand. Maybe he thought she would attack him again. He may also have sensed that her guardian had regained consciousness. She could not be sure.

Jinx sent a telepathic message telling her guardian to resume his post in the outer way. The man before her did not speak until the guardian had turned his back to leave, though that may have been pure coincidence.

"My name is Ash," he began. "I've come here because I'm searching for answers, and I thought coming here might help me."

"And you thought I would be able to help you find your path in life?" she asked. "Your sense of direction?"

"Umm...no. I've sort of lost my identity. I have amnesia."

Jinx looked at him. She was not familiar with this term. This amnesia. He must have realized this, because after a slight pause, he tried again.

"I woke up a year ago and I don't remember anything before that."

"Where was this place?" she asked. She listened as he told her about being chained to a wall. Waking up and leaving. Not knowing his own motives.

"I can only speculate on something such as this," she offered. "What I do know, is that there is something unusual about you. There are some elements that are unpredictable, even to me, which is odd enough to grab my attention. This is no small feat." She paused for effect and then went on.

"When I observe someone or something, especially when they are as close as you are now, I get a sense of who they are. It is an impression of their power or their potential, if you will."

"What do you get from me?" he asked.

"Nothing. Absolutely nothing. But for my eyes and other senses, you do not exist. Even something dead gives off an energy of sorts. You are invisible to that part of me, for the most part. I get a glimmer of you when you exert yourself. I suppose that's a good word."

Jinx had half thought he might corroborate her findings by reaction or voice. A partial reason for her truth telling. Yet he was as devoid of proof, for or against her words, as the blank page he represented to her higher sense. She decided not to tell him how he had awoken her with a manifestation of his power. How at such times, he was as plain as a star in the sky.

"I don't know what that means," he said. "All I know is that I was doing some research and what I found led me to come here. I came here looking for some sort of mystical thing that I thought was a book, but maybe it could have been a person. It wasn't clear. Do you know anything about that?"

Some sort of connection must have brought him here. The self-same affinity that had interrupted her own slumber. Something of importance, as a trivial matter would not tie itself to one such as her, and apparently not to Ash. With this new insight, she needed time to think.

"I have some preparations I must make," she said absently. "I can try to assist you later." She had lowered herself back to the ground and half turned to leave, but turned back to face Ash, almost as an afterthought.

"I do not know what you came in search of. This is my home. It may be that you came in search of me. Who is to say? I will also tell you that the magic you possess is very old and from a source, perhaps like my own, but different. I am very old too and I would hate to ever forget. So, I will help you. In that, it appears that your quest was a success."

Jinx took steps to stand directly in front of Ash, simultaneously willing a key into existence. She placed the medallion around his neck without explanation.

"What's this?"

"When you have need of me, call 'Jinx' into the air and I will find you," she said. "Now you must go."

"Thank you. It was nice meeting you." He started to walk away from her but stopped. "There wouldn't happen to be an easier way out of here, would there? It was sort of difficult to get here."

Jinx waved her hand and then he no longer stood before her. There was much to grasp in a short amount of time. She was still assimilating all the information that Twister had gathered for her, concerning the current age and all the changes she was unaccustomed to. Now, she had this new matter to think about as well. Without any initiative on her part, the source of the strange energy fluctuation that had awoken her, had sought her out. What did it mean?

She sent a mental message to her guardian and told him to wake her in a few days time.

ONE MINUTE, ASH WAS STANDING IN FRONT OF JINX, AND THE NEXT he was outside. Turning around he saw his bike and all his stuff right where he left them. Even his bag was there, along with the ropes and things he had left outside by the entrance of the mountain cave.

How'd she do that?

Checking to make sure he still had the necklace she gave him, Ash mounted up onto Old Faithful, his pet name for his Honda CBR 600RR. He'd paid three thousand dollars for it used. It was mostly black with a little bit of silver painted on for design, and it was his baby. He revved her up and drove away, bound for home.

On the road, he started replaying recent events over in his head. Somehow his research led him to Jinx. Instead of fixing him, she told him that she'd see him later. Could she really help him remember who he was?

ASH CHECKED THE MAIL WHEN HE GOT IN HIS BUILDING. WALKED upstairs and stopped after he opened his apartment door. Completely dumbfounded.

"Hello Kayala," he said after an awkward pause. "I wasn't sure I was ever going to see you again. How have you been?"

"I've been waiting for you," she said. She was standing over by his black leather couch. Apparently, she'd upgraded her wardrobe from the last time he saw her. Tan work boots, and a black sweat suit outfit with a hood. The top had a zipper that was opened, showing a simple white t-shirt underneath. Her golden hair and sparkling emerald eyes were exactly how he'd remembered them.

After closing the door, Ash decided to lean up against the wall as nonchalant as possible, where he already stood. He didn't trust his instincts right now. Even though they were in the same room, he felt that she was too far away and was compelled to all but stand on her feet.

"How'd you get in here?" he blurted out.

"The door was unlocked," she said.

"Oh. I was in a rush, so I probably forgot to lock it," he said, looking at the floor. "How have you been?" he asked his boots.

"I've managed," she replied.

"I'm sorry if I made you uncomfortable. The last time you were here," he stammered, and cleared his throat before continuing. "I didn't mean to."

"I left for reasons of my own. I am not afraid of you," she said. "Come sit with me on the couch. You've been gone for quite some time. You should make yourself comfortable in your own home."

"Of course not," he said. "Why would you be afraid of me? Okay. I'll sit. Thanks." Ash took a seat on the couch.

Kayala sat next to him. She was close enough for him to grab her for a quick hug, which was what he wanted, but he stopped himself. She probably just wanted to talk.

Kayala looked into his eyes long enough that he was more than uncomfortable. He was afraid he might lose himself in them forever, so he looked away, freeing himself somewhat from her magnetism.

"Why'd you come back?" he asked.

"For a few reasons," she said.

"Such as?"

"I need your help."

"Naturally," he sighed.

"And I missed you."

"Of course."

"And..."

"And what?"

Kayala stayed silent. She fiddled with her nails. When she looked up, he tried not to look away, as he felt those green eyes of hers bore into his skull. In those few moments he felt totally exposed to her.

"I never did get to thank you for rescuing me," she said. "And I will. But first, I was wondering if you might do me another small favor."

"Another favor?" he asked. "I don't know. What's another—"

Kayala leaned over and gave him a passionate kiss that lit a fire through him. All his self-control went out the window.

CHAPTER 17

INDOCTRINATION

From far away there was the face of the planet. A smaller part
land and a greater part water. There is no struggle between
the two. Everything is peaceful and serene. Much closer, and
the water goes in all directions. As far as the eye can see, there is
nothing but water and the sky overhead. Just these two.

Much closer and somewhere else, it's a tropical Island and it's beautiful. Water falls from the earth, hurtling down, down, down, to crash
into itself. Embraced by itself. Throughout it all the water and sky are
together. Two birds fly past a single point. Just these two.

Much closer, and somewhere else, it's the taste of salt in her mouth,
but it's also him. His scent is all around her, mixed with her own, as
surely as the intertwining of their limbs.

She wraps herself around him, grabbing tighter with legs and arms.
Pulling. Holding. Enfolding. Within.

The warmth they share is an echo to the passion that rages through
her. He feels it too and knowing that continues to stoke the flames of
her desire. Feeding the embers.

At long last, she finally had someone to share herself with. She treasured the moment. Lingered over every breath and every look. Every
gesture and caress. Every bit of yearning that was the echo of her own,

in the man who shared her bed. Who shared and partook in her body and soul.

They struggle for the heights of ecstasy. All of it coming together, in a culmination of building excitement that reverberates in radiant bliss. Just these two.

$$\sim$$

INALIA AWOKE WITH A START. EXPECTING THE MAN TO BE THERE with her. She was deeply disappointed to find herself alone. The disappointment became stronger, when she realized where she was.

She laid on what was a bear rug of sorts, but a different dead animal fur that was her bed on the floor just the same. She was completely naked, except for the collar around her neck, that was attached to a long chain that resembled a dog's leash. The chain—her chain—was welded to a metal link imbedded in a corner of a wall.

The wall opposite the locked steel door, had a window that was always open but obstructed by steel bars. This little window, no bigger than her head, was set way atop the wall near a two-story ceiling.

The room reminded Inalia of a closet. It was big enough for her to lie in and she could walk a little. Heel-to-toe of her feet, and using her stride, the space was approximately fifteen feet by six. The room was akin to a long queen-sized bed, which allowed it to serve its purpose of giving her enough room to sleep. The walls were all painted in black, which made it feel dark and depressing. It was a little prison cell.

Inalia couldn't tell how long she had been in her sorry circumstances. Long enough to get crying about it out of her system, at least. Things had turned out both better and worse than she could have expected. For one, she was more a pet than the slave she had envisioned herself.

The second, and most important element, was that Inalia Edwards was no more. Her name and identity were ripped right out of her and replaced with Kayala. Since Kayala (this had been her life, whatever you could call it) had no freedom of will or speech, or much of anything, Inalia was privy to the same amenities.

Crunched up bareback on a fucking bear-thing, in a goddamn closet!

Inalia pulled the stupid chain as hard as she could, in a futile attempt to rip it from the wall. It was not freedom, but if it had worked, it would have screamed out her quiet rebellion in a way her lips could not.

Azure had made it more than clear that anything along those lines would end with a severe beating. Though she alone knew the truth about Inalia, with her own life up for grabs if Inalia's 'secret' was discovered. That she wasn't Kayala after all. That she was just an innocent girl from New York City, who had been abducted by a bunch of sociopaths.

Inalia stopped that line of thought, and wiped at the tears that had begun to stream down her face. She sniffled a little and sat staring at one of her walls. The point was, that she knew Azure wouldn't hesitate to kick the crap out of her. She'd already seen her put a guy in the infirmary, for some imagined disrespectful tone of voice. She couldn't remember what started it.

The victim of Azure's aggression had been some burly, massive, construction worker type. At first Inalia thought Azure had bit off more than she could chew, but she chewed that guy's ass all over the corridor, with the blood staining the wall to prove it. At the time, it had been all Inalia could do to stifle a smile. It was exactly what she wanted to do to every last one of these assholes.

Somehow, she had managed to keep a stone face, though just barely. Basically, it was because she didn't know if it was acceptable or not, and also because Azure was in the habit of slapping her, to emphasize what she deemed right or wrong. It was better to err on the side of caution to limit the physical pain. The spiritual pain, on the other hand, was a constant oppressive thing, that never left her for more than a few fleeting moments.

Inalia tried to keep her discipline by Azure's hands down to a nonexistent variable as much as possible. When she first got here, there was nothing she could do about it. Azure was slapping the shit out of her left and right. It was part of her orientation process.

The hardest initial lesson, as crazy as it seems, was getting to a point of not crying after all of those hits to the face. It didn't take much to set Inalia bawling like a baby, but the real Kayala (bless her crazy heart), was supposed to be like a stone. Apparently, she wasn't the type to show much emotion at all, and so neither could her replacement. Inalia was eventually able to keep what she thought of as her 'brave face,' whenever she was assaulted, but it was really motivated by fear.

According to the stories that were her guidelines, Kayala could care less. She was one bad ass cookie, slave or not, and oddly enough Azure even seemed to respect her in some way. Inalia, on the other hand, well Azure could give two shits about her.

Kayala was the Queen's favorite for reasons no one else knew, other than perhaps her own whims. Thank goodness too, because that woman was positively bonkers. She made Azure look like a mild-mannered librarian, which was saying something.

Inalia could totally see why Azure was so afraid of her. She actually had an opportunity, at one of the Queen's whims (she was an erratic woman and these came up with some random regularity), to lie at her side at a sentencing session. The woman had no qualms in regard to human life, whatsoever. It was like she was swatting flies.

The crazy thing was that it got worse. If you did something she took as being against her personally, then she really gave you the business. One poor soul was tortured, cut up, burned, and then finally tied to four horses going in different directions, that literally tore him apart. The sentencing room was actually an arena. It added to the fear of getting caught, because it was a fertile ground for the Queen's imagination and justice, as the place she creatively married the two.

At the time, Inalia was half surprised she hadn't thrown up, but luckily she had already acquired a kind of apathy by then. It made her wonder how far away she was from joining the nuthouse these people would have surely been in back home. This kingdom's worth of lunatics who called themselves Pandorians.

Azure told Inalia, the Queen (slowly becoming Inalia's Queen as well) had obviously borrowed it from Greek mythology, or Greek mythology borrowed it from this place. Either way, it sucked. This whole place sucked and all Inalia wanted to do was go back home. Her real home. She wanted Starbuck's coffee, and pedicures, and television.

Inalia wiped at some fresh tears and went through a new round of sniffles and muffled sobs. She laid back down on her stupid bear, rattling her chains a bit as she adjusted herself, and tried to get comfortable. More tears streamed freely down her face, to run down a single cheek. She didn't even have a fucking blanket to curl into.

WHEN SHE AWOKE, IT WAS BUSINESS AS USUAL. PROBABLY FOR THE rest of her life. She found herself man-handled by Azure, much the same way someone treated their dog.

The lights came on first, as they always did, and then she heard the keys turning in the lock. She knew it was Azure, before she entered, because it was never anyone else. The same way she knew that Azure was wearing her all-leather combat uniform, and that she would soon be unlocking the mechanism that bound Inalia's chain to the metal beam. She was already sitting up, groggy from sleep, in preparation for Azure's command phrase that told her it was time to leave. She had graduated to this state of readiness from being kicked awake, kicked out the door, and kicked along in general, throughout the process.

"It is time," said Azure, and then she turned and walked out the door, expecting Inalia to follow.

As usual, she was briskly led through a series of winding corridors, that would eventually lead outside the castle. At this point, her modesty was long gone, and she no longer hid her nudity from the eager eyes of passersby. Getting used to it, sort of like a stripper, was the main cause. Azure's hard slaps to the face, to make her walk normal, rather than all scrunched up and ashamed, had done the rest.

"You have to walk like Kayala, and she doesn't do that," she had whispered in the beginning. After that it was just five across the eyes, Three Stooges style, without the commentary.

When she was led outside the inner walls that surrounded the castle, it was a sharp left and then maybe a quarter mile walk. Here came the most degrading part (far outshining her usual evening humiliation by the power of two or higher). It was time to relieve herself in the garden. There was a special area picked out for her and everything. Still completely nude, she did her business, with Azure maybe fifteen feet away. About the full length of the chain.

It wasn't so bad this early, when the sun had just gone down, because there wasn't anyone out to see her yet. The afternoon and evening, as she liked to think of them, when she was toilet-walked, were obviously infinitely worse. She had gotten used to it enough not to turn scarlet all over with embarrassment, mostly motivated by Azure kicking the shit out of her every time it happened. Literally.

In the beginning, she thought Azure was having an apoplectic fit or something, and then as far as she knew, she was just getting kicked for the hell of it. It wasn't until after Azure came out of it and had the sense to tell her that she was blushing, that she knew what she had done wrong.

"I'm what?" She had asked, all hunched in while she squatted, trying to protect herself as best she could.

"Your entire body's turning red and I want it to stop now!" Azure had said with sharp whispers, in between kicks.

"How the fuck should I know?" she had started yelling. "I thought you were trying to tell me how to shit, you stupid bitch!"

That hadn't gone over well at all. Inalia woke up sometime later in her room, probably beat into unconsciousness, and worst of all, she still had to go to the bathroom. When Azure came into her little room again, she got caught in the face with 'pieces of feces', that Inalia had hurled at her.

"You better fucking kill me now!" she screamed, in a fit of rage. There wasn't a part of her that didn't hurt already, but she just didn't care anymore. "I don't give a fuck! I'm not sleeping in the same room with my own shit!"

Convinced that she was all but dead, she was taken by surprise when Azure just turned around and walked right out the door, without a single word. A short time later, some servant girl came in and cleaned up the mess. That was how that night went. When she saw Azure again, she didn't bring it up, and Inalia didn't either.

When she was done relieving herself, it was off to the track, for her two mile run at dusk. She knew it was about two miles because she used to run track in high school, in her other real life. The whole thing (the track part) was made out of sand, so it wasn't that big a deal for her to run barefoot.

She loved running because it was the one place that Azure had never gotten on her case. She was already in shape and she bet she could at least run as well as Kayala (the woman she was impersonating), without any extra training from the start. Also, Azure was kind enough to take that damn chain off.

Where did she think she was going to go anyway? The outer castle walls were like three stories high at least, and Inalia was butt ass naked, in some strange land full of crazy people.

The chain had no real purpose, when it came right down to it, no matter what all the crazies thought. But that was something she'd petition for if she lived long enough. To get rid of the damn thing once and for all. First, she had to get in Azure's good graces by becoming 'Kayala.'

Next stop, swimming. After the run she was taken to an indoor pool house, which was what the track was built around. Once inside, she was allowed to swim back and forth for about ten minutes. The place housed an Olympic-size swimming pool for all intents and purposes, minus the chlorine and the floating string things. Also, the pool was a large perfect circle. You just sort of picked an end to get in, then swam to the other side. Next to it was a smaller circle that she would get to bathe in after eating, and there was something like a sauna room behind that.

According to Azure, the Queen had put the whole area together for Kayala, so that she would have a place to play. Just like a pet.

It was time for Inalia to be escorted to the Chow Hall. This was the worst time of the entire day that eclipsed everything else entirely. Why? Because by this time the sun was far gone, with the moon out to full effect, and everyone was just dragging their butts out of bed, which meant... You guessed it. Yes. Exactly. Inalia's naked ass (and mind you everyone else would be fully clothed, as always).

At the same table. Amidst rows upon rows of tables. Filled with rows upon rows of people.

As far as that went, embarrassment aside, it was a very safe experience. Anyone who so much as looked cross-eyed at her and was caught by Azure (her self-proclaimed bodyguard with capital letters, in bold, and an exclamation point), well they wished they hadn't, on their way to the infirmary.

"I rather wish Kayala were still here sometimes," Azure had confided in her ear one day, after one such incident. "She made things more fun."

"Fun?" Inalia had asked, sure that her ears were playing tricks on her.

"Why, yes. I'm only allowed to injure them," she had said conspiratorially. "Kayala," and now she had gone into a little chuckle. "Kayala used to just kill them."

"Oh," Inalia had said, puzzled. "If she used to kill people, why are they still bothering me?"

"It's a game with them. They want to see how far they can get and live to tell about it."

"Even though she was killing them?"

Azure had shrugged her shoulders in response. Apparently, she didn't see anything wrong with it.

"Great," Inalia said, going back to eating her soup.

Thankfully, no one seemed to want to bother her this evening. She got her food and ate next to Azure without any trouble.

In the beginning she had wolfed everything down, desperate to go anyplace else, but she found out that wasn't going to work, after the first couple of nights. No matter how fast she ate, Azure would still sit there at her leisurely pace, and drink her coffee as if she had all the time in the world. While Inalia would sit there with her eyes glued to the table, wishing she was invisible.

It was amazing what a person could get used to. Absolutely amazing.

When Azure was done hanging out, they went back to the pool house, where Inalia had her nightly bath. As always, Azure was nice enough to leave her alone to wash herself and relax in the water. This was also one of the only times that she didn't have to wear that stupid collar around her neck.

Probably so I don't mess it up, she mused.

It was exactly like one of the Calgon commercials that her mother used to tell her about. Total relaxation.

She had just about every kind of scented oil she could imagine. Vanilla being her favorite. It was pretty much like a bubble bath, except that it was like a Jacuzzi, but without the water moving all over the place. It was also at least three times the size of what she'd seen in the movies.

Sanctuary. Quasimodo had his bells, and she had this. It even came with a full twenty minutes of uninterrupted peace, quiet, and privacy. Something that Inalia tried to appreciate with every fiber of her being.

She savored the stream of the scented oils, as they slithered out of the container. Every perfect degree of the warm water, as it swirled and caressed her skin. Washing away all the pain. Every drip and every drop that she heard, felt, or saw. All of it. Entirely.

Azure was always on time and never spared a second when it came to bath time, though she never interrupted and never stuck around. She respected it as Inalia's personal time, totally and completely. This, in turn, only added to the appreciation of the thing. It was like fine wine. Or at least, like the hype that everybody associated with fine wine (something she had yet to experience herself).

When her time was up, Azure showed up with what Inalia was to wear for her audience with the Queen. A red two-piece bikini, which she tried to put on with enthusiasm as thanks for her bath. Azure herself, had gone off during bath time to change out of her leather army gear, into an all-black flowing silk ensemble, with pants instead of a dress or skirt, and black flip-flops. Inalia tried not to put her outfit on too fast, she was half-afraid that Azure wouldn't let her wear it if she was too eager to cover up her naked body. These days she found comfort in putting on what she used to call dental floss, back when she had real clothes to wear.

The audience with the Queen, where she sat beside her (Inalia thought it was more of a show than anything else), let everyone know that she was still the Queen's favorite toy. What other reason could there be? She never did anything, other than post up at her right side, sitting on the floor next to the royal throne.

She did exactly as Azure had instructed her. She didn't speak. She didn't do anything at all really, other than shift into other sitting positions from time to time. Specific ones that she learned from Azure, of course. She pretended not to listen to anything either.

About the only effort, on her part, was when she stopped herself from cringing if the Queen felt like petting her head. She feigned a smile when she received this oh so loving of touches. It was supposed to be such a great honor, because the Queen was about as caring, in general, as a (One of those guys. The ones that put people in coffins and stuff when they died. The ones that worked at like a funeral parlor. Were they morticians?) mortician.

The Queen was wearing yet another long flowing gown, as was her custom. This one was baby blue, with long sleeves that had ruffled lace at the wrists. As usual, the bodice was cut low enough to show as much as was possible, and still hold onto a shred of dignity. Another half an inch and she would have been a common prostitute, even with the crown atop her head. Hair the color of pitch-black night, with pale skin like ivory, and cruel eyes colored an unusual dark gray.

It was hard to tell with the poofed up hairstyle she always wore, but Inalia figured the Queen to be about five seven. Only a couple of inches taller than herself, at five four. Tall enough that she never bothered to wear heels that Inalia had ever seen, opting for lace slippers that always matched her dress. Not the best move, considering how long the gown was, but the Queen didn't seem to care.

The crown at the top was an unusual blend of gold and silver that twisted into one another, with jewels that might be rubies, diamonds, and emeralds, based on the colors. They might have other jewels here that resembled the ones she knew, or (and this was what she was most willing to bet) someone had stolen it from royalty back home. It was always shiny, and the Queen never went anywhere without it.

Other than that, it was all politics this evening. Something that Inalia was glad to see, despite how boring it really was. She didn't think she could handle one of those sentencing things again. The ones where the Queen had people executed.

After about an hour it was off to gymnastics training. Then lunch.

This time around, Inalia was able to finish her lunch without incident, and then it was off to the pool house again. Now she was in the basement learning how to fight with Azure. It was hard work, mainly because her sparring partner was infinitely stronger and faster than her. But Azure was kind enough to comment on the fact that yes, Inalia was improving. Assessing that she was hardly the easy target she used to be, which for Azure, was like giving a standing ovation.

After self-defense, it was on to stretching and meditation. When she was done, it would be back to the Chow Hall for dinner, another bath, and then off to bed in her closet-sized room to be chained up for the day.

For the longest time Azure wouldn't tell her why everyone lived by, what amounted in Inalia's head to be, a backwards clock. Later on, as Inalia acclimated herself to her surroundings better, Azure finally let the cat out of the bag.

The royal Queen was a vampire. A vampire! As such, she had determined a long time ago that everybody was going to live backwards since she, herself, couldn't survive in the sunlight. Also, if you were enough of a cutthroat bastard, to the Queen's liking, then you would get promoted to something that Azure called an Initiate. An Initiate was, you guessed it, a promotion to a vampire. And yes, just like all the stories they ever had in the movies or books back home, vampires drank people's blood and killed them. There weren't that many vampires walking around the castle, but Azure was a vampire too. A vampire!

It explained all her strength, and speed, and her calm assurance that she would easily be able to protect Inalia no matter what happened. But, it introduced a possibility that Inalia had never in her wildest dreams considered. What if Azure forgot to eat one day? What if she was like low on blood and just happened to drain Inalia of a few quarts just because?

Azure, an astute observer of the human condition, having feasted on them for God only knew how long, seemed to understand Inalia's fear. In any case, her master captor, Azure, decided to give her another little tidbit that she was sure would assuage Inalia's fears.

She confided that one of the components of being an Initiate was that you were more closely tied to the Queen, because as your vampire creator she became your master. So when she told you to do something, not only was it an order, but it felt like a decision you originated.

According to Azure, even though these Initiates were by their very nature more dangerous than anything else on two legs, as the most direct representation of the Queen's wishes, they were ironically, the safest bet for Inalia. In that respect, she was convinced that Inalia should actually look forward to having as many Initiates around as possible, as they were all sworn to protect her in the slightest way, from the slightest harm.

This last part Inalia was skeptical on, of course, having been slapped around for God knew how long. To which Azure said they were just "Love taps." A fact that Inalia wasn't ready to dispute.

CHAPTER 18
KAYALA 2.0

On her way to the Chow Hall, with Azure in front and Inalia in tow, a young woman ran up along the dirt path, garbed in the leather army outfit that Azure and the other soldiers wore. She immediately stopped and saluted the moment she was within speaking distance.

"Commander," she said, breathlessly. "I have a message from the Queen." She looked like the perfect soldier to Inalia, with everything crisp and shined and laced. Even her brown eyes and reddish hair seemed to somehow be spit shined.

"What is it, Captain Farn?" asked Azure, with an air of impatience. She didn't seem to notice how hard the woman was trying to impress her.

"Her Royal Majesty wishes that you and the slave join her at a banquet in theatre seven, starting in twenty minutes."

"Why wasn't I informed of this sooner?" snapped Azure, as she leaned forward onto the balls of her feet.

"I'm sorry, Commander, but she only just told everyone." She hesitated and then continued. "She seems to be in one of her moods again."

"I see," said Azure, shifting her weight back onto her heels. "You are dismissed, Captain."

Then she nodded and ran back the way she had come. If she had noticed Azure's change in stance, she gave no notice of it. The only reason Inalia saw anything at all was because of her new training. Something the soldier would have already had a long time ago, so she must have seen it too. Inalia was overthinking things again. It probably had more to do with not being able to fight your boss, and less about a new trainee seeing what a seasoned professional did not.

Back to see the Queen again, Inalia thought. Great.

She didn't have any particular dislike for the Queen, per say. She was, after all, solely responsible for her wellbeing. Hers were the orders that gave Inalia the protected status that kept everyone from doing whatever they wanted to her. Sort of.

It was just that every time she was around the Queen, she had to be on super ultra best behavior. She was always worried that she'd do something to get herself and Azure found out and killed. Not that she cared a great deal about Azure. But if the Queen ever found out that Inalia wasn't really her favorite pet Kayala, two heads would roll. Hers and Azure's. It was one thing to concentrate really hard for an hour to keep yourself alive, but twice in the same day?

With only twenty minutes to work with, Azure had her sprinting back to the bath section for a quick 5-minute cleaning, so she wouldn't be all stinky. Sprinting back to her cell to get a change of clothing. Then finally, to meet the Queen, at a brisk walk.

Inalia had never been to see the Queen in a formal dinner setting and didn't know what to expect. She almost didn't even care, as long as they got there on time. The Queen was as much a late freak as any of Inalia's teachers had ever been, but with an extra temper and the ability to just delete your entire existence. Commanding a great deal more motivation and respect, as far as Inalia was concerned, than any of those hack teachers ever had. So, she didn't even need Azure's usual "make haste or die" speeches. She was already the wind.

Azure must have found the time to get a hold of the required invitation, because she showed one to the guards in front of the entrance, which lead to a long line, that she just blatantly walked in front of, with Inalia in tow, of course. She waited in front of some older gentleman who was really well dressed and gave the invitation to him. He bowed, extended an arm, and told them to enter.

In typical fashion, Inalia was sorely underdressed, in a sheer slip that might as well have been a little nighty. It was a long one that came down to her ankles and was the color of ivory. Everyone else in attendance, from what she could see at the entrance, was dressed to the nines.

There were gowns and formal wear wherever she looked. Not altogether unexpected.

Thankfully, it didn't take long for Azure to spot where the Queen was seated inside, and ferry her over there. At the Queen's side, no one would dare to even look at Inalia cross-eyed, and expect to live to see the following day. So, at least she had that much, in terms of safety. Also, true to form, the Queen ignored Inalia's existence, which allowed her to relax and be a quiet observer.

For the first time, the Queen actually put a plate in front of Inalia, that someone else must have put together. At last, the favorite pet was to eat beside her master. This was a special celebration indeed.

How touching. At least the food was good.

The entire space was quite big, even for a ballroom. It was big enough so that a 747 jet could be parked inside, if of course there was a way to get something that huge to fit. In this vast space, there must have easily been a thousand people moving about, dancing, or standing like statues in conversation. The entire room was the color of ivory with red tapestries of battles or history. At the one nearest her, she noticed there were little babies that looked like cherubs flying around the battlefield, but she couldn't figure out what a cherub had to do with anything. Back home, they were all supposed to be like Cupid on Valentine's Day.

There was a huge chandelier in the middle of the ceiling that looked like it was made of glass. It was big enough to be the size of a moderate dance studio, and reminded Inalia of a comet, most likely because of the sheer size of it. Also, in her morbid fascination, she wondered what would happen if something that huge were to fall to the floor.

It would probably kill a great deal of these bastards. But it wouldn't matter to her. It wouldn't have an affect on her prison sentence here in the castle. Knowing the Queen, she might not even notice, except that the place would no longer be immaculate. At least they wouldn't be in total darkness afterwards, her and the other survivors, because there were little disks that also hung from the ceiling. The disks were suspended by three chains, with a bright candle in the middle.

The motif of the evening was white and red, which were the colors that everyone made sure to wear. She saw that some were dressed in ivory, the same as she, and others wore red. There were a few that wore garments that had a little bit of the two, done in an elegant fashion, but every single one of them made sure to have a rose on their person. Sort of like a carnation for a graduation.

The columns extending from the ground to the ceiling were ivory colored as well, but with intricate designs, that she had trouble seeing because it was all one color.

There was an orchestra off in the north end of the room, up against the wall. It was a concert-sized thing with instruments that looked different than those she'd seen back home, but fundamentally the same. Cellos, violins, horns, and flutes; organized into sections that played music that was in a classical style. Inalia wasn't musical enough to know what song was being played.

Of her guess of a thousand people, she couldn't help but notice how many women there were. The whole affair was only lightly sprinkled with men. She'd heard Azure mention that the Queen favored women over men, in contrast to how society was back home. This amounted to women having higher status and better jobs and positions of authority, and with men being second class citizens.

As expected, everything was top quality and had that expensive air about it. Expensive food on expensive dishes, with expensive cutlery, and expensive tables and chairs. Everything was embroidered in gold and silver, whether they were those actual metals or not. Even the candles along the walls seemed expensive.

She overheard someone mention acrobats and fire-eaters. She had to stop herself from asking any questions. Kayala wasn't much of a talker. So Inalia (the fake Kayala) couldn't be one either. She hoped it was happening tonight.

The most pleasantly unexpected surprise of all, was that her drink was alcoholic. It explained why she was so relaxed. It was a shame they didn't let her drink more often.

She noticed Azure leaning up against a far wall opposite her, seeming to have a good time herself. When she saw her looking, Azure tossed her a genuine smile. Inalia smiled back. Despite any misgivings she might have towards the other woman, it was a party after all.

ALL IN ALL, EVERYTHING WAS COMING TOGETHER NICELY. IF SHE could say so herself.

Azure was in mighty high spirits and quite proud of herself, like the proverbial cat and the milk. It was good to settle into the old familiar routine again. Even though a few minor details had changed.

Poor Captain Pratle had been demoted. Killed, actually. To be replaced by the able Captain Triggs. Any hints about the new Kayala's past, having died with him. "Apparently, this land of New York was a bit more treacherous than we may have originally surmised, Majesty," she had lied.

But she knew the Queen could care less. One boot-licker was as good as another, as far as her Majesty was concerned. She didn't deal with underlings anyway. That was what Azure was around for. The Queen had dismissed her and sent her about her business as usual.

Getting this new Kayala up to speed had been a hard task. The girl had started out as a sniveling piece of fluff. Through sheer force of will, Azure had transformed the girl into something almost decent.

There were still a few small things the doppelganger did that weren't quite right. The fact that Azure's head was still connected to her head, attested to how minor they were. All said, Azure was pleased with the outcome.

It was so good to be home.

CHAPTER 19
HEART 2 HEART

Ash opened his eyes to find Kayala sound asleep in the bed next to him. Relief washed over him. He'd been worried she wasn't going to be there when he woke up.

He eased over to the edge of the bed, careful not to wake her. Something cut into his foot. It was a metal pin from the packaging of a new shirt he bought the other day. The small red blood dot reminded him of a reality he'd forgotten last night.

Ash was a murderer. He would kill again. Just like the women at the bar and just like the original owner of his apartment.

To be fair, he hadn't meant to kill the security guard. It just sort of happened.

He hadn't meant to kill the others, either. Those just sort of happened as well, but he tried really hard to stop himself. That had to count for something.

He decided to go back to bed and just hold Kayala in his arms. Taking in her scent. Trying to hold onto it forever. What if she was his next victim?

When Kayala came back to herself he was gone. A note on the pillow next to her said he had gone down to get breakfast. It left her with some time to think about something odd that had happened.

Last night had brought an unusual dream. One in which she was back to being chained up. She had been wallowing in self-pity. Her face had been awash with tears and she had smelled like a defeated animal.

The dream unnerved her because it felt so real. Also, it was totally impossible. She would never go back, and they would never break her.

Kayala rolled out of bed and went to the living room. Flipping through the channels on the television, she settled on a news program:

Bill Parsons: "A very sad day on the home front, made its presence felt overseas last week, as a top U.N. Rep. withdrew from Sierra Leone talks. Here's a clip of the initial press conference:"

Alexander Edwards, U.N. Representative (PBC): "I will be stepping out of the talks after today, due to a serious personal issue that has come up. I ask that you understand that the severity of this matter is negatively impacting my ability to perform my duties, and in no way reflects on the talks, that I am sure will be resolved amicably in my absence."

Female reporter: "Would you care to elaborate as to what could be more important than thousands of lives?"

Alexander Edwards, U.N. Representative (PBC): "Not at this time."

Male reporter: "Is there any truth to the rumor that this has to do with your daughter?"

Alexander Edwards, U.N. Representative (PBC): "Excuse me, I have a plane to catch."

Bill Parsons: "The NYPD has confirmed that United Nations Representatives Alexander Edwards and his wife Edith Edwards, believe their only daughter, Inalia Edwards, has mysteriously disappeared, and have put out a missing person's report to try to find her.

"Authorities believe it is possible that Inalia Edwards may have been abducted to interfere with negotiations overseas. We ask that you call our toll-free number on your screen, if you have any information regarding to, or have seen this girl:

"Here is a recent photo. She's sixteen years of age, five foot four, about one hundred and ten pounds, with green eyes and blond hair. She's believed to have last been seen attending high school in the Bronx.

"We'll have more on the story later, as Mr. Edwards is expected to address the world, on CNN sometime this afternoon."

WHEN ASH CAME BACK HOME, HE WAS RENDERED SPEECHLESS. HIS TV lay smashed on the floor and there was a huge dent in the wall behind the couch, where Kayala must have thrown it.

"I'm sorry I broke your television," she said. She was seated, curled up on the couch.

"Okay," he said. His eyes scanned the room, taking in the damage and trying to see if she had destroyed anything else. "Would you mind sharing why you broke it?"

"It is hard to explain, but I will try," she took a deep breath. "I saw my sister on the television," she whispered.

"I didn't know you had a sister."

"I don't."

"What? Are you joking?"

"No, I'm not joking," she said. There was another pause. "Let me try again. I found out that I have a sister from the television, but I never knew that I had one before."

"And you know this person is your sister because?"

"She looks exactly like me. She's my exact reflection. My twin."

"Exactly? Exactly? Not just similar?"

"No, not similar. It was like looking into a mirror," she explained.

"Okay, so how come you didn't know about her? What? Did she run away from home or something?"

"When I was made a slave, I was stolen from my parents, probably at a really young age. I don't remember what my parents looked like or anything about them. It looks like I had a sister as well. But at the time, I assumed that whatever family I had, would have been killed by the people that took me."

"But how do you know it's not like some kind of trap or something? That they're not trying to get you back?" he asked. "That group of crazies I rescued you from."

"It is not like that Ash. This other girl's parents work for the government and they are saying that she's missing. It is entirely separate from me and my situation, even though she is my sister. Think about it. There is no way that they could specifically find her in all these millions of people in this city. If they could do that, they would have easily taken me back already."

"Oh. That's weird," he said, sitting next to her on the couch.

"It was on the news. A picture of what she looks like. How tall she is. They could have just taken a picture of me. It would have been the same."

"Okay, so what made you throw the TV across the room?"

"When I saw it—it made me feel so powerless," she whispered.

"I don't understand."

"To find out that after all this time, that I have a sister, and not be able to see her. To have her ripped out of my hands the moment I know of her existence...," she trailed off.

"Well, you know what? It would have helped if my TV was in one piece," he said. "They replay stuff like that all day long. Let me see if I think she looks as much like you, as you do," he said. "And then, if it's true, we can find her together."

Before long, they were downstairs looking for a bar or deli that had a working TV. It was raining hard enough for him to use an umbrella, with his arm wrapped around Kayala to keep her dry too. Eventually they went to an electronics place and convinced one of the sales guys to change the channel to the news. Thirty minutes passed before the report came on again:

. . .

Bill Parsons: "A top United Nations Representative is here with us today. Alexander Edwards speaks out, trying to find his missing daughter."

Janice Monahan: "I understand that the NYPD has some of their top people on this."

Alexander Edwards, U.N. Representative (PBC): "Yes, that is correct. Everybody's been very helpful and we expect to turn something up soon. I've offered a reward of twenty thousand dollars."

Janice Monahan: "And has anyone come forward?"

Alexander Edwards, U.N. Representative (PBC): "No one. They tell me that may be a good thing. She might be a Jane Doe with head trauma in a hospital or something. God forbid. But we're also looking in all the hospitals too."

Janice Monahan: "Because you're on the Peace Building Commission, do you think this might be an attempt to interrupt those negotiations?"

Alexander Edwards, U.N. Representative (PBC): Anything's possible at this point, Janice. I mean, we haven't heard from any credible entities on the matter, but I think it's still too early to rule out something like that."

Janice Monahan: "We're going to show her picture again. Your missing daughter, Inalia Edwards. Is there anything you'd like to tell someone who might be watching now? Someone who can help?"

Alexander Edwards, U.N. Representative (PBC): "Yes. Yes, I do. I still have a twenty thousand dollar reward. Of my own money. From my own pocket. I wish it was more, but it's all I have. If you're out there watching this, I just want my daughter back. Her name is Inalia Edwards, and I want my baby back. I miss her. My wife misses her. We miss her."

～

Right there, before his eyes was a picture of the girl standing next to him. There was no doubt about it.

Outside again, the wind suddenly ripped the umbrella right out of his hand, so that he was left with the handle. The storm was getting worse. Ash grabbed hold of Kayala and ran with her over to the entrance of a building for cover.

"What are we going to do?" she asked, wiping water from her face, when they were sheltered a bit from the weather.

"I think we should call that toll-free number they had up on the screen. I wrote it down."

"And that will bring us to her?"

"No, of course not. Hopefully, we can find some info that can help us find her."

"Okay. Okay. Let's get started then."

"Okay. Let's run," he said, going back out into the storm. He half-turned to see that Kayala was following him, wiping at his face as the rain pelted it. Shielding his eyes with his hand, so that he could see at all.

It wasn't long before she sat behind him, astride Old Faithful. He loved the way she held on, pressed against him, as the motorcycle roared through the streets.

From upstairs in his apartment, he had called the toll-free number listed on the report. That way if they traced the call, they wouldn't have his cell number. He told the operator that he might have seen the girl, but he wasn't quite sure. Was there an office or something he could go to so he could be sure? The woman on the phone had said yes and given him the address.

WHEN THEY GOT TO THE OFFICE BUILDING ASH INSTRUCTED KAYALA to stay outside. She begrudgingly took his advice and went to a Subway's sandwich shop. After a while, the smell of the place woke her appetite and she purchased a tuna sandwich.

She had to find her sister. The thought repeated in her head over and over. It was hard to eat. Hard to sit. Every wasted second was beyond frustrating.

Ash soon returned with what he called a lead. It was like a game where you followed the clues to get at the treasure. Her sister went to a place called high school, and Ash had been able to get the address from a clerk.

"You're supposed to be in high school," he said, as if it should mean something.

"What is high school?"

He explained to her that it was a place where teenagers learned things about life, as she munched away on the remnants of her sandwich, half paying attention. She still didn't see the point.

"Okay," she said when he had finished. "So, what does this high school place have to do with me? I'm from a completely different place, remember? I never went to any school, high or low or whatever." Anger began to creep into her voice. "I don't understand why you're wasting time on this right now." She folded her arms across her chest.

"What I was trying to do was ask you how old you are," he said. He had lowered his voice to speak in a softer, hushed tone.

"Then why didn't you just ask me that in the first place?" It was not easy to understand how people did things over here. "The picture with my sister on it said she was sixteen. Twins, remember? We're the same age."

"Oh," he said. Seeing that she was done eating, he ushered her back outside where the bike was, and she hopped on waiting for him to take them to the next destination. The pouring rain, infinitely more than a nuisance, at this point, continued to soak every inch of her. So much so, that she half-imagined that she was swimming.

Switching to a different outfit, at Ash's behest, had been a wise move. They both wore a leather jacket, covered by a rain poncho on the outside. Underneath they each had warm clothing. If she'd stuck with her hooded sweatshirt, things would have been considerably more uncomfortable.

He half-turned as if he was going to say something but stopped. Then the motorcycle came to life and they were whizzing through the streets once more. With the helmet on and the roar of the engine he wouldn't be able to talk to her, and she was glad. She needed time with her own thoughts.

When they arrived near the high school, as before, Kayala was instructed to wait somewhere else. This time she waited for Ash at a nearby field of grass and trees, under a canopy.

This might have been where my sister played, she thought.

She stared absent-mindedly at the dark clouds in the sky. Something she had rarely seen in her previous life. How beautiful they were, even with the water pummeling the ground from above.

Her sister would probably take something like this for granted and poke fun at her odd ways, but she did not care. All her life she had been made to feel less than whole. A speck on the boot of almost all else. Alone and unloved, she often fancied she had a sister and even had an imaginary friend she called Ina.

Ina was her sister and they were the best of friends and every day she was locked away, they would play together and keep each other company. They made fun of the others and kept secrets together. Ina was probably the reason Kayala did not succumb to the madness beset upon her from all sides. Ina kept her strong.

When she grew older, Ina disappeared. Apparently, her mind no longer had need of her. But Kayala never forgot her imaginary sister and held her close to her heart, deep within, where no one could steal the security of her. All this time, she had a real sister and she grew up here, far away, with a different life.

Deep down she knew her sister was probably ignorant of her existence as well. They would soon be together again and be a family. Kayala was sure of it. Soon her new life would be strong and solid and real. She had a sister.

It wasn't long before Ash returned with more news. She only heard part of what he was saying, completely forgot it and then didn't hear anything after. Kayala's world slowed to a crawl. Every heartbeat, as fast as they had become, was an eternity.

He had said her sister's name was Inalia Edwards. She must have tuned it out when she saw the news report. Inalia, when her pretend sister's name had been Ina? It was true. It had to be true. Maybe they had been together when they were small. Maybe as a child she could not say it right.

"What?" she asked. "Did you say that you know where she lives?"

"Yeah, like three times. Weren't you listening to me? Never mind. Yes."

"We have to go there. Let's go there."

Kayala was already seated on the back of the motorcycle when she asked "Where is it? Where are we going?"

"It's a place called Roosevelt Island," he said. "It's not far. It's actually a small island between Manhattan and Queens. I searched for directions on my cell phone. We'll be there in no time."

"Okay, let's go."

"Don't worry, we're going. Just let me get on the bike first, okay?"

"Sorry. I'm getting impatient. I'm sorry."

"No sweat."

Soon they were flying on the highway, with the rain pouring down harder than before. The strong winds were determined to soak them both down to the very blood in their veins. It didn't matter though. Nothing did. All she cared about was finding her sister. And she was finally on the trail. Nothing would stop her from succeeding.

The Brooklyn Queens Expressway brought them to the Grand Central Parkway, which let them off into Queens, right before the Robert F. Kennedy Bridge. They drove along 21st Street, which lead to 36th Ave, which lead them to a small red bridge, which in turn, brought them directly to Roosevelt Island, which was where her sister lived.

The only thing that kept her from running off when they parked, was that she did not know where to go. Thus far, it was markedly different than any place she'd ever been.

There was only one street that ran right in the middle of it, with buildings on either side, and behind that, water. Across the water was Queens on one side and Manhattan on the other. The entire road was named Main Street and had not a single traffic light. Opting for a series of stop signs instead. The buildings had numbers on them that were painted on the glass.

When they reached 575, they found the doors to be locked, of course, and were forced to wait for someone to let them into the lobby.

The elevator took them to the eighth floor and they walked to apartment 805.

"Now what?" asked Ash. "The door's locked. How're we going to get inside?"

"Ring the doorbell," she said, immediately reaching to do so.

Ash grabbed her arm. "We can't do that, remember?" he said. "If one of them sees you, they're bound to have a heart attack. Also, I seriously doubt you know how to act like their daughter."

"You're right," she agreed, freeing herself from his grasp. She'd just barely stopped herself from putting him right through that door, the moment he tried to restrain her, but he didn't have to know that.

"Go wait around the corner so they can't see you. I'll ring the doorbell."

Kayala walked off to do as he suggested, dragging her feet on the carpeted floor. After two minutes, he walked over to her.

"No one's home," he said. "What do you want to do?"

Kayala ran back down the hallway, and began kicking the door in. She dented the hell out of it, warping the metal more and more with each assault. Eventually, the bent wreck of a door came right off the hinges.

Once inside, she set to work immediately, and discovered her sister's room in five seconds. She ignored the superficial trinkets and concentrated on the scent. With deep inhalations, she took it in and closed her eyes. She took it in until she knew it as well as her own, and then ran out, past Ash in the living room, back to the elevator.

Outside, she found the scent in the air, and she set off at a run. Faint, but as clear as a trail of breadcrumbs, she followed it all the way to its end. The trail died at a train station. How could they have a train station on an island?

Kayala sat on a bench in a park, located behind the station. It was still raining, but she didn't care. There was no way she'd be able to track her now. She'd made the assumption that her sister would at least be above ground, giving her a chance. But there really was none. Not in a place like this. A place so modern.

No!

She threw the park bench she had sat on clear across the field. Ash was staring at her.

"I think I know where my sister is," she said, regaining her composure. She stormed off, heading to where the motorcycle was parked, still oblivious to the downpour.

"What do you mean?" Ash asked from behind her, but she was too focused on getting back to the bike to pay much attention to him now.

Then she was spun around by her left arm and he was right in her face, but instead of the yelling she expected, he spoke rather calm and quiet.

"What do you mean?" he repeated. "You lost me."

"What if my captors took my sister to replace me?" she screamed in his face. "What if the reason she's missing is because of me?"

She didn't wait for a response. Kayala turned right back around and headed towards the bike. It didn't matter if Ash understood what was going on right now. All he had to do was get on the bike and drive them where they needed to go. Nothing more.

Having lost her sister for all these years, she wasn't about to lose her again. She sure wasn't going to leave her in the hands of those monsters.

"It's all my fault. The reason that she disappeared. I think that they were looking for me. My jailors. And they found her instead. They thought she was me," she said, as tears started to stream down her face. "They thought she was me, and now she's gone! They took her!" she screamed.

"Woah, slow down. Just slow. Down. You don't know that," said Ash, trying to console her.

"Yes, I do," she said. "I can feel it. I dreamt it."

"Dreamt it? Kayala, what are you talking about, now?"

"I dreamt that I was still where they used to keep me," she began. "But it wasn't me! It was her! They have her, and she's terrified and crying, and miserable! And it's all my fault!"

"So, you had a dream, and you think that it was her?"

"Don't fool with me," she said, grabbing Ash by his shirt, pulling him towards her. "Look. I just had the dream last night, and then today when I looked on the television, she was right there staring me in the face, through that picture. Of course, it's her. I have to save her!"

Ash struggled to get out of her grip. "Okay. Okay."

Back astride the bike, she instructed him as best she could. No matter what happened or what the obstacles were, they were going to free her sister Inalia, and bring her back unharmed. Even if Kayala had to kill each and every Pandorian with her bare hands.

CHAPTER 20
PANDORIA

As much as they were in a hurry, there was no getting around that they needed a break. They stopped at a restaurant at one of the rest stops.

Ash and Kayala sat across from one another at a booth.

"I'm sorry that you're all wet," he said, after the waitress left.

"What are you talking about?" asked Kayala. "You can't control the weather."

"That's true, but if I had a car, instead of a bike, you'd be much dryer."

"Oh." She ran her fingers through her damp hair. "I'll be fine."

He ordered her a tuna sandwich and chocolate shake. The food automatically came with French fries, and there was a bottle of ketchup on the table. A little white ceramic box held little packets of sugar. They each had a knife, fork, and spoon, lying on a white folded napkin in front of them. There was a low hum of people eating, talking, and taping on their plates with some combination of their silverware.

"I really like you," he blurted out.

"What?"

"I said I really like you."

"Oh. That's good. I really like you too," she said. "Aren't you going to eat?"

"Not right now. No."

It was an awkward moment, only made worse because the food hadn't come yet. They both sat around just looking around at random things inside, or outside of the window they sat next to. He was about to reach over and take her hand, when the food came. So, he rubbed his face instead.

"We're almost there already," he said.

"Oh? How close are we?"

"We should be there in like another hour, or maybe less. It depends on if I get lost or not."

"Oh."

"I'll be right back," he said, getting up to go to the men's room.

When he got inside, there was no one else there. He stood over one of the sinks and looked in the mirror.

What an idiot.

Things weren't going well at all. What was wrong with him?

Every time he tried to tell Kayala that he murdered innocent people, he couldn't do it. Finding her sister was super important now, and she needed to trust him. He knew that. What he didn't know, was if that meant he should tell her now, or wait until after they found her sister.

Ever since she came back, he was so afraid of losing her, he couldn't say the words. Worse yet, how could he ask her to be his girlfriend, without addressing being a murderer first?

His girlfriend. That's what he wanted her to be more than anything. He'd do anything she wanted to make that happen.

If he had any friends, he could ask their advice. If his life wasn't such a mess.

He splashed some water on his face and washed his hands again. With the bathroom still empty, he took about another two minutes to stare at himself in the mirror.

When he got back to the table, she was halfway done eating.

"What's your last name?" he asked.

"What?"

"I was just wondering what your last name was."

"Oh. I don't have one," she said.

"You don't have a last name? Why's that?"

"No one in Pandoria does. The Queen thinks that last names breed animosity, which leads to war. So, back before I came to live in the castle, she had already abolished them."

"How'd she do that?"

"She's like the president over there, except there's nobody else at the top. Whatever she says goes."

"That's pretty cool. For her, I mean."

"For her, yes. It must be nice to have complete power. I agree."

He was so relieved when they were back astride the motorcycle. No more awkwardness. At least not for another hour.

Speeding through the streets like they were, it didn't take Ash too long to get back to the bar he'd rescued Kayala from. Well, where she'd really rescued herself, but they were both back in Monticello New York. It hadn't been too much trouble to look up McGreely's Tavern on the Internet and get driving directions. It was still standing and looking as old and worn down as ever, with no evidence that anyone had smashed right through one of the windows.

"Why did it take so long for us to get here?" he heard Kayala ask, as she dismounted behind him.

"What do you mean?" he asked.

"That night, when you saved me," she began, running her hand across her eyes, after she removed her helmet.

"Yeah?"

"Well, we were on top of one of the buildings in this neighborhood, right?"

"Right."

"And it didn't take us nearly as much time to get to your apartment, as we spent getting here now."

"What? Maybe it's because we came here from the high school, instead of straight from my apartment" he said, through the visor of his helmet.

"No, you don't understand," she said, her green emerald eyes, staring intently. "It took us no time to get to your place that night."

"No time? Compared to what?"

"I can remember everything that has ever happened in my life, but only after I was already a slave," she said. "Everything before is a blur, but everything after my enslavement is as clear as if it were a movie I could watch at my leisure."

"And you remember that it hardly took any time?"

"Look. Think back. Remember when I was first in your apartment and I told you that I didn't understand how it was possible?"

"Yes. I remember. You were in shock because I had rescued you."

"No, Ash. I was in shock because I didn't have any recollection of how we got there. It was like we were here one minute and at the apartment the next."

"Oh." He remembered saving her and being at his apartment too, but whatever happened between the two was just blank. When he couldn't think of an answer, he said "I don't know. Can we talk about it later?"

"Okay. We will," she said, nodding in agreement. "Later."

"For now, though, let's look for your sister. How can we find her from here?" he asked, dismounting the bike.

"Just follow me," she said. Then she was sprinting off to the right on foot. Ash was taken by surprise, but when he recovered, it was a simple matter to tail her. She was amazingly fast. They must have been running for forty-five minutes straight, and still she continued at the same breakneck pace. The only thing that surprised him more than her level of fitness, was that he was still (impossibly) able to run right behind her. A few days ago, he would have been huffing and puffing after three blocks.

Soon they were running through some trees and grass, snapping twigs, and crunching on leaves on the ground. She ran on effortlessly. Jumping over puddles and avoiding mud whenever possible. Ducking under branches and hopping over logs on the ground. With Ash right behind her. Sometimes taking a different path, but always connecting with her a little farther along.

One minute she was running along as usual, right in front of him, and then suddenly and completely without warning, the rain stopped, and it was daytime. It was as if someone had flipped a light switch. Only that switch was connected to the sky.

"The castle grounds are just a little farther along," Kayala whispered, and she proceeded to crouch behind a tree.

Ash followed her lead and crouched next to her. He had expected an underground civilization or one of those compounds that cults lived on, but this was something magical. Something like what Jinx had done to bring him back to his motorcycle.

"Now what?" he whispered when he was close enough to breathe on her neck. She didn't answer. After a brief pause, she was up and running again, leaving Ash to follow.

His plan was a simple one. Follow Kayala wherever it was that she was headed and completely block out his bewildered thoughts. That way, Ash wouldn't have to try to wrap his mind around the fact that an entire shift of time and space had just occurred. Completely turning the laws of nature on its head.

He wanted to grab Kayala and spin her around again like he had earlier, but this time screaming at the top of his lungs asking, 'What the hell was going on? Where were they?' And more importantly, 'What the hell was going on?'

Instead, he ran on in silence and tried to keep the internal dialogue down to a dull roar. Right now, his job was to help Kayala find her sister. They'd be able to talk about other things later.

He continued to keep pace with Kayala as he looked around the landscape. They were now running through unusually tall grass. If it wasn't two stories tall, it was nothing. Which left Ash wondering how Kayala knew where she was going.

Without warning, she stopped, and he almost ran right over her.

"We are here," she said, in between ragged breaths. "This is the castle. This is where we will find my sister."

The stone was dark gray like cement, and was a wall around the castle property that they would have to climb. Kayala told him that this was the first one and that there would be another two walls farther in. It was a good thing he still knew how to do that levitation trick of his, otherwise they'd have had to use the front door.

He thought he saw a bird fly almost right in front of him, but it looked like a green fish. He could swear he saw big fish eyes and gills, and fish wings, not big bird wings. But if that was the case, how could the thing fly?

"Did you see that?" he whispered, trying to conceal his shock.

"What?" she asked, turning to face him for the first time in a while.

"I just saw a fish fly right past me. Or was that a bird?"

"You probably saw a flying fish. Don't you have that?"

"We do, but all our fish need water to breath."

"Oh. Some of ours do that too," she said.

Ash took her in his arms and willed himself up. Here he was, a man floating up into the air, flabbergasted at a flying fish. You'd think he'd have learned better.

Once on the ground, she moved as stealthily as a cat. Hiding behind tree, bush, and rock, as if nature itself sought to conceal her. And then there was Ash, with his bumbling around behind her like an elephant on tiptoes.

He made a point to put a nice distance between them, hanging back out of her way, lest his own clumsy movements give away her position. Compared to her, he might as well have been whistling and stomping around, while screaming at the top of his lungs. She made every twig he stepped on, every scuffle of his boots on the dirt, and even every breath he took, seem louder in his ears, by tenfold.

When they'd gone a short distance in from the third and last inner wall, Kayala motioned him over.

"Not too many people are going to be around right now," she said from behind a bush.

"Why's that? Is it a holiday or something?" he whispered.

"No. Everybody just comes out at night."

"Long nights of partying?"

"No. Everything is closed in the day and opens at night. Everyone's sleeping."

"What, are they all a bunch of vampires or something?" he asked.

"Some. Not a lot. But the Queen is, and she makes the rules," she said.

"Oh. Really? How do you know?"

"Come on," said Kayala, sprinting to a nearby tree.

Vampire? Sleeps in the daytime. I guess that means I've got to be something else after all, he thought, while running after her.

After a little more hide and seek, he saw a huge one-story building surrounded by sand, but it had footprints and was worn, like it was a track or something. It went around the building like a ring around Saturn, without touching anything in the middle.

"Do you see that building?" Kayala asked, when he caught up to her, standing behind another tree.

"What about it?"

"We're going in there."

"Okay."

"I'll explain when we get inside." She looked left, then right, and broke into an all-out sprint for the building.

She caught him off guard, but he recovered fast enough that when she reached the door, he wasn't far behind. She shut and locked the door behind him before continuing.

"Don't worry, there's no one allowed to come in here."

"How can you be so sure?"

"It's an offense punishable by death," she said, raising her eyebrows for emphasis.

"That'll do it."

"There are two guards that patrol the area at this hour. We're going to knock them out and steal their uniforms."

"Sounds like a plan," he agreed.

In the movies, things like these always worked out. In reality, both of the guards ended up being Amazon women that were taller than Ash. And of course, a woman's uniform is constructed differently with a place for breasts and wider hips. Needless to say, there wasn't an item that either of them could wear that wouldn't have them sticking out like sore thumbs.

"It was worth a try," he said, patting Kayala on the shoulder.

"I guess," she sighed. "I was just hoping that with the uniforms we'd be able to move faster."

"We'll be alright," he said.

"I hope so."

They made sure to tie up their captives. Then they stripped off some of their excess warmer clothing, and piled that up inside a steam room, before making their way towards the castle itself. Kayala said they were taking a service entrance and that there probably wouldn't be any guards.

Their short journey was as uneventful as she'd predicted and before long, they were under the castle in a basement, staring at a locked door.

"She should be in there," she said, as she walked over and got on her tiptoes. She pulled a latch that opened a little metal window so that she could see inside. "She's not here."

"What do you mean she's not here?" he asked. "Does that mean they don't have her?"

"No. The whole room smells of her. She was definitely here, but she's gone."

"Where could she be?"

"Follow me. We're going to the Queen's chambers," she said, stalking off down the hall.

KAYALA TOOK GREAT PAINS TO LEAD ASH THROUGH THE CASTLE, AS stealthily and without incident as possible. She was glad to see that whenever they were unable to circumvent an obstacle, usually in the form of a guard or two, that Ash proved more than capable in helping her subdue them.

"That door straight ahead is the Queen's quarters," she told Ash in a hushed whisper. "Be ready for anything. There's no telling what to expect, but with any luck she will be alone."

Kayala crept up slowly to the plain-looking door and tried the knob. It was opened. The door was very plain and unadorned, as a sort of camouflage for security reasons, but also was always locked. She hesitated a bit, wondering if she was walking into a trap. Maybe a guard had regained consciousness. She cleared her mind. It was too late to turn back now.

As she opened the door fully, she found something she had never suspected. The room was empty. This was the first room in a series, leading up to the Queen's actual personal room, but where were the guards? There were supposed to be guards at each of the checkpoints. She ran to the next door and pulled, to find that the room beyond was exactly the same. Empty.

With no obstacles to slow her down, she was in the Queen's personal room in seconds. The furniture and papers and books were there, but absolutely no one was inside.

Ash had crept up behind her to take a peek inside, and seemed to relax a bit when he found what she had already seen. She ushered him in and closed the door behind them.

"So, what are we looking for?" he asked.

"There might be a key somewhere or maybe a book with today's schedule," she said, as she began searching the room. Of course, everything was just how she remembered it. A big bed, writing table, make up area, big bookcase, and a high-backed chair that mimicked the Queen's throne room, for the audience in her chambers. There was also a window behind the chair covered by long purple curtains, which Kayala had always thought unusual. Why would a vampire have a window in her room?

When she pulled back the curtains, she found another smaller room with bookcases lining the four walls. There was a small table in the middle of the room and a reading light, but there were no chairs. It was actually while looking around for a seat, that she noticed one of the bookcases was pushed away from the wall. On closer inspection, she discovered another door to another hidden, smaller room. This one was much like the other, with a small table with a reading light on it, surrounded by two chairs. Unlike the other table, it was covered with books and charts. On these walls there were maps, instead of bookcases.

It was a picture, in a picture, in a picture. All of it set in a deep recess in the wall. Mimicking a small room, within the larger room that Kayala was familiar with. The smallest was definitely a secret room. What was the Queen hiding?

Taking a cursory glance at the table-top, Kayala found a journal. Skimming through it, threatened to send her anger through the roof.

It read:

"Today will be a memorable day, indeed. I've taken the slave down to visit the sacrificial altar as an inside joke of sorts. I view it as a dress rehearsal, but it just thinks it's going for a walk again. The coordinates I have deciphered mainly from 'A Treatise on Sacrifice in History,' and the other manuals, have shown me the correct location. They appear genuinely authentic. I'm optimistic the test run will meet my approval and she'll be dead, according to the earth date of October 13, 2023."

Just when she thought things couldn't possibly be any worse, that's exactly what happened. The journal entry date had long passed, but the date it referred to would be sometime soon.

"We don't have a lot of time. We have to hurry," she said, not really hearing her own words. They seemed hollow to her ears.

"But it's only August now, that's like a month and a half away," said Ash, when she showed him the journal.

"No, you don't understand. Time moves differently here. Faster. I don't know exactly," she said, exasperated. "But it's fast enough that if we hurry, we might get back within a couple of days of that date." Something was distracting her from their conversation.

"No way," he said. "Kayala, are you okay?"

Forever gone and deleted from existence never to...

The room began to spin and Kayala's balance faltered and slid until she lost it. She was having trouble breathing but when she tried to ask Ash for help, she fell, and the world slipped through her fingers.

CHAPTER 21
NUMINA

Chanovalle Remseldorne, Queen of Pandoria, stepped gracefully through The Shimmering Gate. It wasn't often that she came through the portal leading to New York, except to communicate with secret agents and carry out her schemes. Particularly the coordination of their efforts, in searching out the whereabouts of her nemesis Bryne Xarn. A vampire at least as old as herself, that she knew to be in hiding. She had already spent years searching for him on Pandoria and he was NOT there. The only logical conclusion was that he was here. Somewhere.

Most germane to her current visit, efforts searching out certain geographical possibilities, that would yield her the sacrificial altar. And in so doing, bring the Child of Destiny (the one called Kayala, tethered to the chain in her delicate hand this very instant) to a strategic end. A masterful stroke of genius that would increase Chanovalle's power tenfold.

For centuries she had sifted through all the data. The lore. The history. Searching. Always searching. Until one day, she stumbled onto what she had been looking for.

In that moment, Chanovalle's revenge went from pipe dream to fact. Making all the hard work worth it.

Hundreds of years ago, Bryne Xarn had been sucked into a temporal rift that took them both from the loving bosom of their home world, Numina. She was always confident that she'd find him eventually and repay him for his treachery. It had actually been her treachery, but why split hairs?

Centuries before that travesty, she had worked for the High Council. The uncontested government of the entire world of Numina. It was composed of a conglomerate of nations, which were in turn composed entirely of vampires. Excepting of course, those nations not indoctrinated into the government. These were composed entirely of a human population, and thus not recognized as anything more than a grazing land for livestock.

As humans supplied the vampires with their blood. Their food. A subsidiary of the High Council, called Chando Corporation, was exclusively responsible for cultivating the humans for consumption. Also thinning the herd as necessary, from time to time, due to overpopulation.

At that period of her life, Chanovalle served in the militia as a 2nd Magistrate. Something akin to a High Captain. It was hard to get promoted because vampires, especially in a civilized community, have such long lives. As a woman of no small ambition, whose talents and focus had propelled her meteoric rise through the ranks, Chanovalle soon found herself 'stuck' with no place to go. Destined to stagnate in mediocrity for an eternity.

All civilizations have crime and fortunately she was able to busy herself in her casework, which was how she came to know 2nd Magistrate Bryne Xarn. They were peers at the time, bringing justice to the world of Numina. Each in charge of their own contingent, as they righted the wrongs of their world ceaselessly.

Occasionally, she would see him walking through the halls, or talking to someone in the crime labs, and sometimes they even said hello to one another. For the most part, everything was business as usual, with a humdrum existence that Chanovalle, in her naiveté, had become accustomed to.

Years later things began to pick up, as The United Liberation Organization for Inter-species Coexistence, or ULO for short, made itself known. They believed that humans should be freed and that the High Council should cultivate a synthetic blood product instead. Human beings were sentient creatures and should be treated with the same rights as ordinary vampire citizens. Until such demands were met, enumerated ad nauseam in their manifesto, ULO would engage in guerilla attacks against the establishment. Perpetrated by like-minded vampires throughout the world.

Of course, the High Council thought the whole thing nothing but utter hogwash, as did any self-respecting vampire. Chanovalle not the least of them. When ULO started acting out their threats, it fell upon her and her colleagues to rise to the challenge and bring order from the ensuing chaos. It was during this period that she found herself working more closely with 2nd Magistrate Bryne Xarn. He had a reputation of excellence, akin to her own, and they were often involved in missions together.

Numina was a great world to live in, with technology easily rivaling that of New York, which in turn rivaled the simplicity of Pandoria. She remembered feeling so safe within the walls of the Capitol building, which housed the High Council and most of the government branches. Even more protected than the walls of her own castle on Pandoria.

It was a huge building greater than any dwelling she had ever seen since, with a width of as much as a mile on each side. Much like a perfect square, with even sides. From this space it shot up towards the sky to an immense height, before it changed into a narrower structure, more in keeping with a skyscraper in New York. Taller even than the tallest they had to offer. Reaching into the very stratosphere.

Flying high above the immense structure, it looked like a square symbol with a diamond shape directly in the middle of it. This of course was impossible, as nothing was allowed to fly within a fifty-mile radius of the building. (A failsafe etched into the brains of all technology, manufactured exclusively by the government)

Be that as it may, that overhead shape was the exact shape of the militia patch on all government issued uniforms. The shape of the platinum badge used to identify oneself. As well as the emblem on militia vehicles.

The outer square housed most of the government. With the top diamond that rose out of it, housing the High Seat members, who were the pinnacle of authority. Safe in their castle-like spire, rising ever skyward, with all the amenities one might imagine. It was rumored that this upper part of the structure was entirely self-sufficient, and that inhabitants could survive therein, for eternity.

That structure, from the very bottom to the very top, was composed of a very strong steel, at least as hard as diamond. Easily strong enough to protect the vampire residents from any assault. As if that wasn't enough, it was also surrounded by a field of force. A hybridized technology melding the science of man with the magic of the vampire. The field was impenetrable.

Its lower parts could open like a drawbridge at the middle of either of the four sides. Reaching across a miles-deep chasm, the distance of a quarter of a mile. On the other side of the chasm, in all directions, was a surrounding road that bordered the territory in a huge square road. This in turn, connected to roads leading in all different directions, out from the Capitol building.

A vehicle would travel slightly above ground as a hovercraft for fifty miles out before its engines initiated the sequence that would allow it to fly. The fuel source was unlimited. Another hybridized technology, of a water propellant nature. The side effect of which resulted in a lot of rain. There were no threats of water shortages anywhere on Numina as a result of this technology.

Vampires almost never go out into direct sunlight, as most have a severe allergy to it, with only the oldest developing an immunity after some eons have passed. Both New York and Pandoria had a twenty-four-hour cycle with twelve hours of daylight and twelve hours of night. These factors only increased the nostalgia of her own home world, where the cycle was twenty-four hours as well, but with a full eighteen hours of night, and only six hours of daylight. With its two beautiful moons near-constant, and the lone sun, only ever in the sky long enough for a brief sleep. She remembered it all as if it were yesterday.

There was nothing like the rush of pulling up in a militia cruiser to mete out justice to the law breakers. It was like a fire engine in length, but lower to the ground like a sports car, with six doors that opened from top to bottom. Inside however, it was spacious enough to house eight seats. Three on either side as swiveling chairs, connected to overhead turrets, so that the cannons could be shot in virtually any direction. There was a chair in the middle of the front and the middle of the back for the drivers, so that the vehicle was Omni-directional.

There were no windows to allow for vulnerability, but the technology inside allowed you to look about as if the whole thing were made of glass. There were never any feelings of claustrophobia within the vehicle, but ironically, there was the sense that you were, in fact, too vulnerable and exposed. The militia cruiser added to the sense of superiority and righteousness, and motivated her to get out there and do her job with her fellow comrades in arms.

Chanovalle performed her duties as a 2nd Magistrate for two hundred years, fighting against the insurgent ULO faction members. It was a never-ending battle, not unlike a war, that added an excitement to the routine of the previous years. In the beginning she found it refreshing and enlivening, but as time went on, though, even this proved too little.

One day her life finally changed for the better. It happened while interrogating a captured ULO operative, in an abandoned building his members were hiding out in. She was trying to get the fellow to give up his contacts. It turned out that he was of considerable rank. A Captain, if she remembered correctly.

Chanovalle had the room cleared out of her subordinates, so they could converse one on one. She was not worried for her safety, because he had been restrained by titanium bolts, reinforced with force energy.

After a short while he unexpectedly started trying to negotiate with her.

"Are you happy here, Captain?" he had asked.

"What do you mean?" she had replied.

"Are you happy with your job, I mean?"

"Why wouldn't I be?"

He smiled. "Look. Hear me out for a moment. Don't interrupt until I've finished. Don't worry, it's not propaganda."

"Okay, I'll hear you out. But don't start giving me the run around. I'll know if that's what you're doing."

"Deal. Here goes," he paused for effect. "I want to make you an offer."

Chanovalle's face was stone.

"What would you say to working with the ULO?" he asked.

She was about to protest, but he cut her off.

"Don't get me wrong," he said. "I'm not talking about leaving behind everything you've worked so hard for, here in your career. I'm talking about a side deal that won't even affect you directly."

"Go on," she said.

He took a deep breath. "We need a double agent. Someone who can work for us from the inside, totally unsuspected, and without compromising his or her ideals."

"And how do you suppose that's possible?" she was incredulous.

"Look, let me be frank. For all the glory of the militia, there aren't that many perks that go along with it. I'm willing to supplement your income, in exchange for minor intelligence. Or looking the other way. Delaying pursuit. Or even just informing us ahead of time, when the High Council is onto one of our operations."

"Supplement my income how?" she asked.

"How does five thousand credits a month sound?"

"Only five thousand?" she haggled.

"Five thousand for now, and other items in the near future. We're very well-funded and our resources allow for certain amenities that you might not be privy to. And if things go well, you could be looking at a prominent position within the ULO. Far greater than your 2nd Magistrate status, and far higher than you would ever be able to attain, within the High Council."

"And you have the authority to make this happen?"

"I do."

"You do realize that even speculating something of this nature would be considered treason, don't you?" she had asked.

"I won't say anything, if you don't," he had said. "And call me Lucas."

It turned out that he was able to make good on his promise, and Chanovalle had not wasted her time in letting him escape. She later found out that he was, in fact, much higher than a Captain's rank. Maybe even a direct link in the ruling authority of the entire ULO itself. From that point on, she became a double operative working for the other side.

She remained unsuspected for the entirety. Growing richer and richer as the years passed. It turned out that Lucas was a man of his word. Being a long-lived vampire, she had a lot of time in which to put her plans into action. Plans that were once again fueled by her great ambition.

When it came down to it, she didn't care one iota about the opposing side's ideals. Her only concern was entirely selfish. It became all about Chanovalle's increased prosperity and clout. She had more money in private accounts, probably than if she'd been a member of the High Council herself. Thanks to Lucas and the ULO, she was also afforded other special considerations. Invitations to VIP functions. Rubbing elbows with people of power and influence in society. Fine dining, clothing, and decadence. It was as if her whole world had changed overnight.

All she had to do was give Lucas a heads up every so often, when the militia was going to intercept. Or add minor misdirection into a proposed plan of militia action. Things like that. Trivial things that never jeopardized her career in the slightest.

The next hundred years passed in an ease and relaxation that she was born to have. Of course, all the while she kept her eye on the prize, which was to one day sit on the High Council herself. Even if it was as a ULO representative, if they achieved recognition by the government as a member of the conglomerate. But by whatever means, to have a seat for herself high in that tower.

Then came the day that robbed her of everything.

ULO had orchestrated a plan to overthrow the High Council and take the government over by force. They had their guerrilla armies stationed at key locations throughout territories neighboring the Capitol. There was a secret weapon that would knock out the force field that surrounded the structure and allow them to finally penetrate its walls. They would storm the gates and take it all over. For her part, Chanovalle had supplied them with blueprints, the schedule of the security force, and used misdirection so no one was going to be anywhere near ULO meeting points.

Very late in the scheduled takeover process, Chanovalle discovered that 2nd Magistrate Bryne Xarn had accidentally stumbled onto one of the elements. At the time, she didn't know if it was through a snitch, if it had been a gut feeling, or just blind luck. And she didn't much care. All that mattered was that she stopped him and made sure that he did not get in the way of her victory. She tried to reach his team before they left the Capitol building, but she was too late, and was forced to take a team of mercenaries to intercept on site. Over the years, she'd accumulated resources for just such an occasion, so that part wasn't much of a problem.

On the way, however, she found out that things had changed, and the very instrument responsible for disabling the force field was at an experimental compound called, The Taznar Memorial Laboratory of the Sciences. The idea was that with all the inventions and such at the compound, no one would be able to detect the technology of what they called the Destabilizer Cannon, hidden within the signatures of the other items. The Destabilizer Cannon was a long-range projectile of pure genius, that would have surely brought about the desired outcome if wielded properly. The overall idea itself, however, was doomed to failure.

She was too late, and a battle soon broke out with her and 2nd Magistrate Bryne Xarn at each other's throats:

"How could you?" he yelled.

"Oh, don't be naïve, Captain," she'd yelled back, shooting a portable cannon at his hiding position.

"Selling your soul to the humans? What's next, equal rights for human pets too?"

"Don't be so dramatic. I don't care about the humans any more than you do. What I do care about, however, is my career," she said, ducking under a volley of pyrokinetic bullets, he'd shot at her.

"Your career," he asked. "What's wrong with your career?"

"Nothing. If I was human. But we both know that I'm not."

"So, you're just crazy then? Lost your mind?"

"No, you simpleton," she said, annoyed. "I'm talking about upward mobility. There is none! How can I care about the humans or the government, or any of it at all, when they refuse to reward me for my talents?"

"Reward you? Reward you how?" he asked, hiding behind a desk across the room. He'd stopped shooting for the moment, perhaps really trying to hear what she had to say.

"By keeping me as a 2nd Magistrate for the rest of eternity," she said. "That's how."

"So, all this is about a promotion?" he asked

"Well, in case you weren't paying attention, vampires don't die very often. So, I suppose that's it. In a nutshell, for your simple mind, yes. I'm doing this because I want to be promoted."

"And so, you turned your back on the government, instead of trying to change it from the inside? What's the matter, didn't you think you were smart enough for that?" It was his turn to be sarcastic.

"Or, I was smart enough to realize the futility of it, from the start," she had said.

Eventually they ran out of bullets and engaged in hand to hand combat. She was sure that she had him on the ropes, when all hell broke loose.

Somehow, one of the others had activated the Destabilizer Cannon, which in turn interacted with another form of experimental technology on site, and the unimaginable happened. For a brief instant, theory became reality, as a spontaneous temporal rift was created, pulling 2nd Magistrate Chanovalle Remseldorne and 2nd Magistrate Bryne Xarn inside of it.

CHAPTER 22
RESOLUTIONS

When she regained consciousness, it occurred on a new world, which she subsequently conquered and renamed Pandoria. The planet was about a third the size of her Numina but with an odd orbit around the center star that made the days equal to what she would later discover as New York. Pandoria, however, had magical properties. A trait that would come in handy.

She knew what the Shimmering Gate was the first time she saw it, but unlike the rift she was dragged through, this gateway was stable. Unable to find Bryne on Pandoria, she had despaired, but the discovery of the gateway changed that. She stepped through without hesitation.

Channovalle spent what felt like an eternity, searching for Bryne both on Pandoria and in New York. She knew he would be trying to return home as well, so he would not have gone far from their point of entry. She used others, to extend the range of her search. A network of followers loyal to her cause.

She knew he was out there somewhere. She could feel it.

Years passed.

Not too long ago, as time went for one who was seven hundred and seventy-five years old, she had discovered Kayala, the Child of Destiny, as foretold through ancient Pandorian texts. Kayala was the daughter of Thorne Vandar, a noble from a bloodline of great healing and stamina, and Elyse Zin, daughter of a royal family from an equally great bloodline. Each was part of a different side of a war that had raged for generations, so that they were obligated to be sworn enemies by their respective cultures.

Thorne and Elyse chose to be spiteful and fall in love. What they didn't know was that their child, if a daughter, was prophesied to bring about the end of the world. Through a destined sacrifice at a very specific location, at a very specific date. And she had to be a virgin. Something that was assured from the moment she was abducted at the tender age of five, thanks to yours truly.

Chanovalle had been a techno-magic scientist back on Numina, but tossed a career in that field aside in favor of law enforcement. Scientists never amounted to much, except for perhaps an honorable mention. Chanovalle had always wanted more.

On Pandoria, she was fortunate enough to encounter a Light Sorcerer of about two hundred and fifty years old, who would teach her great magics, allowing her to manipulate things around her through spells. She saw this as a natural progression from her earlier years of techno-magic research, and there were many parallels, which allowed her to excel quickly.

After she learned all she could, he died shortly thereafter, without her even having to lift a finger to kill him. The old man was gracious enough to possess all the literature she required on both subjects of good and evil magic. She immediately took to studying to become a Dark Sorceress on her own, against his dying wishes.

The new abilities she gained, kept secret from all her subjects, were used to enhance her thirst for further knowledge. They also greatly contributed to her research efforts.

It was through the old man's resources, now hers to wield, that she was most efficiently able to bring truth to the folk tales she discovered about the Child of Destiny. For it lay in magical texts, that she would not have been able to decipher without her training, hundreds of years earlier. Magical texts all but useless in the hands of someone not possessed of her powers. It was old knowledge that Kayala's people, on either side of her parentage, had long forgotten generations upon generations ago. A divine secret that Chanovalle alone had unearthed.

It had been a simple matter to track down her parents. They were on the run once they found out Chanovalle's interest in them. She caught them, slew them, and took the girl into her possession. For all the good their little rebellion did them.

With her scientific mind and magical prowess, she saw what a lesser mind would not. Yes. Sacrificing the child would lead to the end of the world, but there was so much more when you looked deeper. It turned out that the sacrifice needed to be performed in New York, for a successful outcome.

That meant that all of New York would be destroyed. So what? She could destroy it and come back to Pandoria, with no worries. The most interesting part, which ruled her dreams since before the girl was ever born, was the scope and nature of the magic.

The right person, with the right magic, could harness those energies for personal gain. Once the rites of the sacrificial spell had been completed, initiating the desired outcome, the spell would be effectively over. But the energies would still be lying about until they finally dissipated. A genius and powerful sorceress like Chanovalle, would be able to harness those energies for herself, and in all likelihood, be able to open a portal to Numina and have her revenge.

The plan was to quickly bring Bryne to her location and kill him. Use the remaining energy to open a portal to Numina. Wherein her magical prowess would bring that world to its knees.

She would no longer need to have a seat on the High Council. She'd trump it. It would be Empress Chanovalle Remseldorne, or Goddess of the High Council, if she didn't just outright obliterate the lot of them. It would all be hers. All of it. And if by some miracle she was not able to return to her beloved Pandoria, it was a sacrifice she was willing to make.

Chanovalle smiled to herself, pulling Kayala a little bit closer to her, as they climbed into the bus.

Today's plan was simple. They would appropriate five buses to load in two hundred and fifty persons from her army. Archers, front-line fighters, assassins, and the like. Some of her deadliest. It was a sufficient number.

The buses would be driven to New York City, approximately two and a half hours from Monticello, New York, to the sacrificial location. There everyone would meet and set up a defensive perimeter, designed so that nothing could hinder Chanovalle's destiny. The idea being, that if anyone did in fact try to delay anything, it would be far too late, before they mobilized and negotiated the situation that she had organized.

Chanovalle had Azure, her trusted right-hand Commander, check to make sure that everyone on her bus was dressed appropriately. They were supposed to look like tourists, with the story that if they were accidentally discovered, that they had gotten lost.

Chanovalle had a grandiose nature, and she was constantly fighting the urge to empty out all of Pandoria, to seize the surrounding territory by brute force. She resisted the urge to decimate every living thing for miles around the sacrificial site in preparation for this great occasion. All because she wanted it so desperately to work. Wanted so badly for her dreams to finally be made reality.

Compose yourself, she thought. Your moment is at hand.

WHEN KAYALA WOKE UP, SHE COULD NOT QUITE MAKE OUT WHAT was going on. After a quick look around, things started coming back to her, and she was glad for Ash's arm to steady her balance. Otherwise she might have very well fallen off the desk he had placed her on.

No matter how hard she had tried to ignore her sister's impending doom, the dread of it had caught up to her. Until it rendered her as helpless, as she feared she might be, in saving Inalia's life.

Defeat never felt so numb.

"You're awake," said Ash. "Welcome back."

"I'm sorry. I guess I passed out."

"It's okay. You're under a lot of stress." He handed her a book. "Have you seen this?"

"What am I looking for?"

He explained that it was one of the codex books referenced in the journal entries. In it were details about the sacrificial site, but it was written in code. They didn't have time for all this nonsense. They needed to find the coordinates now. The Queen must have written them down somewhere.

"Let's keep looking, Ash," she said, trying to put a note of optimism in her voice. "Maybe we can find something that shows exactly where."

The information was based on old geography and some kind of riddle. It was so useless and all utterly futile that Kayala was on the verge of losing it, but this time she would smash and destroy everything in the room, instead of passing out. The single thing that allowed her to maintain her composure, was the possibility that she might inadvertently destroy something they needed, to find Inalia.

It was while suppressing one such outburst that she noticed Ash staring at a page in the book of riddles. Something in there had caught such a hold of his attention, that she lost her own focus and was half wondering if some magic of the book had caught him. Apparently not, because he was able to answer her question on the third attempt.

∾

"WHAT ARE YOU LOOKING AT?" SOMEONE ASKED.

He wasn't sure and he didn't care who had spoken. He was lost in a symbol in the book. He knew that shape. He had seen it somewhere. But where?

"What are you looking at?" someone asked again. Ash came out of his meditation and answered the only person it could be.

"I've seen this symbol before," he replied. "It's magic. Real magic.

Like with a wizard and magical powers and stuff. My brain's too fried to make any real sense out of it."

On a hunch, he went into the small room where Kayala found the journal. He started looking around for another trap door or hidden compartment, when he realized that the maps on the wall were parts of New York.

Right there, as plain as the nose on his face, was the one place he was intimately familiar with. New York City. But this time, unlike any of the other maps, the key geography was circled in a red pen. A little island that stood between Manhattan and Queens. It was the one they'd just been to. Roosevelt Island.

Why would the queen circle the place where Inalia Edwards lived?

In his haste, he'd failed to register what his subconscious already knew. It wasn't a circle. It was the same magical symbol he'd seen in that book. It had been hastily drawn on the map, by someone who knew what they were looking at. Someone like the Queen.

Could irony be so cruel? What were the odds that Kayala had a twin sister, that just happened to live right at ground zero?

"I've seen this symbol before," he said, pointing at the half crescent moon with a dot in the middle, but more like an ankh. "We need to go back out to New York City. That's the place that they're going to sacrifice her. I'm sure of it."

STANDING ON THE ROOFTOP OF HIS APARTMENT BUILDING IN STATEN Island, Ash waited for Jinx to appear. Clouds still hovered in the sky overhead, but it had finally stopped raining. Granted, he'd been propelled through time, losing around two months of it when he returned with Kayala through the gateway, but for all intents and purposes it looked like the same day they'd left. From his perspective the whole thing couldn't have been more than a few hours. Lunch time was right around the corner.

The ride back had been uneventful.

When Kayala had walked into the apartment, she went straight to sleep. Leaving Ash with his thoughts. He was tired too, but he knew that he needed help. There was no way they could rescue Inalia by themselves. Going up to the roof and calling on Jinx, seemed the right thing to do. At least he knew that much.

As far as Kayala was concerned, he was clueless. No matter how he played it out in his head, all his options were wrong. Everything he thought to say was stupid. Everything he thought of doing was stupid. He was stupid.

Ash had fed on someone less than a week ago. Sometimes he had memory lapses, but that didn't seem to be happening lately. That meant that he didn't have to worry about killing Kayala in her sleep tonight. Thank God.

If she stayed around him at all, she'd notice that he wasn't eating food. It was only a matter of time before she asked him about it. When she did, he wouldn't be able to lie to her. The truth would come out, and he'd find out if he was meant to be with her or not.

It all made logical sense. Why was he so afraid, then?

Without any warning, he felt someone standing behind him and knew that Jinx had arrived.

"Do you like?" she asked, doing a slow spin. "I copied it from a magazine."

Jinx was wearing denim jeans with black sneakers, a green t-shirt that said 'House Rules' on the front, and a dark blood-red long coat that matched her eyes.

"Very stylish," he lied. Though, he did note that it was a step in the right direction. He had half-expected her to appear completely nude like before.

"I get the impression you have need of my assistance," she said. Apparently, she had caught onto his somber mood, and maybe noticed the book in his hand.

Ash got right to the point.

"What do you know about this symbol?" he asked. He flipped to the page in one fluid motion.

"It is a book of magic," Jinx said plainly. "None other than one who is skilled in such things is permitted to see them or would be aware enough to inscribe them. Or use them."

"Good," he said. "A friend of mine is going to be killed at this place." Ash had flipped the pages over to what he now thought of as coordinates and showed the book to Jinx again. "Can you tell me—or is there a way to find out what this is? I think I already know, but is there a way to confirm it?"

Jinx looked through the book the way a jeweler examined their precious stones. Flipping the pages back and forth. Caressing the letters on the page. At some point, even closing her eyes for a time.

Ash walked away and sat on the edge of the roof, away from her crazy antics. If not, he'd be shaking some sense into her.

"We don't have much time," he told the air.

She must not have heard him, for it was a considerable amount of time before she spoke.

"As you have no doubt surmised, there are magics within this book," she said.

He had surmised no such thing.

She continued, "There is a form of gatekeeper within and other things not readily apparent. Suffice it to say, it is a very old text and I am going to need a bit of time. It is the only way to arrive at an acceptable degree of certainty."

Ash had turned to face her while she spoke and was now slowly walking towards her. "And you'll have an idea of what the spell might be?" he asked, trying to conceal the excitement in his voice. "As far as I know, the person who's planning on carrying out whatever this ritual is, will be doing it on a place called Roosevelt Island, located between Manhattan and Queens, not too far from here. I know it's sacrificial, but something tells me it'd help if we knew its purpose, so that we could put a stop to it."

"These are things that I should be able to find out. When someone creates a spell or manipulates magic in certain ways, there is usually a residue that can be used to map the potentialities," she replied. There was an unmistakable hint of pride in her voice as she spoke.

"How long do you need?" he asked. "Weeks? Months?"

"It shouldn't take longer than twenty-four hours," she said.

"Well, you've got about twelve. According to the calendar it's already the twelfth of October. That means the rite is tomorrow. And since we don't know what time it's supposed to take place, we're gonna be there at around eleven tonight to be on the safe side. What time is it now, eleven in the morning?"

"I believe so," she answered.

"My friend Kayala and I have got to get some sleep. I don't even know how many hours we've been up already, with all the traveling and everything. Can you meet us at the 42nd Street New York Public Library, later today? At about 11p.m.?"

"I will be there."

"Also, it probably wouldn't hurt to bring that little Asian guy for help, especially since we don't know what's going on."

"I will see to it."

"Thanks, Jinx. You're the best."

ASH HAD SCARCELY LEFT THE ROOFTOP BEFORE JINX TOOK A CROSS-legged seat on the floor. Holding the book in her lap, she closed her eyes and freed her mind of all her thoughts. She rose ever so slightly off the floor and began to focus all her attention into her third eye. Formlessness took root, as she merged with the other magic and entwined it with her own.

Even before she got very far in her research, the ancient text spoke of a ceremony that would bring about the end of the world. Something known as Armageddon. It was a transformative representation of impetus. The constant ebb and flow represented in Yin Yang, but immediate.

The magics further spoke of a sacrifice as having to be concurrent with a special planetary alignment that only came about once every three thousand years. The date, according to the Roman calendar, fell on October 13, 2023. It was now October 12, 2023 at eleven in the morning. Ash had reasoned that without a specific time, they would have to assume that it was at the earliest point. Midnight. She saw nothing to contradict his logic. But she continued to delve deeper, searching for an understanding of the monumental event.

Concurrently, she sent a missive to her trusted servant, Twister. Telling him her fears and suspicions on the matter. His response was typical. He would be there. Then, almost as an afterthought, his response changed. Could he bring another as well? An unusual thing, but not unwelcome, under the circumstances. She acquiesced to the request.

Her mistress, The Great Mistenyar herself, had told her of an occurrence that had taken the life of an all-powerful dragon, eons ago. She couldn't remember the dragon's name, but the story told that he had underestimated powerful magics, as he actually let a ceremony reach fulfillment. His plan, at the time, had been to show everyone that even after such a monumental event, he was still the supreme power. Something that had stood the test of time immemorial. He was certain that he didn't have anything to worry about, all the way up until the ceremony ended.

The story went, that one of the high priests had taken great magical energies into himself, unbeknownst to the dragon, who had been too full of his own importance to pay attention. Just when the dragon thought everything ineffectual, flying around and boasting, and full of hubris. Just then, at the pinnacle of his own self involvement, the high priest cast magical energies at him that completely erased his existence from the face of the planet. After what seemed like a huge lifetime bordering on forever, the dragon was no more.

Jinx remembered the story, all these years later. She would not make the same mistake.

MARTHA WAS SITTING IN THE FRONT PASSENGER SEAT OF HER FRIEND Marjorie's Honda. She didn't know anything about cars to know more than it was red on the outside and that it had four doors. Janice and Florence sat in the back. They were on their way to the Bingo game at the Senior Center over on the Upper West Side. She couldn't make out what the man on the radio was saying so she turned it up:

BILL PARSONS: "IN THE NEWS TONIGHT, A CASE OF BUTTER FINGERS.

"A man was gunned down as he attacked police in upstate New York last night. Sources tell us that there was a warrant out for his arrest for killing a State Trooper in cold blood. An eyewitness phoned in the man's whereabouts.

"The man was killed by police in a shootout and transported by ambulance. But in between the location and the coroner's office, the body seems to have disappeared.

"A spokesman for the Sheriff's Department says, this is the first time something like this has ever happened and that the body couldn't have gotten far..."

PRATLE RUBBED HIS FINGERS OVER HIS EYES, WISHING HE HAD Aspirin. He was thankful to be alive, but not for the head splitting migraine that made him want to scream.

His Commander had set him up. That much was certain. Even if he didn't know why.

Just like a woman, he thought, as he laid his head back down on the hay.

Months ago, she'd told him to wait at their hotel for one of the search teams that were on their way. The squad never arrived. Instead, he became the main suspect in a manhunt for a cop killer. For the most part, he'd been able to give them the slip, but a few days ago, he ran into the business end of a lot of angry police and their guns.

Knowing nothing about his hardier Pandorian constitution, they'd tossed him in an ambulance and left him for dead. When he regained consciousness, he snuck outside and into the back of a pickup truck, where he passed out again.

The next thing he knew, he was walking past a sign that said "Bear Mountain" on it and into someone's barn.

He'd live, but healing was going to be a pain in the butt. For one thing, he was going to need a lot of food, and stuck out in the middle of nowhere, he wasn't very hopeful.

All he kept thinking about was why he'd neglected to get ice-cream when he was back in the city. That would have really hit the spot right about now.

CHAPTER 23
TWISTER

Freddy sighed as he looked through the refrigerator for something to eat. It was Martha's Bingo night, which meant he was going to have to sift through the leftovers for something good. He usually went to the restaurant downstairs, but tonight he was craving something home cooked. Besides, the weather had been positively atrocious lately and he'd rather not be surprised by any of its crazy business.

He settled on the beef stroganoff from a few days ago and popped it into the microwave. Freddy noticed his wedding ring as he punched the numbers in and smiled. Even when she wasn't around, Martha was still always taking care of him. Just as much as she'd been all their long years together.

She'd bought him his favorite gold watch. Was the time right? If it was, then his show was on. He flipped the knob to the station, on the radio they kept in the kitchen, while pressing the button that would turn the thing on:

ISAAC STEVENS, PROFESSOR OF RELIGIOUS PHILOSOPHY, NYU: "Throughout time immemorial, mankind has had a fascination with the end of the world. Across cultural boundaries and the division of land or water, this concept has consistently persevered through the test of time...

"EVEN IN THE OLD TESTAMENT, FULL OF THE STORIES THAT ARE THE foundation of most modern religion today. A document thousands of years old. There lies, not far after creation, this presupposition that some divine being is keeping score. Much like Santa Claus, he knows when you've been bad or good, so be good for goodness sake, or you won't get any presents.

"And when you become an adult, the ending changes to, be good or you'll burn in hell for all eternity. This of course, can also be upgraded to, you've been so bad that God's fed up and is going to destroy the entire planet and start over. Or not start over, but it doesn't matter anyway, because you'll be long gone, so it really won't matter from your point of view.

"And just to prove that he's not bluffing, you can read that old story about Noah and the Ark. So behave...

"AND THIS OF COURSE, HAS FURTHER EVOLVED SO THAT BURNING IN hell is the end result of any infraction, where you've ever broken the rules in your entire life. Sort of like divine credit. Unless of course, you're on the right team, in which case you might get a free pass. But everyone claims to be the right one, and who knows who we can really trust, and we're all just going to end up in hell anyway...

"TAKE WHAT'S COMING UP NEXT WEEK, FOR EXAMPLE. ON OCTOBER 13th, 2023, the Cairo Calendar says that a new cycle is coming. But what does that really mean? A new beginning? A new ending? Who's to say?"

Michelle Gardner, host: "So what do you think Professor? Is Friday going to be the end of the world?"

Isaac Stevens, Professor of Religious Philosophy, NYU: "I don't believe so, no. I think it's more sensationalism born out of media hype, if anything. But then, I don't think we'll really know until the time comes."

Michelle Gardner, host: "So, what do you recommend people do to prepare, if there is going to be an upcoming disaster?"

Isaac Stevens, Professor of Religious Philosophy, NYU: "Live your life and enjoy yourself, because life's too short. I think that's what it all really means. Who wants to spend a lifetime worrying about impending doom all the time anyway? It's exhausting. On October 13th, 2023, this time tomorrow, you know what I'm going to be doing?"

Michelle Gardner, host: "What's that?"

Isaac Stevens, Professor of Religious Philosophy, NYU: "It's a Friday. I'm going to take the wife and kids to the movies, just like always."

Michelle Gardner, host: "There you have it. Professor Isaac Stevens, from NYU. Thank you, Professor."

Isaac Stevens, Professor of Religious Philosophy, NYU: "Thank you for having me, Michelle. It's been a pleasure."

ALYSSA RUNNING DEAR AWOKE TO FIND THAT SHE'D FALLEN ASLEEP in her leather recliner again, in front of the seventy-five-inch LED TV. According to her watch it was about one in the morning. She stifled a yawn, as she got up and made her way to the bedroom, and her comfy king-sized bed with the down comforter. It had been a long night at work, and she was in desperate need of some shut eye, which explained why she had dozed off in the first place.

Some months ago, it had come to her attention that a corporate venture had been formed between the Supreme Council of Antiquities. Egypt, their affiliates, and the famed actor-turned-philanthropist, Michael Evans. The cooperative thought it rather intriguing to publicly display the riches of the prominent Sheik, Marcus Silvi. (The Americanized name of Madrinot Solimar Verdi Sumar, self-proclaimed descendant of the Pharaoh, Ramses the Great.)

Quite wealthy, despite his delusions of grandeur, Mr. Silvi created a treasure trove of his own, out of pure gold. Inspired by his ridiculous number of greats, grandfather on his mother's side.

The collection, aside from busts of his face and a gold coffin containing his mummified remains, was said to boast many depictions of modern life. As if an actual modern Pharaoh had passed onto the next world.

Long story short, Evans, along with his partners, thought it would be a hoot to house the collection in a real Egyptian pyramid.

Alyssa took it as yet another form of sacrilege, where little minds were once again disrespecting the history of great nations, and their people, in the name of entertainment and profit. The event immediately made it to the top of her hit list, prompting an immediate flight to Cairo.

The first few nights there, she performed a thorough reconnaissance of the target pyramid. Not hard, given that the artifacts had not yet arrived.

The next step had been to formulate her plan, while getting a hold of any necessary equipment. It presupposed that due to the location, it wouldn't be state of the art. And that they were more likely to focus on simply guarding the entrance and perhaps installing a couple of security cameras. In that case, she could probably drug the guards and have carte blanche of the entire place.

As it turned out, her plan worked perfectly, as newspapers around the world lamented about how the great fortune had disappeared. Naturally the Council, their affiliates, and Evans blamed one another, saying it was a scheme to get the insurance money. Accusations flew, as everybody tried to sue everybody else.

After the dust settled a bit, they began to collectively wonder where all the treasured possessions of Madrinot Solimar Verdi Sumar, self-proclaimed descendant of the Pharaoh, Ramses the Great, could have disappeared to. How was it possible that someone had walked out the front door? It had to be an inside job. Again, the accusations flew.

In the end, only Alyssa knew the absurdity of it all, and that in fact, the front entrance wasn't the way the treasure had been stolen at all.

Obviously, the sheer manpower required to move the entirety of it would never allow for such a thing. She'd simply done what came naturally to her. Trust her instincts. She'd buried it.

That's right. Why waste the time trying to move all that treasure if she didn't have to?

She'd buried it right there in the same pyramid, in the grave she dug, right there in the dirt. It had been a simple enough matter to create a faux stone floor before anyone ever started moving the items in.

Alyssa installed a camouflaged hydraulic lift weeks in advance, so that once the treasure was situated, all she had to do was press a button. Even now, all the items were safe and sound, and had never even been moved from where they were originally placed. Everything was simply lowered to a secure location under the floor. Life was so much easier when you already had your own money.

In a few months she'd decide if she wanted to melt down any of the items and turn them into gold bars. Maybe she'd even give some of the money to charity this time.

In the meantime, she was safe and sound, in her fluffy bed, after a long flight back to the states. All she had planned on her to do list, was a nice day of pleasant pampering, starting bright and early.

In Alyssa's dreams she was the Queen of all Pharaohs, and her Egyptian Empire had successfully conquered the globe.

~

AT NINE IN THE MORNING, ALYSSA WAS SITTING AT HER FAVORITE salon, 'Tidbits of Pleasure,' having her pedi-manicure combo, while sipping a latte. Today she felt like hot pink.

When her nails were done, she had her bikini line, upper lip area, and legs waxed, along with the threading of her eyebrows. Soon followed by a full-body massage, mud bath and herbal facial treatment. Then her hair was washed and cut, and she had an artificial tan applied. Unlike her ancestors, she wasn't a fan of the sun and wrinkles.

With the beautification process complete, she went to her afternoon yoga class and then to her lunch reservation at Nobu, for some sushi. After that, it was a short cab ride to 5th Avenue for some shopping, as she window shopped at her leisure. Occasionally stepping into places like Saks, Donna Karen, or Tiffany's. Every so often, she emerged with another bag to add to her collection. There was a time when she used to have it all delivered, but she stopped when she realized how much more she ended up spending as a result.

It had stormed while she was shopping, and now only a light rain remained. She had a giant black umbrella with her, that could have probably fit three more people underneath. It was so good to be back in New York City.

Almost home, after a fun-filled day, Alyssa hopped out of a cab. On the way to her building, she noticed a little man sitting on the roof of a car, right at her entrance. As before, he smelled as if he didn't exist, except that she caught a whiff of soap this time, which meant he might be clean. But his hair was still the same terrible mess.

"You," she said, surprised to see him again. "What do you want?"

"Can we talk?" he asked, comfortably seated atop the car. "Something very big is happening. Something monumental, that I think you should know about."

"Monumental, huh?" she said, studying the expression on his face. Would she hit him with curiosity or disinterest? She thought about their last encounter. He'd been rude that night, but he did obey her, when she'd kicked him out.

"Stay put, small fry," she told him. "I'll be right back." It looked like curiosity had won out, so that after she went upstairs to drop her bags off in her apartment (she couldn't bear to have her doorman carry it), she actually came back outside like she said, about five minutes later.

"Alright, spill it," she said, approaching the car. "What's monumental?"

"The world is going to end tomorrow," he said.

"Oh? Yeah, I'm up on that already," she said. "Saw it on the TV. You should buy one." She turned around, to head back into her building.

"You already know?" he asked. "We just found out yesterday. How did you find out?"

When she turned back around, she found that he'd slid down off the car, so that he was standing. It meant she had to look down at him.

"Who's we?" she asked. "You're the only one here."

"My master and I," he replied. "And two others that brought it to our attention."

"Did they make you wait this long for the punchline too?"

"I'm not joking. There is no punch line."

"For somebody who speaks perfect English, you sure are stiff. Where are you from anyway? China?"

"Yes. I am five hundred and sixty-seven years old."

"That's a lot of birthday candles," Alyssa said with a smirk. "You look good for your age."

"As do you," he said in an admiring tone. "You are physically the exact same as when I saw you in France in the year 1924."

"I see," she said, running her fingers through her hair. "And what, pray tell, was I doing?"

"Running from the authorities."

"And why exactly, would I do that?"

"I believe you got caught stealing a really big diamond from the Louvre."

Alyssa was about to respond, but he cut her off.

"Please," he said. "I only need five minutes to give you the information I have."

"Okay, small fry," she agreed. "But let's walk. All this standing in one place is killing me."

It took about twenty minutes, before she finally extracted the information he was trying to give.

"Okay, let me get this straight," she said, when he was finished. They continued walking down 11th Avenue. "You're telling me that the Cairo Calendar thing is real, and that a woman's getting sacrificed to make it happen, like forty-five minutes away from where we're at right now. But you don't know what's going to happen?"

"Yes."

"And that the group who's responsible is from another dimension, but they all look like regular humans. And they may have an army with them to make sure this thing, whatever it is, gets done."

"Yes."

"There's one big hole in your story, though," she said.

"What is that?"

"In front of my building, you said you'd only just found out about this like sometime last night." She paused for emphasis.

"Yes."

"So then, what the hell were you doing at my apartment a few months ago?" she asked, stopping dead still to stare down at him.

"I was trying to get you to retrieve something for me," he said.

"Steal something, you mean. Why don't you just steal it yourself, tough guy?"

"A long time ago when I was a child," he began. "My village, composed mostly of farmers, was attacked by Mongolians. Historically, we know that this was not an uncommon thing. My people would have been entirely wiped out on that day, had it not been for a fighting hero who defeated their assault—"

"You?" she asked, cutting him off.

"No. As I said, I was only a boy at the time." He took a deep breath before continuing his story. "Like many before me, I sought to be just like him.

"I followed him and begged to be his apprentice. But he would not hear of it. He told me to go back to my farm, but I would not listen.

"On the night that I almost starved to death, sick with a fever, I told him that I would refuse his help. That I would rather die than not learn what he alone could teach me."

"You know, you're like my grandfather, with these stories," Alyssa teased, leaning up against a parked car.

He went on. "He agreed. I learned to fight, and I killed many men over the years, before I finally joined the monastery and became a monk. Even my new home, as a sacred place, was attacked.

"I was forced to fight again to save the lives of my brothers. But I was so ashamed at renouncing my vows of nonviolence, that I left the monastery. Determined to live in town, somewhere below our mountain."

He cleared his throat before continuing. "It was in town that I discovered the reason behind the attack. One of the brothers who liked to sneak out at night had accumulated a gambling debt, and to pay what he owed he stole a sacred gold scroll.

"Delivering it into the hands of disreputable men. Who in turn, killed him and attacked the monastery. They acquired more treasure, as they looted and killed in our sacred temple.

"Over the years I found everything, except the most sacred. The first item that incited the attack was forever lost to me." His eyes refocused and the history lesson ended. Alyssa stayed quiet.

"On the night I saw you at your residence," he said. "I had come for your help. I found the scroll, but it's too well protected."

She waited until she thought he was truly done talking before she said, "I'll tell you what. After this thing pans out tonight, I'll give you a hand with this treasure of yours too."

"Then you'll come?" he asked. "You'll come with me tonight? To save the world?"

"You know, you're a bit over dramatic. Anybody ever tell you that?"

"I don't think so. No."

"I do have one condition though," she said, looking past him, across the street.

"What's that?"

"What's your name?"

"Please excuse my rudeness," he said, bowing respectfully. "In English, I am called Twister."

Alyssa put out her hand. "Alyssa Running Deer, at your service."

Twister beamed a smile up at her that would have parted the gray clouds in the sky.

Saving the world. She thought it had a nice ring to it.

CHAPTER 24
PLAY DATE

"Strap her in!" yelled the Queen.

But it was a thing she did not associate with herself. Even when she was summarily lifted off her feet and set onto a stone wall. When she was aware of having chains tied to her arms and wrists. It was still not something that touched her.

She dreamed that she was finally home on Roosevelt Island. But that was impossible, because the Queen was here and Inalia had never told her where she lived. She was dreaming that she stood on top of the old lighthouse. She Looked down at the water from an angle she had often fantasized about, but had never been able to achieve, because the old lighthouse was always locked.

There were so many of them. As if the entire castle had been emptied to re-establish itself in the real world. She couldn't see them from up here, all tied up, but she knew they were there.

How did they know where she lived? She never told anyone because it didn't matter and because Azure would have beat her mercilessly if she had. So how did they know?

For a moment, her mind shifted ever so slightly back to reality. She knew that the Queen had drugged her. She knew that something bad was going to happen, but she had to wait for the events to unfold. It was like watching a movie. One in which Inalia Edwards was as much the star, as the audience.

ALYSSA RUNNING DEER SAT AT THE STEERING WHEEL OF A WHITE Chevy SUV. There was an additional row of seats in the back for a total of three. The driver and front passenger row, and two others. More than enough for her four expected guests. She adjusted the mirrors for the second time. The car was a rental and she was still getting used to it.

She'd already punched the destination into the onboard GPS, waiting for Twister to return with everyone else. She drummed her fingers, tapping them against the steering wheel, before she turned the radio on. The tiny dial spun until a rock song filled the air. It was an old one by the band Queen.

It had started hailing outside. She was fiddling with the wipers switch, when someone opened one of the rear doors.

Alyssa shut the radio off and turned to see exactly who she'd be driving around. A bald-headed woman with red eyes stared back without a word, fearlessly sizing her up immediately. She knew this to be Twister's master before he introduced her.

The next one to enter almost made her jaw drop. It wasn't because of her great beauty, with hair the color of the sun, or emerald delicately slanted eyes. It wasn't even the way that she carried herself with barely concealed danger. It was her scent.

Wonder of wonders. Here was the woman she'd smelled in the park that night, when she saved that woman from those men.

Right behind her came the final addition. An unremarkable bald man with brown eyes. It had nothing to do with his looks. He was probably about her height and more than handsome enough as a male. It was the complete lack of menace that he represented.

That couldn't be right. The oddness of that alone, told her there was something special about the man. At least as special as Twister, the scentless, who had resumed his seat next to her. She'd have to keep an eye on that one.

On all of them, she reminded herself.

Twister introduced them as Jinx, Kayala, and Ash, respectively. He offered up her full name of Alyssa Running Deer.

"Am I the only one with a last name?" she asked Twister, in mock petulance.

"Looks that way," said Ash. "Is it true that you're a werewolf?"

"Yeah. Why do you ask?" Twister must have told everyone all about her, which was annoying, considering that she didn't know much about any of them. She noticed that Ash didn't smell scared of her. Most people were always scared of her true nature.

"It's a long story. I hope you don't get offended, but I used to think I might be one. A werewolf."

Alyssa couldn't help but smile. "And you're not?" she asked, using her disappointed voice.

"No, I don't think I am," he said, and then leaned a bit closer excitedly, "Do I smell like one?"

"Nope. Sorry."

"Thanks. Just figured you'd probably know if I was or not, just to make sure."

"What are you then?" she asked, trying to get the exchange of information going.

"I still haven't figured that one out. Probably not human," he replied. Then he lapsed back into silence.

Knowing that they were pressed for time, Alyssa pulled the car out onto the street and started their journey.

"Turn left in four hundred feet," chimed the GPS. The automated voice was useful for a change. On a night like this, with the snow and rain combination falling from the sky, it was difficult to see street names. There wasn't any time for wrong turns tonight. Not if the world might be ending.

No one spoke. It put Alyssa on edge. She put the radio back on to calm her nerves.

Eventually, the trip led her across a small bridge and down a spiraling ramp. At the bottom of it there were two directions to choose from. Left or right. She turned the radio off.

"Which way?"

Jinx stepped out the back, leaving the door open, and walked up front to stand directly in the middle of the road. Neither the cold nor the hail seemed to bother her. Which might explain why she didn't care about the heat seeping out of the car, or the wet slush trying to gain entry.

After a few seconds she hopped back inside, and closed the door.

"To the right," she said, and then added, "Don't any of you feel that?"

"No," answered Alyssa. "Feel what?" It must have been rhetorical, because everyone had lapsed into their usual silence.

With the GPS turned off, there was only the constant hum of the windshield wipers, and the fan of the heater, as the warm air blew. Despite seeing Twister in her periphery, or the others in the rearview mirror, she might as well have been alone. Only the blonde one even looked around to see where they were headed.

At some point the road split again and Jinx instructed her to continue going straight. In a short distance, the road ceased to exist, ending at small stone columns, to keep cars from driving farther in. The river was immediately to their right.

"What do we do now?" she asked, turning to look at the others.

"We walk," replied Jinx, hopping out the back door. This time she was nice enough to close it behind her. Ash and Kayala got out on his side, behind Alyssa, who shut the engine off and stepped out into the cold herself. Twister stood next to his master.

The wind was blowing in gusts from behind them, so Alyssa couldn't get any scents from up ahead. For the time being, she was reduced to eyes and ears only, which was why she didn't smell the policeman before she saw him.

"Sorry folks, the park's closed. We're filming a movie." he said, struggling against the wind.

"What?" asked Ash.

"I said the park's closed!" He put his arms up to bar the way. When Kayala stepped forward. He said, "How'd you get loose?"

Kayala was on him in an instant, with two swift strikes, before she tackled him. She smashed his head onto the cement for good measure. When she stood up, she hurled his limp body into the river.

"Definitely not prey," Alyssa mumbled.

"What'd you do that for?" Ash asked.

"He's one of them," she told him. "They're already here."

As if to confirm her words, the wind shifted, bringing Alyssa's nose to life. Whoever they were, there were a lot of them.

Kayala must have smelled it too, because her eyes grew wide and she turned directly into the wind. After a brief pause, she took off running. Jinx took to the wind as well, but she flew instead, with Twister running after Kayala. Only Ash hung back, next to Alyssa. Maybe he was distracted by the broken sky.

It was the only way that she could describe the shimmering lights that flickered in the heavens. It reminded her of what she'd heard about the Aura Borealis, but this wasn't the North Pole. This was New York City. She'd spent most of her life in the city and had never seen anything like it. If this was the end of the world, then she had a front row seat.

Alyssa pulled her mind away from the sky and jogged forward. The path straightened out, with a lighthouse at the tip of the island. Shielding her eyes against the storm, she saw a large crowd of people spread out, with the lighthouse as the epicenter. There were hundreds of them.

She thought she saw Jinx, with her dark red long coat flapping in the wind. A big ball of energy streaked down from the sky, bringing daylight to night ever so briefly. Unless her eyes deceived her, it had come from Jinx.

Whatever it was, it threw bodies around like matchsticks. Another smaller ball shot out towards the lighthouse, soon after. But unlike the previous success, this one reverberated off at an angle into the water.

So quick, Jinx was struck by a bolt of lightning out of the sky. With smoke coming off her body, she hurtled into the river, like a fallen cloud.

Alyssa hid behind a bush, stripped off all her clothing in the freezing cold, and began the change.

~

ASH FELT THE ENERGY IN THE SKY WHILE HE SAW IT. THERE WAS NO denying it. This was magic.

In computer-like fashion, he calculated the people standing before him at two hundred and forty-nine. One of them was Twister and the other was Kayala. Both were running in a direct collision course, to meet the other two hundred and forty-seven in combat. The newest addition to their group of misfits, Alyssa, was standing a bit up and to the left of him, probably figuring out what she wanted to do.

Jinx had taken to the sky. Even through the storm, his sharp eyes allowed him to see her as if he were looking through binoculars. She gesticulated and shot a burst of magic down upon the army on land. Another was bounced off a spell of protection. The magical retaliation sent Jinx into the river. It's source? Probably the one responsible for the ritual.

That was the one that they had to confront, to save the world and Kayala's sister. But first, he had to make sure that Kayala herself survived.

He began to call his own energy to the fore. The same one he felt coursing through him that night in the bar. Instinct warned him to move. Now!

He dove forward, just as a bolt of lightning struck. Unscathed, his eyes were drawn to a woman with a crown on her head leaning over the top of the lighthouse. Their eyes met.

Something about her was familiar. She knew him too. The recognition on her face was unmistakable.

She quickly moved away from the edge and his view.

~

MAJOR GORDON WATCHED IN DISBELIEF, AS HIS MEN WERE TAKEN apart by one fiftieth their number at least. The flying one in the sky had been taken care of by the Queen, so he didn't worry about her. To see the three that remained, going through his men like they were children, was beyond disturbing.

Two of them with the artful grace of accomplished warriors. The third was a force of nature in her own right. Fighting like a wild animal. Like his Caymon, for instance.

Then he spotted something that put a smile on his face. Something that he hadn't noticed, because it was lower to the ground. Apparently, the opposition had a canine in its midst.

"Looks like someone brought you a playmate, Caymon," he told the wolf. "Go get em boy!"

Caymon was off like a shot, with Gordon jogging at the rear to see the sport of it. The canine was quite a specimen. Arguably one of the largest he had seen. Size wasn't an issue when one side had an ace in the hole. While larger, it didn't have vampire blood coursing through it like Caymon did, and so stood no real chance.

Caymon would play with it, as he always did. Just a bit of sport. Making it think it had a chance. Then when he lost interest, it would die like all the others.

When he got there, the two were already locked in combat.

The opposition had snow-white fur and gray eyes. He thought it might be a female, but if it was, she was huge. Caymon looked almost like a puppy standing beside her, with his own dark brown coat and blue eyes. Though only mortal, his opponent was a wolf too, so it should be a good fight.

They circled one another, feinting as they took exploratory nips. Both growling savagely. With vicious strikes at leg or body, as openings were presented. Then Caymon made his move and leapt at the female, going in for the kill. She accidentally knocked him aside when she turned to run away.

He was right behind her. His blood hot with pursuit. He had her for sure and she knew it.

The white wolf jumped onto a picnic table and leapt off, circling back around on the ground. Then up on the picnic table again. Instead of jumping back on the ground, she turned, using her longer body to advantage and locked on, impossibly to the back of Caymon's neck. He let out a sharp yelp and then was still, before Gordon had scarcely stabbed the white one with a spear in her belly.

"You bitch!" he yelled in defiance. He freed Caymon to see that he was okay.

ALYSSA LAID ON THE TABLE. THE BLOOD POURED OUT OF HER. HER injury hurt, but it was nothing compared to what she'd done to the other wolf. From the moment he'd confronted her, she knew him for what he was. It was as plain as the nose on her face. A vampire. His master must have turned him when he was made, so they could be together forever. He was probably the one that had stabbed her, crouching protectively over his pet.

In his hubris, he failed to realize that his pet was dead. She'd snapped his neck in two the very moment she bit into him. With meat, tendons, and fur probably the only reason the head was still attached. These same character flaws prevented him from realizing that Alyssa was only playing possum while her wound knit itself back together. The spear was regular metal, not silver, and that would cost the vampire his life.

Alyssa leapt off the table, striking purchase, and made for the old man's neck. He probably never even saw her coming with that stupid eye patch of his. By the time he realized she was on him, it was too late. Vampire man and vampire dog, together forever, just like he planned.

CHAPTER 25
THE LAMB

Ash slammed into another two bodies, protecting Kayala as best he could. She stood to his left, hurtling forward. Twister was fighting to his right. They were running out of time. He didn't know how, but he could sense it. They had to save the girl and they had to do it soon, or all was lost.

"What happened to Jinx?" Ash shouted, dodging a blow meant for his head.

"She's alright," replied Twister, after executing a series of moves that knocked three soldiers to the ground simultaneously.

A blast of energy struck at the heart of a mass soldiers directly in front of them. It was Jinx. She dropped out of the sky to land next to him. "Sorry, I got held up," she said.

"That's okay, but we're running out of time!" shouted Ash. "We've got to get up there and we've got to do it now!"

"Do you see how no one's touching the lighthouse? Not a single soul?" Jinx asked.

"Now that you mention it, I do," replied Ash.

"She's got a shield around it, but I think I can bring it down. If I do, it's only going to be temporary."

"That's the plan, then," Ash told her, loud enough so that Twister and Kayala could hear him. "You get that shield down, and we're going to the top to rescue Kayala's sister."

"I'll stay down here and hold them off," offered Twister.

"Are you sure you can handle that?" asked Ash. "We're not looking for any martyrs tonight."

"I can," replied Twister.

Not for the first time, tonight, Ash wondered if this was what it was like to have friends. He was proud to be among them. "Alright, let's do this," he said.

"You'll know when it's down," said Jinx. And then she took flight.

Now that she had brought it to his attention, Ash could make out the outline of the field of force that protected the lighthouse from intruders. From high above, Jinx threw a blast of energy, but she directed it at the base of the structure this time. The shield faltered and disappeared.

Next, she threw two balls of energy. They hit into the crowd ahead of them, raining down destruction. Now there was a clear path to the lighthouse.

"This is it!" he shouted, and reaching for Kayala, he flung her as far forward as he could. She sailed over the heads of her would-be assailants. Ash ran in her wake. A blur of motion, stiff-arming anyone that got in his way. Unfortunately, the door was locked.

Again, he flung her. This time straight up. She was able to grab onto the metal railing and he was immediately tackled.

KAYALA WAS A WOMAN POSSESSED. WITH EVERYTHING SHE HAD, SHE leapt at the Queen. Knocking the dagger out of her hand, and throwing the Queen back, so that she nearly fell over the edge. The woman was at first confused, and then furious. Kayala stood in front of her sister. Ready to defend her to her dying breath.

A bright flash passed by her from above and her sister was suddenly released from her chains. The Queen turned around to see what was going on. It was Jinx.

Kayala used the distraction to her advantage and clutched her sister to her. Helping her to climb over the metal bars at the edge. She was unresponsive, and Kayala feared the worst. She lowered her sister as far as she could and let her fall, before jumping down herself.

At the bottom, she checked to make sure that her sister was okay and hadn't broken any bones. There was only blood on one of her forearms, where the Queen had likely cut her for the ceremony. Otherwise she was unharmed.

"I've got you, sister," she told her.

WITH TWISTER'S HELP, ASH HAD BEEN ABLE TO FREE HIMSELF IN time to be at Kayala's side, before anyone could assault her at the bottom of the lighthouse. When he got there, he found that she had her twin in her arms. Despite a nasty gash down Inalia's left arm, she was alive and breathing.

"I am victorious!" screamed a woman a little distance above. It was the Queen and she was positively delirious. Her ramblings weren't what had suddenly caught Ash's undivided attention.

Something was happening. He could feel it through his entire body. It was something very powerful and extremely magical. The earth began to rumble.

"Earthquake!" he shouted, putting his arm protectively around Kayala, as she in turn had her sister. "We need to back away now!"

Jinx had suddenly joined them as well. "Something's coming!" she shouted. "Something big!"

"I know!" he exclaimed. Ash grabbed Kayala's sister from her and cradled her in his arms. This wasn't the time for walking. "We've got to get back to the car," he told Kayala.

The earth continued to shake all around them, with the river's waters spilling onto the island.

"We've run out of time!" yelled Jinx. "Look!"

Every instinct in Ash's body compelled him to stop walking and turn around. Then he heard something that eclipsed even the tragedy of nature around him.

It was what he could only describe as a powerful roar. It was the sound of a thousand lions roaring in unison, but with a giant microphone. It came from out of the earth itself. No, the river! The creature soared into the heavens and joined the lightshow overhead. It roared again, and the earthquake stopped.

So, this was the end of the world Jinx had been talking about. This was Armageddon.

"We are too late. All is lost," said Jinx's familiar voice. Apparently, she was just as surprised as he was. They all huddled close to one another and braced for the unknown.

All those myths with their descriptions of them, had not done them justice. It was a dragon. With wings and scales and the whole story come to life. Except this story was big enough to fill Union Square completely. With its white hide somewhat subdued in the night. Amazing.

Any minute now Jinx would teleport them to safety. Any minute now.

"Umm, Jinx?"

He was all alone. Not even the girl in his arms remained. They had all mysteriously disappeared, leaving him with the remnants of the Queen's army. They were either staring up at the sky lost or running away as fast as they could.

The dragon continued to bellow in the night sky. It breathed fire ahead of it, but the energies shifted in color until they matched exactly with the Aurora Borealis effect, in the heavens. Soon the storm broke so that the sky was completely clear, except for the light show.

Now that it was clear, he noticed the Queen taking to the air herself. She flew up, to meet the all-powerful dragon. The two of them took on the colors of the energies in the sky. They both shone. Became brighter. Ever brighter. The Queen grew in size to proportions similar to the dragon's.

The spectacle became too bright for Ash to watch and he turned away. Focusing on the magic, he felt the two energies intersect.

At long last all her years of planning and scheming. All the anguish of waiting and the insults she had suffered. The tree she had planted was finally going to bear fruit. Chanovalle was awash in an ecstasy she would not have been able to describe. She had found the Child of Destiny, and here and now, her own long-awaited destiny was upon her.

No longer would she have to fear the sunlight or being staked through the heart. In mere moments she would be immortal in ways she had only dared to dream.

All those early years of magical-physics science back home had paid off. All the magical training. All her calculations on Pandoria. All the suffering. All of it. Even Bryne awaited her below. She'd seen him earlier trying to stop her with his friends, but they were ineffective. Oh, the sweet agony of victory!

The transformation was almost complete. She continued to absorb the last of the dragon's energy. All of it. Eradicating the soul of the great beast, so that only she remained.

She was reborn. Anything she desired was the simplest act of thought. She floated in the sky, a woman the size of a tremendous dragon. She willed herself back to her normal size and took a deep breath. It was effortless.

Down below, she could see Bryne as clearly as if he floated beside her. She glided down to meet him.

"2nd Magistrate Bryne Xarn," she said in her sweetest voice. "How nice to see you again."

He looked around like a buffoon and then he said, "Are you talking to me?"

"You wound me, Magistrate. Who else might I be talking to? Who else, do you suppose, might really know me in all this pathetic world? Who else could I ever talk to about Numina?"

"Who's Numina?" he asked. "Am I supposed to know her too?"

"What are you playing at, Bryne? All these years in New York must have addled your brain, if you think this a time for games. You and I have unfinished business, do we not?"

"I don't know," he replied. "You tell me."

Chanovalle was fit to obliterate him right here, this instant, but she restrained herself. That was her old way. She wasn't the same woman she had been, and she'd have to start acting like it, if she was to bring in her new world order.

Ever so subtle, she worked a truth spell on him. "Why don't you remember me?" she asked, when it was complete.

"I have amnesia and I can't even remember anything about myself, let alone some random woman," he blurted out before he could stop himself. He looked shocked and took half a step back. "How did you do that?" he asked.

Chanovalle took to pacing in front of him, ignoring his question. This was a most disturbing revelation. The spell she cast was infallible. That meant he was telling the truth. That her own nemesis didn't even remember who she was, troubled her greatly. She could still destroy him, but somehow it felt like an empty victory.

"You are so much below me now, but I will humor you," she told him. Then she closed her eyes and stood before him, casting an intricate spell in her mind. When she uttered the word "Remember" he dropped to his knees and began to shake.

CHAPTER 26
REVISITED

The sound of steel on steel rang out, as he deflected a blow meant for his face. A false step a second later, and he fell.

Hold onto your sword, he thought. Just hold onto your sword and everything will be okay.

He landed on his back, and a second later his assailant fell on top of him. The other man's weight was smothering. The stranger's fearful eyes accused Bryne, as the life drained out of them. Where a man had been, there was nothing but a corpse. Bryne rolled the body off and got to his feet as quickly as he could. It was a struggle to pull his sword out of the chest cavity, but he succeeded.

With a few battles under his belt, experience had kept him alive. The same couldn't be said of the others. Somewhere in the forest, were men from his hometown. He'd talked to Randy and Percival on the ride over here. A set of brothers with red flaming hair, freckles, and blue eyes. The three had promised to stick together and watch each other's backs but had been separated during the battle.

The world spun. The rocks were not kind when he hit. He saw. He heard. Nothing.

He was lifted off the ground, with his feet dangling in the air like a child. His eyes began to blur, and he knew that to lose consciousness was to lose his life.

Get a grip, he thought. There was time enough for idling in the grave. How could anyone be so strong?

His mind began to wander again, but he brought it back through sheer strength of will. Focus!

Fetid breath assaulted Bryne's nostrils. A down-sloped forehead with red eyes below—and below that razor-sharp teeth—belonged to what might be a man. Wearing a suit of black plate mail that covered all but its hands and head. It held him aloft with no discernable effort.

"Prepare to die," it said.

Bryne let out a battle cry in response. Fighting with everything he had left. Reanimated limbs punched and kicked at the monstrosity. Hitting both metal and flesh. Until all feeling left his limbs and he was completely spent. Unfazed by the attack, the beast bit into Bryne's neck, who could only yell into its ear in defiance. The whole earth swallowed him up, as the consciousness he had fought so hard to hold onto left him. Darkness reigned.

Sometime later he awoke. Looking around, he saw his opponent, mysteriously decapitated only a few feet from where he sat. He was in a cavern, with a dim light streaming in from the opening overhead. Trying to get up, he collapsed a few times in pain and dizziness. Eventually he climbed up the steep hill leading to the surface. Black spots floated before his eyes.

In the light of the setting sun, Bryne saw mangled bodies tossed about like leaves. Blood was everywhere. A strong gust of cold air stole the last heat of his body, and with it, whatever tenuous resolve that had kept him on his feet. At last his body relented, succumbing to weariness, and Bryne's grip on reality slipped away.

WHEN HE AWOKE AGAIN, THE STARS DANCED OVERHEAD, WITH NO clouds about to hide their mischief. A shiver ran through his body, and he realized he should find shelter. He noticed a large shadow moving in the distance. He thought it was his horse Prometheus, but he passed out again before he could be sure.

~

BRYNE FOUND HIMSELF WALKING ALONG DARK ROCKS IN THE NIGHT, heading towards the sound of the ocean. He didn't remember how he got there. When he could finally see the water it was all red, which he thought was an odd color, but he didn't know why. Closer to the shore now, it seemed to ooze more than ebb and flow, and made him think of blood.

When he looked up at the night sky, he realized it was the same deep red color as the water, which he thought was odd as well. There were no clouds in the sky, and no stars either. He couldn't remember if that was how it was supposed to be.

Looking back down at the water brought a wave of nausea, and bile threated to come into his mouth. The entire ocean was filled with corpses floating in it. Why had he not seen that before?

The empty sky coalesced into millions of winged red bats, swooping down, in mass, upon the ocean of bodies. Feasting and gorging on them.

Horrified and filled with terror, Bryne turned from the ocean and ran deep in-land as far and as fast as his legs could carry him. He stumbled and fell along the way, but the bats seemed too engrossed in their appetites to take notice of him. Distracted, he hadn't noticed the burning sensation that had begun in his ribs and the side of his neck. A new panic set in when his body felt like it was on fire.

God in heaven, please help. "The ocean," he said.

Heedless of the danger, he ran back to the ocean like a madman. Ready to dive in despite the hungry bats. Stumbling about and falling along the way. Picking himself up when necessary. His skin felt as if it had melted away.

Nearly at the vast bloody ocean, he saw one monstrous bat at the coast, feasting almost right next to where he stood. Even so close to the salvation of the water, it held him transfixed.

There was something eerily familiar about it, though he had never seen anything of the sort. Easily as big as a man. As if to answer his thoughts, it stopped feasting and turned to look directly at him.

Its eye contact poured a freezing-cold draught into his blood that threatened to put frost into the very veins that carried it. Shocked simultaneously with fear, horror, and loathing, he fell over backwards. His entire body shook with convulsions, despite his in-vain attempt to drag himself away. There he sat as impotent as a newborn babe.

The creature had sharp razor-like teeth, blood-red eyes, and a feral-monstrous mad hunger that seemed to emanate from it. Burned off it, like the fire that burned through Bryne now. But it 'was' him. A warped, evil, corrupted version of himself.

It nodded its head beckoning him over in a friendly gesture.

Bryne screamed from the core of his being and passed out.

∼

HE WAS WALKING IN AN OPEN FIELD WITH LUSH GREEN GRASS THAT stretched out infinitely in every direction. There were no trees or bushes. There were no hills or mountains. Everything was flat as far as the eye could see. The sky was a vibrant blue, with only the thinnest wisp of cloud in some spots, and an unrelenting sun. No matter how far he walked the landscape remained the same.

Bryne continued to walk until he felt an aching pain in his side, and neck.

He turned back the way he had come, hoping to get some sort of bearing. A lion was there, with a shaggy red mane. The lion was seated on the grass some twenty feet away, lazily staring back at Bryne, with what he hoped was complete disinterest. He decided he had better move along and not upset it. Hopefully, it wasn't hungry.

He turned to continue walking, so as not to attract undue atten-tion, and saw two more lions with shaggy red manes, twenty feet off that way. Turning to his left brought an additional three, and a swift ninety-degree turn, another four.

What is going on?

Turning to the right, where he had seen the single lone lion, now stood five. He was surrounded, with nowhere to go but through them. It was obvious that he had been in the sun too long and must now be suffering a hallucination.

Bryne closed his eyes and tried to calm himself. This was not real. Everything was fine and he was completely alone. He felt the hot sun on his skin and a breeze gently ruffled his hair, and he heard the grass move.

He counted to three. When he opened his eyes however, the hallucination had grown. Now he was surrounded with what must have been a hundred lions sitting all around him. All pressed together, leaving him a twenty-foot circle of space, and all looking directly at him.

What might have been the first lion slowly came to its feet and roared, causing Bryne to flinch.

This, he thought, was the signal. Sweat began to pour profusely down his neck, as much from the heat as the fear he tried not to show.

He braced himself for his final moments of agony. Any second now he would be food. But nothing happened.

After the first lion was silent, a second stood next to it and the two roared in unison. He tried to master his increasing fear but succeeded only in stopping his weak knees from buckling. The terror was overwhelming.

A lion let out a loud powerful roar and held it. Impossibly, another joined in and their combined musical note held and did not falter. His heartbeat was furious. His mind expanded. His entire body was afire.

The roars mounted and continued to grow, as more lions joined in, and he was soon buffeted by the powerful sound of all one hundred.

Fit to bursting, the pressure mounted. Cleansing. Enhancing. Building.

The great magnificent roar all around him that seemed to shake the heavens, met its boundless match, mysteriously in the being that was called Bryne. It coursed within his veins, engulfing the darkness, til it shone like the sun itself.

He closed his eyes to compose himself and the deafening roar was replaced with a deafening silence. When he opened his eyes again, he was kneeling on grass outside, with his body soaked in sweat. There were other things in his surroundings, but he found that he couldn't concentrate on them. He only had eyes for the woman hovering in the air above him.

CHAPTER 27
A VICTORY

Amidst the casting of a new spell, she heard him speak down below.

"The memories are still flooding back, but I remember you now, 2nd Magistrate Chanovalle Remseldorne" he told her, still hunched over, and shaking, but looking directly at her.

"Now that's the Bryne I remember," she replied when the spell was complete.

"You've accomplished quite a feat here today. I can feel your tremendous power," she heard him say. "What will you do now?"

"Now I go back home and claim what's rightfully mine," she explained. Spoken ever so softly, she added "It's amazing that I can still be so petty."

"What do you mean?" he asked.

"This!" Chanovalle Remseldorn hurled a destructive blast of energy at her foe, while simultaneously opening a gateway that would lead her back home. Not to Pandoria. No. This one would see her to her second revenge, on her home world of Numina.

Chanovalle, who would probably be referred to as the Goddess Chanovalle from now on (yes, she did like the sound of that), did not bother looking down at Bryne's end. Such trivial things were beneath her now. She stepped through the portal without a backwards glance, into the start of her new life.

STUNNED BY THE ONSLAUGHT OF HIS OWN MIND, HE NEVER HAD A chance to get out of the way of the energy blast. He moved, of course, but the diameter of the thing was like a small meteor. Still the memories of his long life poured into him, even as Chanovalle's spell threatened to snuff out that life.

Anyone else would have already been destroyed, but he fought on. The energies she'd hurled at him were too much like his own nature, and so he understood them. He caressed them. Looked for the string that would unravel the spell, like the great ball of yarn that it was.

Finally, it happened.

He remembered. Everything. And. Was. WHOLE!

He screamed at the world from the core of his being. It was the great defiance that was his by right of birth. He was an ordinary man no more. He had been made over centuries ago by his teacher. In his image. The image of the great dragon Xarn E' Xarn. The source of his surname.

More than the vampire he'd been poisoned by, in a battle long ago. More than the energies that Xarn E' Xarn had invested into his very cells. He was an amalgam of them. Combined into something that was greater than the sum of its parts.

A vampire. Imbued with the very essence of a powerful dragon. During the infancy of his change, so that all the elements combined into a cohesive element that was housed in his DNA. For all intents and purposes, he was a dragon in human form. Not dissimilar to the creature that Chanovalle herself had become, but perhaps stronger because he was actualized through a gift freely given.

The point was, that she could not destroy him.

Ash brought himself to a complete state of relaxation, accepting the energies that continued to assault him, and diverted them with everything he had left, into the river.

He lived. Only barely. The old vampire hunger was upon him, so that he was mad with bloodlust. His will evaporated. It was the hunter's madness.

HE WENT BACK TO WHERE THE ROAD WAS. PASSED THE PARKED white SUV that he'd been driven in and grabbed anyone who crossed his path. Draining them all dry.

It didn't matter who they were. He was starved.

HE CAME BACK TO HIMSELF MAYBE AN HOUR LATER. HE DIDN'T know how many he'd killed. Ten? Twenty? All he knew was that the hunger was finally satiated. He blamed Chanovalle for his severe lapse in restraint and vowed to hate her more than ever.

It was the very reason he'd stayed away from the humans and locked himself away all those years ago. When he first came to New York, in around the fifteen hundreds. Afraid that something like this might happen, with no governing body to tell him what to do, as there had been back on Numina. As he felt horribly unjustified at the time, in feeding on the humans in a world that was all theirs alone.

And here, hundreds of years later, she'd made a mockery of his wishes. The same way that she'd made a mockery of his life. As her blind ambition pulled the two of them through the portal long ago. Effectively robbing him of a life with his wife and children. As well as the rest of the life he could have had back home.

Ash attempted heading back to the lighthouse but fell onto the floor instead. Bouncing off a park bench, before he got that far. He screamed at the top of his lungs, as he was born again for the second time.

From his perspective, it was like he exploded. Instead of dying, he went up into the sky and merged with the stars. They accepted him as one of them. Joining him to them so that they formed a constellation.

At first, he was one of them. Then something shifted and they were all part of him. The constellation was in the outline of his own body. He was the constellation. A huge one. Composed of millions of stars.

And then he was back in his body, picking himself up off the ground.

It was like seeing the world for the first time. He knew that he was more powerful than he'd ever been, back on Numina. Because of what he was and his refusal to feed, he'd hidden himself. From himself. That was how he'd lost his memories.

Finding Kayala and her sister Inalia. Being at the right place at the right time, just in the nick of time. What had seemed random and lucky, was not. He'd known where to go to find them. The group of people that surrounded him, collectively, drew him like a moth to a flame. Being lonely, his spirit had sought out powerful beings for camaraderie, leading him to investigate spikes in ambient spiritual energy. Even if he wasn't consciously aware of his true motivations.

Finding Twister and Jinx at the mountain. The research he'd done was a sham. A hallucination for his waking mind to justify the journey his subconscious had set for him. He had gone to the library. He had read through scores of books. If he went back, he would find that none of it added up. There was no trail leading to the mountain, other than his subconscious curiosity. In reality, he had felt Jinx's power when she ceased to slumber. Pinpointing the location of one so strong had been easy.

Discovering the site of the sacrifice. As before, his subconscious mind, along with his sensitivity to magic, had led him like a bloodhound's nose. Even the residual energy was strong enough to blot out anything less significant, let alone any of the fireworks earlier. Speaking of which...

He sensed something he must have been ignoring before. Ash ran to the foot of the lighthouse. He moved so fast that he was here one moment, and there the next.

The waters of a whirlpool spun ever so gently. Falling into a crater in the earth below. It had probably been created by the dragon's exit from a dwelling underneath. Above it hovered a small sphere of white light, that glowed as though it was invested with moonlight. Shades duller, so that he could look upon it without being blinded. It was like a fine mist. To his eyes, he saw it connected to the colorful waves in the sky, by a strong magical connection that could not be broken.

Magically, it was constructed like a portal. One that didn't seem to go anywhere. Its purpose was unknown to him.

He wondered if Chanovalle knew what it was, or if she even cared. If he knew her at all, she was back on Numina wrecking all sorts of havoc. He had no desire to follow her. She'd be back of her own accord soon enough, and he'd be forced to deal with her then. For good or ill.

Ash reached out to the world and tried to find where his friends had gone. As he found them, he discovered why they'd left him.

A film coated his body that served to ground him to the earth. So that when Jinx willed everyone to safety, he was left behind. A minor component in a spell that probably prevented Jinx from returning to their battleground as well. Chanovalle must have done it when she first saw him from the lighthouse. After she missed him with the lightning bolt. With the slightest effort, the film evaporated into nothingness.

Ash discovered that they were back at Jinx's lair in Delaware. A familiar place that she would have been able to return to quickly. He checked for defenses that might prevent his entry and found none.

He relaxed. Gathered his energies. And teleported.

EPILOGUE

We later realized that a great deal more had happened that fateful night, than any of us could have possibly been aware of. We knew that something monumental had occurred, but we didn't know what. We thought that this magical being of indeterminate power had awoken from a long slumber. End of story.

I myself thought I had witnessed the creature's subsequent destruction. That most selfish and hateful Chanovalle, condemned it thus, to reach her own power-hungry ends.

I thought it was all over and I thought wrong.

How was I to know what that white glowing orb of light, emanating from the ocean floor might be? How was any of us?

Imagine my surprise, when the news was flooded with a deluge of similar occurrences peppered across the entire globe. As other energy anomalies winked into existence. Rome, Italy. Paris, France. Cairo, Egypt. On every continent, in every country, it seemed to be the same thing.

But there was more. Much more.

Things were coming out. Strange things that mirrored old myths and legends. Supernatural things. Others that defied description, or comprehension. From the unknown, came all manner of beings and creatures, into our naïve little world. With them, came terror and a subsequent worldwide panic.

The people asked their governments for answers, but there were none. Governments around the world opted for a wait and see approach. Others said it was the end of the world. That the hell on Earth promised centuries ago was finally here.

My friends and I, with our more direct knowledge, began to speculate differently. The ritual we had all witnessed, had been the catalyst that set it all into motion. An untold number of gateways had been opened leading to other worlds. Like my own unfortunate happenstance, that had taken me from my home long ago.

Thanks to Chanovalle's petty vengeance, I had my memories back, and knew for a fact that such a thing was possible. Unlike my own accident, these gateways were permanent.

Here then, was a new element that was destined to change the face of the Earth. Maybe beyond all recognition. There was no telling where the gateways led. So, anything could happen.

Jinx had been right after all. It was the end of the world. But unlike her original interpretation, it was more accurately the end of the world as we knew it.

It wasn't until a week later, that I saw a program on TV that claimed the whole thing had been foretold. October 13, 2023. The date of the Cairo calendar Armageddon.

In the end, the Egyptians had gotten it right after all.

----A MAN CALLED, ASH

COMING SOON

EARTH TORN

ABOUT THE AUTHOR

Step**h**an F. Rogers is a New York City native. He holds a Bachelor's degr**ee** in English Creative Writing, from Hunter College. He also spen**t** a few years as an English Teacher to middle schoolers. With all that **p**ractice writing stories, it didn't seem too far-fetched to "write some **t**hing worth reading" like ol' Benjamin Franklin said.

He enjoys martial arts, meditation, and video games.

instagram.com/stephanfrogers

patreon.com/stephanfrogers